Whiskey

Whiskey

Bruce Holbert

 MCD   FARRAR, STRAUS AND GIROUX   NEW YORK

MCD

Farrar, Straus and Giroux

175 Varick Street, New York 10014

Copyright © 2018 by Bruce Holbert
Printed in the United States of America
First edition, 2018

Portions of this book originally appeared, in somewhat different form, in the
following publications: *The Anthology of Lilac City Fairy Tales, The Antioch
Review, Cairn, Crab Creek Review, Del Sol Review, Hotel Amerika, Inlander, The
Iowa Review, Mary, New Orleans Review, 94 Creations, Other Voices, Quarterly West,
RiverLit, The Spokesman-Review, Tampa Tribune, West Wind Review,* and *Word Riot.*

Library of Congress Cataloging-in-Publication Data
Names: Holbert, Bruce, author.
Title: Whiskey / Bruce Holbert.
Description: First edition. | New York : MCD / Farrar, Straus and
    Giroux, 2018.
Identifiers: LCCN 2017040456 | ISBN 9780374289188 (cloth) |
    ISBN 9780374716387 (ebook)
Subjects: LCSH: Loyalty—Fiction. | Domestic fiction. | GSAFD:
    Mystery fiction.
Classification: LCC PS3608.O48287 W48 2018 | DDC 813/.6—dc23
LC record available at https://lccn.loc.gov/2017040456

Designed by Abby Kagan

Our books may be purchased in bulk for promotional, educational, or business
use. Please contact your local bookseller or the Macmillan Corporate and
Premium Sales Department at 1-800-221-7945, extension 5442, or by e-mail at
MacmillanSpecialMarkets@macmillan.com.

www.mcdbooks.com • www.fsgbooks.com
Follow us on Twitter, Facebook, and Instagram at @mcdbooks

1   3   5   7   9   10   8   6   4   2

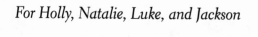

For Holly, Natalie, Luke, and Jackson

It was the last that remained of a past whose annihilation had not taken place because it was still in a process of annihilation, consuming itself from within, ending at every moment but never ending its ending.

—GABRIEL GARCÍA MÁRQUEZ,
One Hundred Years of Solitude

Whiskey

1

EXODUS

August 1991

This time, Claire did not depart all at once but after a series of diligent, daily efforts to prove her affection to Andre—notes in his lunch pail, fruity desserts he favored, VCR Mafia movies, bubble baths, a ferry cruise to Alaska, and a television the size of Rhode Island—all of which moved him tremendously, though he couldn't escape what motivated her largesse. She would argue through the morning hours he was reason itself for her heart to beat, but the necessity for her to pursue her case proved more evidence against it. There was no last straw, no camel's spine, no argument or slammed doors or broken saucers or vases, none of the theater one associates with a marriage's dissolution. Instead, their home darkened until neither of them could light it alone or together. One weekend during which he'd scheduled a fishing trip, she, with his blessing, boxed his books and clothes and organized his papers in a suitcase and added a share of their photographs. Two high-school boys toted the lot to a pickup truck and transported it to an apartment Andre had rented a week earlier. She paid them ten dollars each.

After, Andre would encounter his brother, Smoker, at the tavern each evening. They drank beer—Andre was off whiskey once more—and dined on Smoker's tab, which Smoker squared each sitting, an inclination Smoker entertained only recently.

Their last evening in the tavern commenced like any other: Andre entered the place and Crazy Eddie peered up from his novel and slapped the griddle with a burger for Andre and another for Eddie's dog, Desdemona, a mixed basset with legs no taller than beer cans and a long fat tube of torso that serpentined as she tottered inside. Her head, though, was as square as a Labrador's.

Grease popped and a meaty aroma rose from the grill and reminded Andre of his childhood; he had no fondness for his youth, but he appreciated the meals. Eddie spatulaed the patty onto a bun and extracted tomatoes, lettuce, and sliced pickles from a Tupperware box. With an ice-cream scoop, he plopped potato salad on a plate and added the sandwich. The dog took it bread and all but had no inclination for toppings or fries, so Eddie ladled her the chicken and noodles remaining from the lunch special so as not to short either of them.

By then, the old-timers had yielded their booths to the pool players as the clientele's volume had bested the TV's. The juke was full of quarters, which meant Andre must endure metal-clang and pop tunes that sounded like TV commercials before his Merle Haggard hit the spindle. He poked his meal and glanced at the mirror while the evening regulars milled about the billiard

4

table or piled behind a pair of upright video machines. He could have ordered to go and at home played tapes, but alone and off whiskey the songs just cooked him into a stew.

Desdemona, beneath the stool, feasted until she cleared her plate then harassed Andre until he surrendered the remnants of his hamburger.

"Goddamned communist," Eddie scolded.

The dog retreated to the door and Eddie put her out. No more than a minute later, Darrell Reynolds, one of two lawyers who served the coulee, allowed the dog back inside. Reynolds rotated his head to scan the room, an act that appeared rehearsed, then ordered a beer. Eddie poured and placed the full glass on the bar. Reynolds chose a stool beside Andre, where Desdemona had curled beneath his stool.

"Is that your dog?" he asked.

Andre shook his head. The man wore pressed gray slacks and a blue polo shirt and leather loafers with wine-colored socks.

"Seems friendly."

"Anything's friendly if you feed it."

Reynolds laughed and inspected a scar in the wooden bar.

"I'm Darrell Reynolds," he said. He maintained a mustache to fit in, but trimmed it too carefully.

"I've seen your ad in the paper," Andre said.

"I've been doing some work for your wife."

Andre pointed at the bar then held up two fingers.

Eddie blinked. "You sure on that?"

"I am," Andre said.

Eddie delivered a pair of jigger glasses along with the whiskey under the counter.

"Oh no," Reynolds said.

"You work for free, Reynolds?"

"I charge a fee," Reynolds said.

Andre poured whiskey into the shot glasses and shoved one toward Reynolds.

"What's this?" Reynolds asked.

"It's the fee." The glass had spilled a little. Andre hooked his finger across the puddle and dangled it for the dog, who showed no interest, then downed his glass.

The lawyer smiled and drained his whiskey too then wiped his mouth with the back of his wrist.

"Your wife wants to dissolve your marriage."

"It matter what I want?"

"Of course, there are two sides to anything like this."

"Good. I want to stay married. Tie score keeps the game on." Andre replenished the glasses. His stomach fluttered awaiting more alcohol.

"I'm afraid the law doesn't see it as such," Reynolds said.

Andre hoisted his glass and indicated Reynolds do the same. They drank. Andre poured and lifted his glass again.

"Fee's doubled," he said. "After hours. Pick up your liquor."

Reynolds relented and drank.

"I don't want to see you in court, Mr. White," Reynolds said.

"Well, you won't want to encounter me out of it, I guarantee you."

Eddie threw Andre a warning look. Andre ignored him. Reynolds unzipped a cowhide purse and carefully placed a blue envelope on the bar.

"You can sign these and avoid the courts or hire your own lawyer."

6

Andre poured two more. "I'm hiring you," he said. "Drink. That's an order."

"You can't hire me. Your wife already has."

"I'll pay more."

"It doesn't work that way."

"Goddamnit, how does it work then?"

Reynolds tapped the envelope with his index finger. "You sign the papers. That's how it works. You save yourself some money. You get divorced." He excused himself for the bathroom.

Andre plucked matches from a wicker basket between the salt and pepper shakers and set the envelope on his dinner plate. He struck a match then admired the flames. Only ashes remained when Reynolds returned. He clasped his hands before his chest to demonstrate his patience. "It cost money to draw up those papers," he said. "The courts have to process them."

"Guess she'll have to pay for another time through."

"You don't understand. Once they're processed, they belong to the court. I served them to you. They're your responsibility now. You'll have to pay for another summons."

"For what?"

"The documents."

"Documents?"

Reynolds smoothed his mustache with his thumb and forefinger. "There are witnesses. They will testify to what occurred. You," he said to Eddie.

"We don't do that here, mister." Eddie opened the sink spigot.

"If I subpoena you, you damned sure will. I'll be prepared with perjury or contempt charges, otherwise."

Eddie withdrew a plate from the soapy water and rinsed it,

then another. "You thought you were prepared when you walked in here, didn't you?"

Reynolds switched his attention to Andre. "I'll serve you at work, in front of your students."

"It's summer," Andre said.

The lawyer drew a deep breath. "I can see why she's leaving you."

"So can I," Andre said. "I just don't want her to."

"It's my job," Reynolds said. "Nothing personal."

"No offense taken. A little more fee?"

"My wife's going to shout bloody murder."

"Better make it a double, then."

Eddie let the dishes sit and paged through the phone book nailed to the wall. He punched some numbers.

"Mrs. Reynolds," Eddie said. "This is Eddie at the tavern. Yeah, Crazy Eddie, though I'm not much crazy anymore. Your husband, he wanted me to inform you he's with a client."

Reynolds pleaded for the phone. Andre hushed him.

"No, I'm not covering for him," Eddie said. "He's a good man, now, everybody with any sense knows so. He's with this hard drinker is all, and they're working something out, so he's indulging him to grease the skids. You'll want to taxi him home when he finishes here. I won't have an educated man arrested for drinking on my watch." Eddie paused to listen. "No, ma'am. If there were women, why would he ask you to pick him up? He'd have one of us drop him off. That's how it's done. Thank you, ma'am. I'll call you when he's ready."

Reynolds whistled.

"He don't cost a hundred dollars an hour, either," Andre told him.

They had put a significant dent in the bottle when Smoker arrived and sat on the opposite side of the lawyer. Eddie retrieved him a beer. Smoker nodded to the whiskey bottle and Andre slid it past the lawyer to his brother. Smoker hoisted the bottle and pulled.

The brothers were heads and tails on the same coin. Andre had trouble meeting another's gaze. His eyes drifted about a room, measuring occupants uneasily. His rounded shoulders folded forward over his chest like he expected a blow, though his reputation made the event unlikely. He cut his black hair short to disguise a stubborn cowlick. As an adolescent, he'd suffered acne. He still washed his face three times a day, but his skin shone with oil in any light. His brow shadowed his eyes and a bent Roman nose. He had straight teeth; still he rarely smiled; he appeared at times pensive and at others bilious. Living alone had left him with intuition like a woman. Sometimes it served him well. Others it hardly mattered.

Smoker shared the same black hair, though not the cowlick. He wore it nearly to his shoulders. In certain lights it appeared purple. Stronger lines than Andre's delineated his face, as did a genial countenance. He was as tall as his brother, but he carried his shoulders more horizontally. Though Andre was a capable high-school basketball player, Smoker was the one who looked the athlete. He walked like his limbs were half air, and if he decided to leap it appeared he could decide when to come down.

"Seen my good-for-nothing woman?" Smoker asked.

"Not since the last time you asked," Andre told him.

"Check with Eddie," the lawyer suggested.

Smoker lifted an eyebrow. "How's he know about Eddie?"

Eddie wiped the counter under his glass. "Every sinner finds the Lord sooner or later."

"What about it, Edward?"

"Haven't seen her since Flag Day," Eddie told him.

"She's probably just making a wide loop," Andre said. He reached across the lawyer and confiscated the whiskey.

"I ain't finished with that," Smoker complained.

Andre paused. "You stop to wonder why a lawyer is my drinking partner tonight?"

Smoker stared at the french fries in ketchup and the lettuce leaf blackened with the letter's ashes. He didn't reply. They listened to the beer lights tick.

"Who's watching Bird?" Andre asked. Smoker's twelve-year-old daughter was named Raven, but Smoker called her simply Bird.

"Dede's got her."

"You never said nothing about that up till now."

Smoker shrugged. "Didn't know till this afternoon. I thought Vera was watching her."

Andre glanced at Smoker. "Where you looked?"

"At that biker she used to shack with and Vera's, like I said."

"Neither's seen her?"

"That or ain't saying."

"There's a child missing?" Reynolds asked.

"Damned straight," Smoker told him.

"Is there something I can do?"

Smoker pursed his lips. "Might be good to have a member of the bar in our corner. We could roust Vera and Biker Bump again."

Smoker bummed Eddie's cigarettes, lit one, and put it between Reynolds's fingers. "It'll make you look meaner." He hooked the lawyer's arm and steered him to the door. Andre followed. Outside, Andre paused at his rig for a .38 pistol. In Smoker's pickup

10

cab, Smoker unholstered a snub-nosed Luger then tossed Reynolds a twelve-gauge from the window rack.

"Don't shoot it," Andre said.

"But if you do, get close," Smoker added.

The lawyer crawled into the pickup bed and propped himself on the wheel well. Andre joined him.

Their first stop was Smoker's live-in's sister. Vera was as husky as Dede was thin. She looked like a legged ham. Twice she'd whipped her husband into the emergency room. Finally he countered by half scalping her with a posthole digger then lit out for Ephrata and the county hoosegow where he awaited the morning turnkey. But Vera declined to charge him and they had lived amicably since.

Smoker pounded the door and Vera answered.

"You should keep an eye on them better if you want a family, Smoker." Vera was loud enough for the neighbors to come to their windows.

"She's got the child."

"Girl's as much hers as yours."

"And if you were God above, who'd you want looking out for her, Vera?"

"Neither of you."

She shoved by Smoker and marched to the truck. She inflicted a curt look upon Andre then bored her eyes into Reynolds. The lawyer opened and closed the breach of the double-barrel.

"That don't scare me," Vera said.

"I wasn't trying to," the lawyer told her.

"Good, because I'm sure armed threats are against the bar."

She turned and found Smoker. "I don't know where she is," Vera said. "I'd get the girl myself if I did."

"You see her, that's what I want you to do," Smoker said.

"It would be for the child's sake," Vera told him.

"I don't care why," Smoker said.

Smoker turned for the pickup.

Vera raised her voice. "You know our mother's place?"

"Up Metaline?"

"Still summer," Vera said. "The roads are manageable." The place had been Dede's parents'. The old days, their father skidded logs the warm months and winters tugged green chain at the mill, and their mother cooked in the school kitchen. Both passed some time ago; they left the place to Dede and Vera and a brother who manned a Louisiana oil rig and pronounced no word to the sisters even for the funerals.

Smoker reversed the truck from her driveway.

"You think bikers are tougher than fire?" he asked Andre.

"Tough ain't the question. Stupid is," Andre said.

"Let's hope this Bump is a lot of one and not much of the other," Smoker replied.

"You could drop me at home," Reynolds shouted from the truck bed.

Smoker opened the back slider. "Not yet."

At the trailer court, the biker's porch light glowed. Smoker dropped from the truck cab and clubbed the front door. Bump Rasker opened it.

Smoker put the gun muzzle to his forehead.

"I ain't seen her, goddamnit."

Andre fished a gas can from behind the seat and soaked the skirting beneath the manufactured home. Smoker tossed him a matchbook.

"I'll call the law," the biker shouted.

12

"We brought us a lawyer." Smoker aimed his flashlight at Reynolds. "I guess we'll do as we please."

Bump approached the pickup bed. "You a real shyster?"

Reynolds nodded.

The biker scratched his goatee. "I got to tell?"

Under the streetlight, Reynolds appeared white and holy. "It seems prudent," the lawyer said.

"You won't burn me down?"

"Not if I'm satisfied with your answers," Smoker told him.

"Last I seen either Dede or the girl was three weeks at least. They was with Harold the Preacher and his whacked-out son."

"I recognize that Harold's name," Andre said.

"First I heard of them was when they knocked on the door."

Andre lit a match, which threw a watery light on the grass and low shrubs. "Seems to me a long way from answering my question."

"Give me a minute, goddamnit," Bump said. "They were hunting Peg."

"She's dead."

"I told them. But they kept around. They had cocaine and money, so I didn't argue."

"So how do we find them?" Smoker asked.

Bump shrugged. "I don't know. The boy's drugs dried up and so did his money, but he claimed he had more. Harold read his good book and watched TV news the whole time. Drank a beer or two but didn't put out spending money or partake in the cocaine. Dede decided to follow the son and took the kid. I wasn't invited."

"You're not telling me anything useful," Smoker said.

Bump eyed Reynolds.

"In Spokane. A place off Wellesley. Heroy, I think. Twenty something's the address."

"How do you come to know this?"

"Dede wanted her unemployment forwarded."

"He spilled it all, you think?" Smoker asked Reynolds.

Reynolds said he sounded genuine.

Andre extinguished the match and pocketed the rest.

They returned to the tavern where Eddie phoned Reynolds's wife.

When Reynolds's wife arrived, she wore white, which left her tanned skin darker. She was fully aware of the effect. Her short hair was practical. She did little with it, maybe because she wasn't required to. Reynolds kissed her hand like a sailor long at sea might. She laughed. A man could go a hundred years without hearing a sound so pleasant.

Smoker and Andre watched their lights go. A grassy strip lay between the curb and sidewalk. He walked to it and sat. The cool of the earth swirled around him like water. He wanted to slump into it and sleep. Smoker kicked him in the shin, hard. Andre rolled but Smoker booted him once more, then grabbed Desdemona and lobbed her at him. The dog yipped and her claws drew blood through Andre's shirt. Smoker dodged backward but Andre caught his shoulder and thrust him to the pavement.

Smoker glared up at him. Andre punched his belly.

"That hurt?" Andre asked.

"Not as much as you want it to."

Andre rose and kicked Smoker between the shoulders.

Smoker grunted. "Want to go for a ride?" he asked.

"Sure, why in hell not?" Andre replied.

Smoker navigated the truck through Grand Coulee's Main Street. The place was a coupling of Colville Confederated Indians, construction men hard-hatting at the dam, and locals between jobs or disability checks. The coulee towns lost a kid every other year to poor driving and poorer drinking. The high school had exhausted athletic fields to name for them, so the last funeral paved the student parking lot.

They crossed the lit dam's mile span then steered for a road few remembered existed. The truck wound between the riprap, stones bigger than the vehicle. Andre felt like a child in a dream of dinosaurs. Farther, a boneyard retired the contractors' ten-foot cable spools, bent and rusted crane booms, and a scrapped loader minus tires, the Bureau emblem barely visible on the door. Another hundred yards, fifteen years of Christmas trees lay against an ancient retaining wall, their dead needles still piped with tinsel.

Smoker maneuvered them along a wide trail to an abandoned park on the water. The government had let the place go after the third powerhouse. Water-blackened pylons held a log boom the drawdowns had stacked against a half-sunk swimming dock. Smoker and Andre listened to the water lap the park's pebbled beach.

"You ain't Jesus Christ, you know," Smoker said.

Twenty feet upriver, a deadheaded tree lay sideways in the sand, its dry roots spread like a gray star against the water's darkness. Andre chucked a stone at it and missed. Smoker tried with the same result. Andre lobbed another, closer.

"You got to turn everything around, don't you?" Andre said.

Smoker sorted through a handful of gravel for the rocks that would fly best. He hit the deadhead on the bounce.

"Don't count," Andre told him.

"I know it," Smoker said. He threw another, shorter still.

Andre plunked it his next try. Smoker emptied his hands.

"You'd have found someone else to drive the nails," Smoker said.

"You saved me looking."

Smoker lit two cigarettes and offered Andre one. Smoker exhaled. The smoke broke up around him. He was quiet awhile.

"Zebra can't change its stripes, can it?" Andre said.

"Don't make it right," Smoker replied.

"No," Andre said. "But it keeps it from being a surprise."

A typical summer haze, wheat-harvest chaff and dirt trucks and combines in the fields smeared the halved moon. Its light winked in the reservoir waves.

"Don't change the matter at hand," Smoker said. "I can't leave Bird in the wind. Dede alone, I'd not ask."

Andre nodded.

"But this lunatic is religious to boot."

"That's troubling," Andre agreed. Lately religions had become unruly. Most had organized into megachurches where hucksters suckled from the masses' fears and otherwise normal people crowded into warehouses to shut their eyes and lift their quaking hands toward heaven as if their football team had just scored a touchdown. At the other end of the trough, a north Idaho sect was rumored to have eaten a wayward cross-country runner a few summers ago.

Andre listened to the wind press the reservoir waves into the bank.

"What do you want?" he asked.

"Need," Smoker said.

"Need, then."

"Someone to ride shotgun."

"What else?"

"Money. Couple thousand probably." Smoker lit a cigarette. "I won't pay it back." He dragged from his smoke. "Even if I scraped that much together, I mean, something will keep me from getting it from me to you."

"That ain't news."

"I'm tired of lying to you."

"Maybe you ought to keep the truth easier to tell," Andre told him.

Before light, Andre woke to eggs snapping on his stovetop. His head ached from the whiskey and too little sleep. The coffee had already perked when he discovered Claire at his stove at a quarter to four.

"Bacon's in the oven," she said.

"Smoker has visited you."

She leveled her gaze at him from the stove. Andre sipped his coffee. She brewed it better than he could, though they had employed the same blend and kettle.

"You corrupted my lawyer," Claire said.

"Only a little."

"I told him you had a stubborn streak."

She carried the pan to the table and slid two basted eggs onto his plate. "Can you get the bacon?"

Andre retrieved it with an oven mitt. He set two strips on his plate and left her the same.

"It doesn't make any kind of sense," Claire said.

"Keeping married?"

She nodded.

"You got prospects?"

"No," she replied.

He drank his coffee.

"Do you see us together somewhere ahead?" Claire asked.

Andre peered into his cup.

"That would require too much, wouldn't it?" Claire said.

"Too much?"

"I don't know. Forgiveness. Optimism. Faith."

"All words I can't comprehend, you figure."

Her brown eyes reflected the light, and the breakfast grease made her skin shine. "I don't want to fight."

"But you want to put me in the skillet then blame me for cooking."

"No," she said. Andre thought she might cry and if she did maybe he would, too, and if that happened, this moment might be the one to lift them past history, both recent and ancient. He heard the clock; waiting had become his lot and the rest was just supposing. He finished his coffee and Claire refilled the cup then poured more for herself. She sipped it then set the cup down and blew on the surface.

"Don't let Smoker twist you into something you don't want to do," she said.

"There's a child involved. My niece, in particular," Andre replied.

"That child's in trouble whether Dede or Smoker raises her."

"You don't know that."

"Anyone with eyes knows it," Claire said. She sighed. "Look at you."

"I had a chance once."

Claire surveyed their plates. "She's not your daughter."

"Child don't need to belong to you to require your help," Andre said. "I'd thought you might have considered that."

Claire winced. "That is a mean thing to say."

"It is," Andre agreed.

"I suppose I deserve whatever hurt you mete out." Claire rose and dumped her coffee in the sink then rinsed the cup. "I don't guess there's anything I can do to talk you out of it."

"I been trying to talk myself out of it all night," Andre said. "Part of me isn't listening."

"You need anything? I have some money."

"No, I got enough. Smoker tell you different?"

"No," she said. "He never told me as much as you thought."

"Wasn't about that, was it? Telling, I mean."

"It wasn't about that, no," she said.

Andre nodded. "Have Reynolds make another paper. I'll sign it if that's what you want."

A passing car's light stretched their shadows on the wall. In it, Claire's tight jaw and the tired corners of her mouth came clear then the light slid from her and she became the yellow of old paper. She bent and kissed his forehead.

LAMENTATIONS

September–December 1983

Andre met Claire when he was, of all things, sober. She accepted a teaching position in the middle school adjacent to the high school where Andre taught math. Her first day, she lurched into him in the yearly orientation. On her binder spine she'd scrawled her name. He had never known a female with such poor handwriting.

Their classrooms were opposite each other, and early on she inquired about attendance reports and lunch-money accounting. October, they sorted through a playground row together. At lunch that afternoon, Claire sat at Andre's table and attempted a conversation. Behind her, in a long window, was Andre's reflection: He was a homely man; it left him little to say. He lumbered through his life's social burdens as someone might morning traffic, acknowledging the red and green lights and free right turns, distracted and polite. Occasionally, though, Claire observed students enter Andre's classroom after the last bell, sometimes in pairs or groups of three. They conversed about personal concerns: parents who hollered too much, boyfriends too needy or inattentive. He countered with pragmatic suggestions they thought wise or comic but avoided judgments, which put them at ease. The other teachers knew Andre as broken; to his students, however, his wounds were noble and his suffering added gravity and comfort to his advice.

Faculty meetings, Andre tarried until Claire entered the room and then hunted a seat behind or across from her. Making notes, she employed a pencil but didn't erase, instead slashed through words and scribbled on. She whispered as she perused handouts, a habit common to reading teachers. Her high cheekbones and narrow jaw pinched her mouth in a pretty way when she spoke and her nose remained out of matters, which was the best that could be said of a nose. Her chestnut hair was cut to her shoulders. It curled when she rose early enough to use an iron and lay straight when she did not. She was appealing either way; Andre longed to say so and save her the trouble.

Nights when he'd climbed far enough into the bag, Andre

would press his hands together as if in prayer, then undo them until his palms separated and he could conjure her face between. He had encountered prettier women, but none that made him ache so clearly for a life other than his own.

After the time change, the evenings grayed early and, from a quarter mile behind, distance enough to argue denial or coincidence, Andre began to trail Claire to her duplex two hills behind the school. She marked themes while she hiked the incline, chewing a red pencil between notes, and didn't divert her attention, even while she unlocked her door.

Soon, despite cold winds or spitting snow, Andre lingered in an alley's shadows where he could view Claire's front window. Evenings she often halted before the glass to gaze at passing cars or her neighbors exercising their terrier. She typically changed to a T-shirt and sweat pants. Her hands clawed her hair like she'd had a nap or been stirred from a book. Seeing her embarrassed him and he pitched his eyes away, down the hill where the house roofs below collided geometries.

A month into his vigil, he unwrapped a meat-loaf sandwich for his dinner and ate, comfortable, until Claire gulley-whomped him from behind with a two-foot icicle. His stunned skull sang like a tuning fork as Claire's soap smell passed, so simple it seemed impossible. He lay bleeding until police tumblers approached. A cop's flashlight wand striped the dumpster where he'd taken refuge. Andre stood and hoisted his hands.

"What are you surrendering over?" the cop asked. His name was Marcus Popp and he was two years behind Andre in high school. Answering to him seemed one more injustice.

"You decide," Andre said.

The cop wagged his light at Andre's cleft scalp. "You know the woman in that building?"

"Yes."

"You going to have a go at me?" the cop asked.

A minor tavern legend to regulars, in a scrap Andre accepted blows without regard and offered his own until he grew too tired to lift his hands. Recently, he'd pinned an ironworker's ears to his skull with a stapler. While the man attempted to claw the staples out, Andre splattered his nose and uprooted his front teeth with the handle. The honyocker was new to town. No one local or sober had tried Andre for years.

"I'm inclined not to."

"Okay," the cop said. By then Claire had pulled open her door. Oily light from inside spread across the snow-blanched yard. She proceeded in slippers toward them.

"You," she said.

Andre nodded.

"You deserved to be hit."

"I know it."

The cop didn't move. He was enjoying himself.

Claire's brow creased and she blinked. The blood bank took a pint and Andre guessed he'd leaked nothing less. It warmed his cheek but froze in his hair.

"I did that?"

Andre shrugged. "Head wound," he said. "They always bleed worse than they are."

———

The cop signed Andre in at the hospital emergency desk then suggested he review his manners. He saw no need to cuff him or offer him Miranda. Andre had not even made a successful crime of it, which demoralized him further.

Despite much study, Andre had not acquired the element most necessary for romance in this world: the capacity to appear detached in the tragic and compelling manner that presses a woman to discover why. Instead, women saw Andre as plain country, a flat lot on a town road, like any other. An abundance of heart and a scarcity of self-regard served him poorly, but a man suffering such who hadn't swallowed a gun barrel was likely not just dirt and rock and scrub.

An hour later the doctor knit Andre's eyebrow with fifteen stitches then sheared half his scalp so he could add twenty more. Andre listened to the scissors snip and contemplated the four miles home. He could phone Smoker but only after assembling a tale that justified his injuries. He'd narrowed the possibilities to brawling Californians or a slow-moving four-by-four on the icy streets by the time the hospital released him and he found the exit. Local urchins had shot out the parking-lot lights with pellet guns so Andre didn't recognize Claire's approach until she was too close for escape.

"Should I be flattered?" Claire asked him. "Or were you just in it for an eyeful?"

"I hope you're not armed," Andre replied.

She reversed her jeans pockets to demonstrate she was no danger. But there was still the jacket so Andre steadied his feet and loped for town. Twenty yards and the frozen sidewalk spilled him to all fours. Claire's hand hooked his elbow and steered him up.

"I'll see you home," she said.

In her car, Andre pointed toward the trailer court, but Claire traveled another direction and parked at a Stop-N-Go. Inside, she bought tall coffees, which left Andre the prospect of bearing his embarrassment both awake and sober.

Claire dipped her face into her cup, while Andre waited for the cream to cool his own.

"Our first date," she said.

"This isn't a date," he told her.

"Why not?"

"Because if it was I'd be worried about getting kissed at the end."

Claire arched her eyebrow, then bent across the emergency brake; their lips clobbered bluntly and Andre lost a good share of his coffee in his lap. Scalded, he gasped and his legs straightened, which scuffed his scalp against the roof. He put his hand to the wounds, but the stitches seemed to hold.

Claire retreated to her seat. She tipped herself over the steering wheel and her hands latched her knees. A long hair clung to her ring finger; the other end twisted in the heater's exhaust. Light through the window flickered in the strand. Andre extended his finger to touch it. Claire hurried her hand away then changed horses and plunked it in his.

"I'm sorry," Andre said. "I'm not accustomed."

"Me neither," Claire told him. "Please, don't think I am."

Claire fit a straw through her coffee top. The radio played a commercial, though Andre couldn't make out what for.

"I never saw you close to naked," he said.

Claire gazed out the windshield. The market lights made the snow more starry than the sky.

"I went home early. Before eight always."

"You scared me is all." Claire unjoined their hands and stroked a finger on his split hairline. He winced.

"I used to pinch my brothers until they'd bleed," she said quietly. "I guess I have a mean streak." She returned her hand to the shifter ball. Her fingers tapped the enamel. He wanted them to doctor him.

"You spied on me in school," she said.

"I guess I'm none too sly."

"Someone else pointed it out to me. Stack." Stack Edwards was in charge of PE and wore T-shirts, even in winter. Andre hadn't seen them as much as sit together.

Claire took Andre's hand in hers then raised them both.

"He didn't like public displays of affection."

Their coffee depleted, Andre excused himself to refill the cups. A Williams girl tended the till; she had a gabby bent and the line went three deep, and when Andre returned, Claire's eyes were closed and her head rested on the window. The temperature had dropped near zero, a hard freeze that would require ranchers like his father to ax creek beds to water stock.

A yellow mongrel crept from beneath the streetlight; her steps rasped the still air like a sawyer's saw. She paused to sniff an empty can and her ribs fluttered. For a moment she eyed Andre, then vanished in the dark. Andre perched the coffees on the car top. Back in the grocery, he paid for a handful of jerky then fished five straps from the jar. He exited through the back door and sat on the concrete steps.

Outside, Andre regarded the highway from the coulee out. He'd traveled it a hundred times, if once. College returning home, Highway 2, first, you hit the air force base, then Reardan, then the Lincoln county seat of Davenport, then Creston in the scablands. Andre recalled seventh-grade basketball, a balcony extended over one of their gymnasium's corners, where the Creston team would force the ball out of bounds then blanket the inbounder with their tallest player. Opponents had to bounce a pass between his legs or risk the balcony. Eight miles later, Wilbur, and more wheat country, million-dollar land. From Wilbur, you divert for the coulee through more wheat until the highway descended into the rocks. Once an Ice Age glacial dam near Clark Fork stopped a Montana full of water. A thaw blasted the country into a mile-wide gutter. The place looks ravaged by giants.

The highway drops and the coulee walls rise and the sky becomes just a block of blue. Then you see the river, the reservoir, and farther, a mass of concrete that backs the Columbia into Canada.

The dog whimpered in the shadows then squatted and leapt for the open dumpster. Her claws scraped the metal. The sound doubled in the cold stillness. Andre skidded a jerky piece across the frozen lot. The dog halted. She inched herself to the meat, sniffed then ate; he offered her more, each closer until she arrived at his feet. Andre held out his hands and she licked them clean. A piece of him knew Claire would be asleep in the warmed car when he returned and it would be as if he'd never left her, while another remained certain she would be absent and whatever had happened between them had not.

Claire awoke an hour later, Andre's shoulder pillowing her cheek; her mouth wet a line on his sleeve.

"Your coffee's bad," he told her. "You want more?"

Claire shook her head. "It keeps me awake, as you can tell." She yawned. "Do you see anyone?"

"Just the doctor there when I'm down with something."

"To date, I mean."

Andre didn't reply. Finally he piled the two empty cups on the floor into his own then stuffed them with the napkins that remained.

"You do," Claire said.

"What?"

"See someone."

Andre laughed. Claire wrapped herself in the arms of her jacket.

"Why are you cleaning my car, if not to go?"

Andre stopped.

"I told him to shove off because of you. Stack, I mean," Claire said.

She dipped her shoulders under her coat then offered her hand to shake and make an end of it. Andre took it. Her skin was as smooth as when he first touched it and his as thick. Her words were all he'd had of a woman's voice outside grocery checkers and barmaids in two years, and the kiss his first not inflicted by alcohol or mistletoe since high school. The wadded napkins had unfolded inside the cup like petals on a flower, their slumping middle soaked with the dregs. He undid one and let it float to the carpet then another until she joined him, laughing, and soon the floor was cluttered with their mess and more when they rummaged scraps from the glove box and under the seats.

After a time, Andre returned once more to the market for fresh coffee. In the bathroom, he twisted the water to hot, then clamped his eyes shut and scoured his face with powdered soap and stared into the mirror over the sink. Once, in high school, he had scored eighteen points in a basketball playoff, yet near the game's end stood at the free throw line, certain he would miss. In the second before he directed the shot forward and watched it careen off the rim, everything came clear and he understood that he'd arrived at the boundary of himself and would progress no further.

The back door was next to the restrooms and he employed it again after swapping the two coffees for a six-pack of stout.

Outside, the dog looked at him woefully. Andre opened a beer and ignored her. He filled his pockets with the others then lit out across a field for a road that led to another that led to his trailer and the whiskey there.

GENESIS

October 1941–November 1950

Neither Andre nor Smoker had access enough to their mother's history to determine where the conflagration she was began. And she was as confounded as the boys.

As a child, summers, Peg spent many days with her mother's aunt. In a small house overlooking the dam, her great-aunt baked or steamed or braised exotic foods for her neighbors just to satisfy her curious palate. All hours, she maintained a picnic table lined with meals and quantities a business concern would envy. She had cut back the lawn to construct a series of gardens, which held leeks, cabbage, jicama, radicchio, peppers, legumes, squashes of many kinds, turnips, yams, carrots, radishes, onions, chives, endive, dill, sage, turmeric, fennel, and marjoram. Peach and apricot trees shaded carrots in rows and a potato patch. Each summer evening with an

air rifle she plunked the raccoons that ventured up the cliff's twilight to rob her. She reared chickens in a roost on a fenced side
lot and two goats for cheese and fried kid. She had tried sheep
awhile and a Guernsey but could not hush them enough for the
neighbors.

As a toddler, Peg pulled weeds for quarters and when she wanted
to ride the carnival coasters. Perhaps, if she had lasted longer, she
may have kept Peg sorted out, but she died from a brain aneurism
before Peg enrolled in first grade.

By then Peg's first-blood aunts had scattered like dandelion
hair under a hard breath: Bernie, the oldest, into three short-lived
marriages and, finally, the low-level political toil in which widows
and intellectual divorcées engage to remain of consequence. She
once said men were far more satisfying as well-dressed ideas than
hairy-legged chimps with no pants.

Martha, the youngest, as dramatic as Bernie was aloof, her
mouth a lipstick smear and her mascara-penciled eyebrows wings
in flight over smoky gray eyes, burned through her days like a
prairie fire with a tailwind. She clipped flowers and put them in
her hair and donned loud-print blouses and frightened everyone
but her children, whom in summers she deposited with her mother
for the season. Peg's father would permit her to camp with them
under the stars where they smoked and hyperventilated and sniffed
model glue from paper bags.

Together, the sisters were open wounds and Peg's father, born
in the middle, would flit from one end of the yard to the other at
family gatherings, like a bee trying to pollinate warmth between
the two. Their hard feelings troubled him more than either of the
principals, who counted their anger as only another fact in the
world and saw nothing lost in saying so.

Peg had a series of uncles, as well, though none were blood: mechanics and construction cohorts of her father without children of their own to stir or coddle. Edgar, her father's best friend since grade school, was an orphan. He collected Peg three times a week after dance classes when her parents were otherwise occupied. Peg was a beauty already and aware of it. But when she flirted with him, as prepubescent girls will do, he simply offered her a Tootsie Pop and tuned the radio and sang in falsetto to Frankie Valli, all of which struck Peg as strange as most of her father's friends leered at her from behind beer bottles and harassed her with Indian burns and tickling if her parents left the room. She prepared for such visits by stuffing her blouse and underwear with toilet paper. As a last resort she pissed her pants and hurried off to change.

Another uncle, Quantrill, limped as if tipped forward into an ever-present wind, due to a bullet Owen the Cop planted into his spine years before. The month following the shooting, the doctors expected Quantrill to die, then, after he was out of the woods, to remain wheelchair-bound. But fishing season Quantrill hobbled to Osborn Bay and cast in a line. Two hours later he'd landed a stringer of crappie.

By then he was out of surprises, though. Using a shovel was impossible and driving heavy equipment for more than ten minutes numbed his legs so he couldn't operate pedals. He was a skilled engineer and accepted occasional state survey contracts, but smoked and drank coffee on his house's covered porch mostly, alternating between two chairs and a swing to remain comfortable. He once attempted to coax Peg to jerk him off, but she found his hairy fist of balls and dick humorous and laughed, and he quickly zipped his canvas trousers and neither the subject nor his loins were raised again.

When Peg was eight, a neighbor woman hired Quantrill to paint her living room. Quantrill delivered Peg a brush and paint-filled coffee can, told her to go at the walls, then left for the tavern. Peg coated anything within reach. The woman lit into her but Quantrill claimed she was just being thorough. Quantrill did not appreciate argument. The next weekend, Peg found him by the fire pit in his back lot. Next to him was a matchbook and a heavy family Bible. He snapped a stick on a stone edge, watched it light, and then tossed the match into the pit. It died at the hole's bottom. Quantrill ripped several pages from the Bible and sailed them into the pit, then struck another match. It caught. The pages yellowed with heat and released granite-colored smoke. Quantrill added more then tugged his lower lip like he was figuring. The flame burned low. He wadded several pages into a ball and tossed it at the coals.

"This book, it means something to that woman," Quantrill explained. He tore another page. "Burning it means something, too."

Quantrill arranged kindling sticks over the blaze and, when it pinked to coals, added a quartered tamarack. His skin appeared to soften as morning lifted. He set a grate over the fire and a skillet on it then added two ropes of sausage and scrambled the better part of a dozen eggs, then divided them onto paper plates and they drank orange juice from the carton and they breakfasted like gladiators.

On the other hand, Peg's parents' home appeared to possess a stability many of her peers' lacked. The police only visited to inquire concerning Quantrill's whereabouts. Her father drank occasionally and her mother not at all. Alcohol made her violently ill. The two spoke to each other civilly and when they disagreed didn't empty the cabinets or clobber one another with frozen hams or ketchup bottles. Her mother grew petunias and dug weeds because the neighbors expected it. Her father rose at the hour the auto parts manager demanded and returned when the man turned him loose. He derived his most pleasure Saturday mornings, when, in jeans and a plain T-shirt, he tugged at bolts and hunted sticky lifters or bleeding gaskets under the hood of his '41 Mercury Straight Eight. Several times locals offered twice what it booked and once a collector put up a '45 Chevy and a '38 Pontiac Streak to no avail.

When Peg was nine, her father fell from a ladder. With no insurance, he was compelled to sell the car to Quantrill, who let it sit in his driveway. Her father, though, walked the ten blocks separating their houses and ratcheted the braces and nursed the water or fuel pump just like he still possessed it. It was the history he could not face: the parts missing, the misfiring motor of his life.

By fifth grade, though, Peg either rained vitriol and blows on any adult or child who twisted her tail or stewed at her desk and piled bilious clouds in her mind in order to do so. She was mean weather, not a misguided urchin. Her teachers, good women, attempted to coax potential from her. She loathed the word. She'd rather be called an elephant, rather *be* an elephant—then she'd only have to pack weight, which was not nearly as bulky as other people's convictions.

The principal resorted to a retired crone who isolated Peg inside a tiny room for special-ed kids. The woman hissed and plunked Peg's ear with a ruler whenever she lifted her gaze from her worksheets. "I've set straight the likes of you many times, dear," the woman told her.

The second day Peg sniffed at the woman when she neared her desk.

"What," the woman said.

"I smell something spoiled," Peg told her.

"You smell nothing of the kind."

That evening Peg rustled half a dozen bad eggs from her uncle's refrigerator. She hid two in an unused desk.

"It's you," Peg told her. "You smell like female problems."

"I do not." The woman huffed, but any time she approached, Peg grimaced. The woman spent twenty minutes searching the room for odors.

After class, Peg added two more eggs to the radiator vents. Next morning, the woman lined an air freshener and two cans of Lysol on her desk. Peg twisted the thermostat to high.

"Don't you bathe?" Peg asked the woman.

"You just keep to yourself," the crone replied, but the authority in her had departed. The next morning she arrived in disarray and applied her lipstick skittishly in front of the coatroom mirror, then rearranged her gray hair and bobby-pinned it in place, but it fell apart before she crossed the room. Peg walked to the board. DOUCHE, she wrote in perfect capital letters.

The woman scurried from the room. Through a window, Peg

saw her enter her car and drive from the parking lot. Peg collected the eggs and threw them into the back lot. An hour later the principal escorted her to her regular classroom.

That evening, after an hour detention, the high-school sports bus delivered her home. An overcast sky drizzled. Peg traversed the damp lawn to her family's front porch and shook herself dry. In the big window, she recognized her parents' heads. Her father nursed a beer and nodded with the TV news. Her mother scratched at a crossword puzzle. They were accustomed to Peg's late returns and teacher's notes and principal's phone calls.

The end of the light leaked from the sky. Inside, her parents and the room grew yellow and warm in the house lights. Her father extended his arm across the recliner arm and held her mother's hand, his thumb circling the tiny bones in her mother's wrist. Peg locked one hand upon the other and searched out the same places, but finding them, felt nothing.

The television anchorman talked but from outside he was just a huge, understanding face she couldn't hear. Her parents' hands remained joined and Peg recognized, with the kind of sudden intuition children possess, that her parents, unlike the newsman, were genuine and ordinary, a thing to be proud of compared to a man in makeup reading news at a camera. They aspired nothing past tending each other's needs and looking after her. Peg knew, if she decided to, she could come through the door and crawl into her father's recliner and he would loop an arm over her so she could burrow into him and be less separate. And her mother would scurry into the kitchen and fetch her a meal with a glass of milk. Peg would devour the food while they peppered her with questions about her day and she would have a different life, one with quiet and holding hands. It was not some promised land a desert and forty years off. All it required was to twist the knob and lean on the door. Part of her wanted to be warmed and fed by these good people. They were strangers, yes, but everyone was a stranger to everyone else. Her mother and father didn't intend their strangeness toward her nor she to them and perhaps faith and goodwill could wear a path to each other.

Peg remained on the porch a long while. Her parents' hands separated. Her mother set out the TV trays and delivered silverware and salt and pepper to her father, then a plate full of roast and potatoes and carrots in gravy. Then she did for herself. They ate carefully, as if eating mattered, and it did; everything mattered for them: the garden, the carburetor float, the silverware in order, and the end wrenches lined accurately in the shop cabinet. And Peg, she mattered as well, most of all, maybe. Each night, separately or together, her parents entered her room after they thought she was asleep. They straightened the dresser drawers, lined underwear and socks in one, blouses in another, T-shirts and pajamas in another yet. They organized her disheveled knick-knacks on shelves her father had constructed and tested monthly for level. They repeated the behavior like prayer. And like prayer it was as much for them as for her, Peg knew.

She circled to the backyard and smoked a cigarette. The neighbors' tabby cat leaped from the slatted fence and approached. It rubbed her legs and purred. Peg scratched it and the cat tipped its nose to the sky with a look past joy—not ecstasy, she knew about that from Quantrill's stag films—it was, she decided, certainty. The animal was happy and before or after did not penetrate now.

Peg backhanded the cat and watched it roll then scramble to its feet and examine her, blinking. Then it trod forward and again wound through Peg's ankles. That was what hope looked like. Peg petted the cat for half an hour until a noise inside startled the animal and it bolted for the fence and home.

Peg checked the kitchen from the back window. Her mother had lined the dishes to dry in the Rubbermaid rack and retreated to the living room. Peg carefully inched open the back slider and descended the stairs to her room in the basement, where she turned the music up and leafed through a *Cosmopolitan*. Above she heard her parents' footsteps and felt their worry and it didn't much concern her.

2

EXODUS

August 1991

Smoker had mounted his hunting camper onto the pickup bed. The roof was patched with tar twice a year and the tin seams resealed a dozen times. Inside, it stank of mold and male sweat and fried meat. In the cabinets were boxes of stale cookies and soda crackers. Rivets in the walls kept the plywood paneling from splitting. Andre added his ditty bag to the mess.

"Where's your gun?" Smoker asked him.

Andre patted the pistol under his jacket.

"The rifle, I mean."

"I'll require a rifle?"

Smoker walked into Andre's apartment and returned with Andre's Model 70 and a shell box. He slid them behind the seat.

"It'll be a concealed weapon now," Andre said.

"Good thing it's hid, then."

Past town, Andre tuned the radio to an old country station that played Conway Twitty then Sammi Smith. Smoker switched it to news.

"You don't want to do that," Andre said, though his eyes were closed.

"Thought you were asleep."

"I sound asleep?"

Smoker drove on. He guided the wheel with his right hand and, with the thumb and forefinger of his left, tapped a rhythm audible only in his head. He'd always trusted intuition and instinct and dumb luck, the latter of which he seemed to possess in heaps.

"What happens when we find her?" Andre asked.

"We bring her home."

"To what?"

"I know how to take care of her," Smoker told him.

Andre drank his lukewarm coffee. "Why'd you lose her then?"

"Her mother is responsible."

Andre chuckled. Smoker stayed quiet.

"You want Bird back because she's yours," Andre said. "You ought to want to look after her and if you can't you should hunt for someone who will."

"You don't know. Having children changes you," Smoker said.

"I don't believe it's changed you at all."

Smoker remained quiet a long while.

"I'm going to change," he said. "Once we get her home. Remember when she was a baby. I hauled her everywhere with me."

"Same can be said about a puppy," Andre replied.

Smoker declined to argue more. Men are homeless in this world, Andre thought. Bibles and legends try to make them into heroes but their repetition just emphasizes a man's impermanence. Last names, most times that's all a man leaves. Women, on the other hand, are steady as earth. A woman, her home is inside her. Wherever Smoker lit was separate from who he was and where he wanted to be. It's why he kept moving, Andre realized. His biggest fear was being found out, especially by himself.

Andre uncapped Smoker's thermos and freshened his coffee. Above the coulee, the brothers watched the sky come up on the wheat flats. Farmers loaded grain into semis, their cargo worth more than some houses. Stubbled wheat traced the arc of the seed drills that planted it, waiting to be burned or plowed for next year's crop.

Highway 2 sped them through little towns, each with a grocery, a tavern for the hands, a bank for the farmers, a crosswalk and a school with a basketball team to argue over, along with gas, which everyone needed so the price was a dollar higher than in cities.

"I always thought I was better than you," Andre said.

"Don't be too hard on yourself," Smoker replied. "You set your sights mighty high."

An hour later, the freeway dropped over Sunset Hill toward the city of Spokane. Maple was the first downtown exit and Smoker signaled for it. They crossed the toll bridge and paid a quarter in the basket. Andre pointed at the far bank. "That's a big damned dog."

Smoker replied, "That's a bear."

Sirens approached and three police cruisers, lights tumbling, rushed over the bridge the opposite direction.

"They might know shoplifters but they got bears wrong," Smoker said.

"How's that, Wild Kingdom?"

"Bears don't like heights," Smoker said.

"They climb trees."

"Because they got something to hang on to. I can't imagine why he'd try a bridge once, but he ain't doubling back."

Smoker directed the truck onto a gravel service road that switched back twice then stopped where the bank bent steep as a blade. Their boot edges skidded as they scrambled the incline and clawed at weeds and rocks to avert falling. At the riverbank, basalt blocks, mossy from the falls' spray, formed a shelf that led to the water. Andre whacked an ankle and hobbled behind Smoker, who loped toward a locust copse. Halfway up one of the trees, a yearling black bear stared at them. The cops' blue lights lit a park on the river's other side where they searched the arcade and food trucks.

A wind gust bent the gaunt tree. The bear scrambled for balance.

"Stay put," Smoker said.

"Me or the bear."

"Just watch him," Smoker said.

Smoker hiked from the canyon, ten minutes later reappearing with a picnic ham, his rifle, a skinning knife, and a hundred feet of nylon rope. Smoker sawed a tunnel under the ham bone, strung one rope end through, and knotted the loop. He lobbed the ham at the bear and missed. The bear sniffed. Smoker tried again but threw low.

"Quit throwing like a girl," Andre said.

Smoker handed Andre the ham. "Jim Thorpe it up there then."

Andre clocked the bear in the head. It roared and batted the air. Andre flung the rope again and once more clouted the bear. It clung tighter to the tree.

Smoker demanded the rope back.

"Go over that way a little and hoot," he ordered Andre.

"What?"

"Hoot," Smoker said.

"Distract him, you mean?"

"Hoot. Maybe it'll remind him he ain't an owl."

"He forgot and flapped up there, you figure?"

Andre circled the tree toward the river. He cupped his hands and called. After a while, the bear gazed at him, querulous. Smoker sneaked closer and tossed the ham over a near branch. Andre slowly replaced himself next to Smoker. The bear's eyes tracked him. When the rope entered the animal's sightline, Smoker tugged enough to rattle the leaves. The ham moved and the bear sniffed it and leaned forward. Smoker jerked the rope again. The bear tipped then tumbled from the tree. The ham landed nearby and the bear bit into it. Smoker tugged the meat from his mouth. It bellowed. Smoker shoved the rope at Andre then scurried ahead.

"Lead him."

Andre ascended slowly, not interested in antagonizing the animal.

"Don't let him catch hold of the food," Smoker hollered.

"Better it than me," Andre replied.

Smoker hurried farther up then traversed the steepest grade on all fours much like the bear might have. He extended his hand for the rope. Andre threw it to him and followed, as did the bear, which managed better traction than the two men. It encircled both paws around the ham and nearly took Smoker off his feet. Smoker yanked back and tore the meat from the bear's embrace. It sniffed again. Its rib bones expanded, then faded under its loose skin. It rocked its woolly head. Wind rattled and clacked the ditch weeds. Above, passing cars sounded like the ocean in a seashell. The bear reversed himself for the river. Smoker poked his fingers between his lips and whistled. The bear's ears pricked. It plopped down, breathing heavy.

Smoker unholstered the revolver looped onto his belt. "I was hoping to lead him to the rig and save us dragging."

A few feet beneath him on the hill, Andre stood between the two. "You aren't going to shoot this bear."

"Them cops give him better odds?" Smoker asked. "Besides, I ain't slew a bear in three years."

Smoker drew from a cigarette and exhaled. Andre scooted the meat down the grade to the bear. The bear flopped the ham, then rolled to his side and licked the salty fat.

"We could haul him," Andre told him.

Smoker laughed.

"In the camper. Fool him up there just like we were doing."

"He'd tear it up and us with it."

Andre shook his head. "We'd keep him in feed. He'd just eat and shit and sleep."

The bear ripped some meat from the bone and rolled like a dog.

Smoker blew a breath into the sky. "I didn't set out to rescue no bear."

"You're the one steered the rig here."

"I was just hoping for a little amusement."

"Well, I ain't leaving that bear for them to shoot and I ain't allowing you to shoot him. That don't leave much."

"Jesus," Smoker said. "You think we ought to get him laid, too?"

LAMENTATIONS

December 1983–February 1984

Before she accepted her teaching position, Claire had researched the coulee environs. The town bordered a reservation. Unlike the surrounding communities, whose economic and social lives orbited wheat ranches, steady for more than a hundred years, Grand Coulee was a construction town. Erected to build the great dam, the place boomed and busted depending on the whims of government contracts. The uncertainty transformed crisis into the commonplace, so much so most of the residents mounted little energy to deter it. Between jobs, they subsisted on one another's generosity until they themselves found work and turned benefactors.

The other portion worked the dam or union somewhere or taught school or served as bank employees or linemen or read meters with county utilities. They escaped the chaos by avoiding those who had not.

The reservation, though, she'd had no notion what to expect. Her exposure to things Indian ranged from a grade-school book report on Chief Joseph to a Monument Valley vacation, where she bought a Hopi blanket. What surprised her most was the little difference the reservation seemed to make. She heard nothing of police profiling. No one noted interracial dating.

The tribe, twelve tribes mashed together for practicality by the government on one reservation loosely governed by the Bureau of Indian Affairs, operated a pole plant and attempted to market a uranium mine at Mount Tolman until the details gummed the bureaucracy gears and the project collapsed.

Many did well. They managed ranches and hired neighbors, some the best cowboys in the country, to work stock. Some rarely left the reservation except their four years of high school. They neither joined clubs nor played sports; they attended no school dances and found the bus home at the end of school every day as soon as possible. The girls, though, often turned into stars of powwows or rodeo queens; others looked after younger siblings.

Just as many ended up in the coulee. They played basketball, football, ran track. The boys were beautiful, she thought, dark complexions, sleek black hair. Others were blocks of stone, linemen, strong forwards, shot-putters. The girls were just as pretty and just as athletic. And meaner.

Andre was the exception who went to college and stuck. Many kids possessed the intellect, but though the coulee was not too far from the anchor of the reservation, most university towns were. Even Andre, who stuck out college four years, eventually returned.

The towns—Nespelem, Keller, Inchelium—were somber and occasionally dangerous. People recounted to her tavern killings initiated by slights that few would notice sober. But the reservation families, despite their troubles, kept one another stitched close.

Indian beer was Lucky Lager; white people laughed at it but drank it, too. Indian time was a standing joke. Indian kids habitually arrived tardy for class. Claire once inquired of a portly girl as to why. The girl told her she was talking to Sandra and the bell rang. Sandra hadn't finished. Should I leave her hanging for a bell? I don't know the bell. I know Sandra.

After a week, Claire visited Andre's classroom at the last bell to borrow construction paper. As for his exit from the market, she pretended it had not occurred. Most afternoons following, she feigned a need for commiseration or materials or advice.

A former student often joined him, as well. Carl, a senior, was applying to universities. The counselors had ignored him because he'd suffered mononucleosis freshman year and had to retake classes in summer school; his health still came and went so he only managed Bs in the make-up courses. He didn't sit for the SAT until fall as a senior. Andre had sprung for the fee. Carl missed only one math question and only half a dozen on the language portion. He made the paper and his school mail delivered applications from Harvard, MIT, and Caltech. The principal summoned him from class once a week to press him toward Stanford, but Carl didn't trust the sudden interest, so he enlisted Andre to collect recommendations and navigate his forms.

The boy carried bags at the Safeway, so he excused himself before four. Claire always found her way to Andre's classroom at a quarter till. At the end of the first week, after the boy exited she kissed Andre, then after each visit, the first few times on the cheek, then on his lips. Finally she asked him to dinner at her apartment, which turned into a habit. He didn't drink there and remained late enough that alcohol afterward made little sense. Soon he was seeing her every night and rarely drinking at all.

It was following one of these pleasant evenings that Andre's father, Pork, phoned him at half past two in the morning.

"You drunk?" Pork asked.

"I am not," Andre said.

Pork ignored him. "That Model 70? You got it still?"

"Sounds like you're mid-bender yourself," Andre said. "The gun's in the closet."

"Thought you might've pawned it." He paused. "You never could shoot much."

"If you called to insult me, you might've waited till it was light out."

"There a window faces the street in your place?"

"Bedroom does."

"Streetlights around?"

"One or two. You'd get caught stealing something."

"I don't intend any theft." Pork's end rattled as he rearranged the phone. "I'll set up under them lights then you go ahead and shoot me. Left is the heart, remember. My left not yours, goddamnit."

"Depends on how you're facing."

"I don't want to see it," Pork said. "I'll face away. West from your building."

"That's south."

"South?" Pork said.

"So where'll your heart be again?"

Pork spent a second calculating. Andre could hear him shift inside a phone booth. "I'm facing south now, looking at them blinking towers."

"From where?"

"Safeway parking lot. Across from that video place that won't sell pornos."

"You're looking east."

"Why the hell they call it Main South then."

"It ain't south of everywhere."

"Give me a minute," Pork said.

Andre listened to him light a cigarette and draw.

"Seems to me it don't matter what direction I'm faced."

"Sure as hell does. Bullet makes a bigger hole leaving than heading in."

"You mean facing you or looking away?"

"Both."

"I'm talking north-south. Compass-type."

"That, too," Andre told him.

"You're worse than a woman."

"Maybe. But I'm not going to shoot you no matter how early in the morning it is."

"I'm coming anyhow."

"You want me to make coffee?"

"I want you to shoot me, goddamnit."

"Why?"

"It's the civil thing to do."

Andre perked coffee anyway. Sleep now was out of the question. He marked math problems and examined the rows of hesitant, jotted numerals, attempts by his students to abandon calculations for hope. Unlike other math teachers, Andre refused to identify these as flaws of logic. Too many ways existed to conceive a thing and shape it into sense. He weighed only a capacity to create order on a piece of paper.

Outside, a taxi's brakes wheezed and Pork stepped into the streetlight's halo. He turned toward the apartments, not recalling where Andre resided. He raised his hands and sang out "Now, now, now."

The next morning, Andre phoned Smoker at Crazy Eddie's, the only number he consistently answered.

"Now he wants to be shot," Andre said.

"He should have called me," Smoker told him.

"That would have solved his problem, but then you'd have one."

"No court would convict as long as the jury knew Pork." The line went quiet while Smoker chewed some sausage. "We could hang him from a tree," Smoker said finally. "Save a bullet and the noise. Be like recycling."

"Might hurt the tree," Andre said.

"Find a big old bough and a soft hemp rope. None of that nylon shit. Tree will grow a hundred more rings and not be bothered."

"Maybe you misunderstood. The old man requires some redirection."

"I heard fine. My way helps you, helps me, helps him, definitely helps anyone in the future that encounters the bastard."

"There's the law to consider. Patricide."

"Law's just a blind lady with dope scales."

"Cops, then."

Smoker paused. "You're right, they're a handful."

"And the Bible. Respect thy father."

"Moses couldn't have predicted Pork."

"No, not likely," Andre said. "Still, we're his sons."

"Sons of bitches," Smoker said.

"Now you're bringing mother up," Andre said.

"Mother delivered us into this mess. Pork worst of all."

"Well, I am not going to shoot the old man, so he'll come to you and you're too damned lazy to shoot anything that you don't eat, so we'll be here again, except with a three hundred dollar bar tab and I've tired of drinking and mustering bail for those still at it. Might as well save the money and the hangover."

Smoker agreed to meet Andre the next evening, though he was irritated by the venue: a local public greenhouse. Opening the door wet Smoker's face. He undid his jacket. He passed hydrangeas bigger than fists and women coddling them. Andre rested on a bench that circled a small tree. A woman next to him read a plant-food bag.

"She why you're sober?" Smoker asked him.

"Maybe I'll be reason to drink later on," Claire said.

"You're bolder than I figured," Smoker told her. "My brother usually likes his women quiet."

"Usually." Andre shook his head.

Claire spoke over him. "I prefer sassy," she said.

"Sassy. Now there's a word you don't hear much."

"It's on loan from my grandmother. It's perfectly acceptable in a woman."

Claire carried a basket and removed a thermos and poured a third coffee. She had specks for blue eyes and short, darkish hair that eased the blunt lines of her long jaw. Her thin lips seemed as inclined to argument as kindness. Under, she looked to him like a child's drawing of a stick girl—nothing to quit alcohol over.

She'd keep Andre in steady work, Smoker thought, but lead to an uninteresting life.

"Well, word is Eddie's closing down," Smoker said.

"What in hell for?" Andre asked.

"You were half his take-home."

"Maybe he'll become a florist," Claire said.

"All those bartenders tending flower beds instead of drunks." Andre chuckled. "I might like that."

"Make the next morning more tolerable," Smoker allowed.

Claire twined her hand in Andre's, which encouraged him.

"Maybe I'll try dieting next and close Safeway."

"They deserve it, charging what they do for a pound of hamburger."

"Another penny saved," Claire said.

She was sharp, Smoker could see, reining Andre like a horse but allowing him to feel in the lead. Too much bridle or too little and Andre would spit the bit and she and Smoker might be stuck talking to each other.

"How's Bird?" Andre inquired. Andre loved his niece dearly and monitored Smoker's parenting. He knew Dede could not find the straight and narrow on her own, even if she had an interest, and he knew, too, his brother, though he loved his daughter without reservation, was subject to distraction.

"She's smart as a whip," Smoker said. "Gets As in everything without kissing the teacher's patootie." Smoker paused. "Speaking of, how goes school and corrupting taxpayers' children?"

"School bus driver shook them up last week. District is down to hiring kids fresh out of high school again, and one, well, his buddy squealed his tires enough the gravel rattled the bus fenders. The driver didn't like to see government property mistreated, I guess, because once he hit the grade he got that yellow dog loping fast enough to keep respectable. Fourth graders said the speedometer passed eighty and apparently he swapped some paint with a guardrail." Andre pointed at Smoker. "Kind of story they'd tell about him."

"You'd not catch me in that predicament," Smoker said.

"You stole one once."

"I just hid the thing. Somebody else got it out of the yard."

None of them spoke.

"So you're scraping roads still?" Andre asked finally.

"The country no longer needs my services according to management," Smoker told him.

"It's winter still. They figure it will stop storming?"

"What they think is all that matters," Smoker said.

"You get enough time in to collect rocking chair?"

"Not according to the unemployment woman."

"She's a stickler." Andre hauled his checkbook from his pocket.

"If you ain't buying something put that away." All his brother understood of belittling was from the other end, Smoker knew, and if a woman hadn't been present, Smoker would have found the pen himself. He felt sullen not enduring his brother's kindness or sorting a better way through it. "I'll remember you before I miss a meal," Smoker told him.

Claire bent and sorted her basket for three thick sandwiches wrapped in butcher paper. She offered Smoker one. "As long as the subject is food," she said.

Smoker unwrapped the paper. Inside was a bakery poor boy bun, thin cold cuts carved from whole meats, unlike the processed slices Smoker piled onto his own lunch sandwiches. A bite required his full attention; Smoker tasted mustard and jalapeños along with fresh lettuce and tomatoes. Andre and Claire laughed out loud at his effort. Andre opened his pocketknife and Smoker divided the sandwich into manageable portions.

"I can see why you keep her on," Smoker said.

"Your brother is the architect of this fine repast," Claire told him.

"She turn you deli man, too?"

"You used to eat my food, if you recall."

Nights their parents closed the bars, Andre had concocted meals large enough he and Smoker couldn't finish them, which guaranteed fodder for their parents' bellies. Pepper steak with rice. Roasts with any available vegetable or tuber in the broth. Crockpot chickens and dough dumplings the size of fists.

After their sandwiches, Claire deposited their trash into a metal wastebasket then walked toward a low-ceilinged portion of the greenhouse where a bare bulb lit the rose blooms. Her dark hair reflected the light. Her shoulders remained straight, like good posture might offset being ordinary. Through the opaque glass, Smoker could make out smoky shapes where the county prisoners had shoveled sawdust to insulate the dormant perennials outside and dipped the gunnysacks in concrete to anchor them. The light flattened under low clouds and the dropping temperature.

"The flowers don't smell," Smoker said.

"They've got to be outside to be perfumey," Andre told him.

Claire spooned nitrogen pellets into a plastic cup and spread them below a sickly rose.

"So, you're gardening in winter," Smoker said.

"Good trick, ain't it?"

"For those that way inclined," Smoker said. "Maybe flowers aren't the point."

"What is, then?"

Smoker chuckled. "I do believe I'll have me a smoke, if I can beg your pardon."

Outside, the clouds smudged the moon yellow. Falling snow collected on Smoker's jacket. There wasn't much profit in determining which weather approached if you had no power to will it forward or ward it off. Like predicting a hangover, knowing it's pending didn't make it any less due. Smoker searched his jacket for cigarettes and matches but had no luck. After a time, Andre joined him. He hauled a weathered pack of Marlboros from an inside pocket. One slid free when Andre tapped the top. He directed the package to his brother then struck a match and watched Smoker pull the cigarette's end to an ember. "Thought you might have given these up, too."

"I have," Andre said.

Smoker laughed. "You're oddly equipped then."

"You remember the last time you bought cigarettes?"

Smoker examined the package. The cellophane caught the light. He shoved it and the matches into his coat.

"So what do you want to do with Pork?" Smoker asked.

"Detox."

"Again?"

"Hard to convert a believer," Andre said. He shifted his legs against the cold.

"I suppose you enjoy a steady cook," Smoker said.

Andre buried his hands in his jacket and straightened his arms.

"Breakfasts in particular," Smoker went on.

"I wouldn't know about that," Andre told him.

"Got to keep up schoolteacher appearances, I suppose."

"That's not it," Andre said.

"You tell me what would drive you out of her warm bed then?"

"Not residing in it in the first place," Andre said.

Smoker smoked awhile. They both studied the snowfall. Smoker said finally, "She's a little shy likely." He inhaled his cigarette ash red then watched it darken. "Women are supposed to be reluctant. Keeps them from thinking badly of themselves." He threw his cigarette onto the gravel and ground the ash out, then lit a second one and flicked the burning match at Andre. "You need a ruse," Smoker said. "In football when they fake a handoff and throw the bomb. Keeps the defense occupied. You know the plumbing, don't you?"

"I graduated college. They did require you pass a science class or two."

Smoker tapped his cigarette and watched the falling ash pock the snow.

"Getting her drunk is out of the question, I suppose."

"Seems unlikely," Andre said.

"You never inquired with her. Just asked, I mean?"

"No, and I never asked NASA to put me on the moon, neither."

"That's too bad," Smoker said. "I'd like to be brother of a man that stepped on the moon. Might get me laid sometime if I was to meet a woman who liked planets and such."

"Moon isn't a planet. It's a satellite."

"And you ain't sleeping with your woman, no matter what we call the lights in the sky."

The snow carpeted the pavement and the grass walk to the arboretum. Smoker breathed a deep breath. "She ain't a math problem," he said. "Six and six will make twelve all day long, but a woman turns fourteen or fifteen or eleven depending on what time of day you do the figuring."

Andre took the cigarette pack from Smoker's jacket and struck a match. Smoker watched him draw one lit.

Andre said, "We shouldn't speak about her like schoolwork." He returned the cigarette package to Smoker.

"You stubborn bastard. You're already goddamn calculus; you just dress up like two plus two." Snow collected on his boots. He moved a toe and snowflakes slid into the gravel. "She's no magazine model," Smoker said. "She's likely as skittish as you."

"Not good enough for you to look twice, you mean."

"I never said that."

"It doesn't matter how common we are."

"I never said you was common," Smoker told him.

Smoker watched Andre lift his foot and press his cigarette into the sole of his tennis shoe. His brother was not inclined to bend, not even in elementary school. He did not look for fights, but he was uninclined to give ground if someone crossed him. On the playground, children often turned to fists. The crazy ones you never knew what would make them laugh one minute and have them throwing hands the next. Andre had boundaries. His rules were like those of a knight, though of what order no one knew, including Andre himself.

"You'll be at Eddie's later?" Andre asked.

Smoker glanced up. "This ain't reason to drink."

Andre disappeared through the hothouse door. Through the fogged glass, Smoker watched him unhook an apron from a peg. Claire knotted it behind him. They selected tools from a rack then tilled the shining, damp earth. Andre opened a faucet and settled its hose in a box, alternating sides to prevent water gullying the dirt. Claire pruned another flower with shears, determining which branches to let bud and which were too tired to merit going on.

Smoker finished his cigarette in the cold then another. His mind searched but he could figure nothing to do but follow inside. There, he heard Andre question Claire about fertilizer. Claire hunted a spray bottle for the blossoms. She adjusted the nozzle and aimed it and a place in Andre's T-shirt dampened. His face remained still despite the assault, and she put the next stream between his eyes. He blinked. She laughed and kissed him and Smoker worried Andre might cease being at all if she dropped her gaze. When they saw Smoker, they shied awhile then returned to misting the rose petals, and Smoker realized the only happiness he himself knew was the absence of worry. He plucked a claw from an open drawer and drew it through a flower box. The dirt parted into rows. The clean lines pleased him and he repeated them. A gray-haired woman finished with a watering can. He accepted it and the water blackened the dirt over the root mass in the box. The soil inundated, Smoker scooped fertilizer from a bag with his hands. The nitrogen stung, and after he scattered it onto the dirt, he plunged his fingers into the water to soothe them. Across the room Andre worked the lilies, which apparently kept their perfume indoors; he passed one off the bloom to Claire, who cupped the flower, then closed her eyes and inhaled and suddenly turned nothing plain at all.

An hour later, the three exited the greenhouse. Half a foot of snow had piled against the building's windward wall. Claire's duplex was a mile away. She and Andre had walked the gravel road to the park, but considering the weather, they accepted Smoker's offer to deliver them home. His unstudded tires couldn't keep to the grade, however, and the pickup skated broadside into a cross street, them laughing.

Behind them, a patrolman hit his lights and stopped. He chatted with Smoker about other storms, in December of '68 and January of '79. The cop had radioed the incident so was required to run Smoker's license. The snow climbed the windshield while the defrost fan cleared their breath fog. Smoker hit the wipers. Through the glass he could see the cop withdraw his radio receiver and speak into it, then write, then wait for a return call, which seemed a long time in coming.

"Give me your billfold, brother," Smoker said.

Andre handed his wallet to Smoker, who removed the cash and a credit card and gave them to Claire.

"I could just run a tab," Andre said.

"Nope," Smoker said. "I used your credit up. Eddie won't take anything but green money or good plastic from either of us."

The streetlights turned vague and seemed to hover in the snow-crowded air. Tomorrow, following the storm, the temperature would drop near zero. Smoker liked the cold. It numbed his skin but put a skitter in his chest the same as a whiff of fresh tobacco or the first card in a poker hand. The patrolman opened the squad car's door.

"Claire," Smoker said, "you tend to my brother, now. See he wakes up with the alarm and makes you coffee before he leaves for work and such. And he needs to be put to bed early."

Claire stared at Smoker. The cop rapped the window and Smoker cranked it open. Someone Smoker's description had torn the tire stems from four county graders.

"I heard that, too," Smoker said.

Outside, the squad car radio squawked, and the cop read Smoker his rights and applied the handcuffs.

"You all got a King James?" Smoker asked.

The cop said as far as he knew.

"Good, them New Internationals read like school board minutes."

Andre and Claire stepped outside the car and huddled. Claire turned toward Smoker and the cop. Her eyes glistened, but she wasn't crying. She uncrossed Andre's arms so that she could get herself inside them.

Andre said, loud, "Morning, I'll go your bail."

The cop replied, "The judge has already been to town this week. Be another at least before he comes back."

"Told you I'd make meals," Smoker said.

Andre nodded. "You want me to fetch Bird?"

"If Dede slips up. You see her in the tavern check Vera. Dede usually has enough sense to leave her there. You can offer to spell Vera but I'd wear a helmet when you inquire."

Claire laughed and Andre did, too. Smoker was glad to bring it from them. Snow the consistency of flower petals stuck in his hair. It gathered on his shoulders and arms and covered the cop's uniform. It had turned relief, getting caught, part of the whole of the country going white and fair.

GENESIS

September 1950–November 1957

As a teenager, Pork did not appear to pine for girls' sweet faces and private parts. Despite this, his cousin Delbert felt compelled to educate him on such matters and saw Sophie Andrews as the cure. She had bloomed to a pear-shape after middle school and remained only middling in the face, but Pork was no prize himself so Delbert did not aim higher. He convinced Pork to meet at the reservoir. The beach was cold and deserted.

Delbert beckoned, whiskey bottle in his fist. Sophie demanded the whiskey then after a long draft set the bottle in the sand. Delbert lifted it and strolled for the spindly locusts out of the wind. Sophie clamped Pork's hand and dragged him along the beach. Half a moon smeared with clouds was all that lit them. Sophie plopped onto the sand, but Pork kept upright; his eyes tracked the mile of lights where the dam held the river. Beside him, Sophie's dark hair was long and straight; her face brooded under its swooping shadow, her eyes, a little white crowded the brown in the middle. Sitting would reduce Pork's heart to coupled plumbing while not would leave him stupid about what everybody wanted to know.

Delbert had built a fire with driftwood, and Sophie, finally bored, rose and began for it. A few minutes later, Pork followed. Closer, he saw another girl had joined Delbert: Pam. Her auburn hair was tugged back with a comb; it yellowed in the light. Her face was as delicate and smooth as museum sculptures.

Opposite her, Delbert drew circles in the sand with his boot. Sophie took the whiskey and disappeared. Delbert chased after.

"You ever beat anyone up?" Peg asked him.

Smoke tufts undid against the cold. Pork recognized a blinking beacon, unsure if it was a satellite or airliner. He had been in two fights in his life, both the same day. In a pickup basketball game, Jasper Hart flung an elbow into Pork's throat. Jasper was a minor nuisance, but he had been throwing himself into people like he was Rocky Marciano. Pork's patience finally thinned. He dislocated Jasper's jaw with a single blow then kicked in two ribs. Jasper's partner hauled him to the emergency room and an hour later arrived with Jasper's older brother, Arlo, a wrestler who graduated two years before. The brother was only half out of the car when Pork threw his shoulder into the door and pinned his leg. Arlo hollered. Pork grabbed a handful of scalp with one hand then collected the ball, still bouncing, with the other, and shoved it into Arlo's face. Blood pocked their shirts, the car window and door. The boy driving hit the accelerator and cranked the wheel while Arlo clutched the open door, ankles dragging.

"Maybe they got a dog you could whip, too," an onlooker said.

The girl in front of him shifted her legs. Each step loaded her sandals until she unloosed it with the next one.

"Some girls like that," she said. "I wish I could beat someone up."

"Find somebody littler's all the trick to it."

Her lips, neither thick nor thin but some pretty and animated place cut between, parted and her teeth looked to have been straightened by braces; they weren't perfect but looked better for not being. A dimple pooled beside her mouth. Pork rotated the fire's top stick to the bottom. Her shadow crossed his like a weight and she bent to peer into the flame while the fresh wood snapped and took. The fire spat a coal into the wind. It smoldered and Pork scooped a handful of sand over the cinder. He piled more until he had built a hill and thought nothing at all, which, beside a beautiful girl, seemed quite a trick.

Pork was not altogether surprised when Peg applied for a ride the week after. When he was thirteen, he spent his harvest wages on a '55 Chevy Bel Air and devoted three years to scrapheap it past cherry.

Pork had no delusions when the rides became habit. The car and avoiding a long walk led her to him at the school day's end, and her beauty paid the fare, nothing more. She operated the heater and he the radio. They both scraped if the windows frosted. The first time he hit the filling station, she offered to share gas, but Pork declined. Afterward, he topped off outside town to spare her the awkwardness.

Pork saw her only on school days and never after dropping her off. Occasionally, evenings, he'd circle her block but never caught her as much as peeking from the window. She told him she suffered bad dreams and that was why she drew her curtains. Younger, a series of his own nightmares had set Pork back in a similar manner. He'd filled his bottom lip with coffee grounds like a tobacco chaw, which kept off sleep altogether until his vision went lacy and time was only a skinny stick chasing a fat one. The school found him out when he spelled "Kentucky" aloud instead of solving the multiplication problem the teacher had proffered.

Rumors put Peg as born-and-bred Wenatchee, but Wenatchee had not fit her and she departed in a haste that appeared beyond choice. The law didn't permit newspapers to print juvenile cases, so, outside that, her past remained conjecture. Pork allotted it to the gossips. Peg was no assistance regarding them. When foolhardy boys risked advances, she wagged her chin at them like a man would. They felt more likely to end up in a fistfight with her than survive long enough for a kiss. To the girls, she was beauty multiplied by boldness, and evil was the product of that sort of math every time. In class she was as mouthy as the worst hellions. She'd been kicked out of American Literature three times, the last for composing an essay on *Don Quixote*—which she hadn't bothered to read—in Spanish and then arguing for extra credit.

Just before Christmas, she arrived at the car with ice in her hair. Pork hurried her into the backseat and closed his eyes while she stripped to underclothes and covered herself with a wool blanket he kept beneath the seat. The next day, she threatened her Home Ec teacher over a dinner-roll recipe and was suspended. After school, she ordered Pork to trail the woman home. Peg saw she kept cats and proceeded to scheme.

"Those animals don't know dinner rolls from toilet bowls," Pork told her. "You want to bust on them, you're on your own."

He carted her to the uncle with whom she resided and retrieved her each morning of her punishment so as not to give her up. During school hours she hid in the car with sack lunches and read novels, then rewarded him the next week with a dozen cookies so salty they threw them to the dogs across the street.

"Maybe that teacher had a point," Peg said.

Valentine's Day, Pork detected Sophie and Delbert climbing an eave above the parking-lot double doors armed with water balloons. Peg's class was nearest the exit and first out.

"Let off, or I'll crease you good." Pork glared at Sophie. "I ain't above hitting girls," he said.

The two released their balloons. They skidded across the frozen shingles and broke on the gutter. The school bell clanged. Peg walked past Pork into the parking lot then recognized Delbert and Sophie above. In her uncle's driveway, she kissed his forehead before exiting the car.

March, Peg offered his taxi service to others: girls, usually pudgy or beany or funny-toothed. Some chattered as they had since third grade, aiming their jabber at him or Peg or both or neither, others thanked him, then rode mute, like quiet kept off looking peculiar.

May Day, Peg invited him on a picnic. Pork collected her late morning along with another girl, Ruth. The wind gusted Peg's hair; she laid the backseat blanket on the sand. Pork anchored it with four stones and they ate their sandwiches and fruit. Ruth huddled against Pork for a windbreak. Seeing it, Peg made for the swing set and outbuildings across the park. Ruth entwined her pinkie finger with his. In grade school, her blond hair had reached her waist but frayed most of the way. She'd pruned it as a freshman, which softened her cheeks and she became prettier. Now she tipped her face toward Pork's and kissed him. Far off, Pork heard Peg's swing squawk.

The trip home, Pork hiked the radio volume to avoid speaking or listening to either of them. After he let off Ruth, Peg moved up front.

"She likes you," Peg told him.

Pork didn't reply; instead he planted his hand onto hers. Her eyes gathered him in without a crumb of malice or ardor. He did not retreat, however, and after a time, she tipped herself across the shifter and inclined her head into his shoulder.

"Get a six-pack," she told him.

Pork's youngest uncle agreed to bootleg and, after, they parked in a hidden maintenance road atop Almira hill. Peg uncovered her basket. Inside lay a whiskey pint. She cracked the seal and drank. Pork sipped a little, too, though he was not yet inclined. He occupied himself with his beer. The coulee bottom darkened and the town lights came up. Pork examined his hand in Peg's, square and scarred from the beating work required. Her ring finger tapped him nervously. He glanced up and her dry lips whispered. He bent to hear. She stroked the fleshy underpart of his jaw, then his throat. His blood circled beneath her fingers; air passed, too. She was making herself like them.

Pork slanted his face to accommodate hers and, as her mouth descended, he shut his eyes. She kissed him tenderly and for a good while, then took a breath and clobbered him with her mouth hard enough to split his lip, which was little price to pay for such a kiss.

Peg drew back, her lips rosy with his blood.

"You take it, but you won't dish it out," she told him. "That's your problem."

"Thought the other way was what you had to watch for."

"Well, it's not," she said.

Pork daubed his lip with a jacket sleeve. Peg looked through the windshield at the silver sky.

"A boy," Peg said. "It's why I moved here. It's why I'm not interested."

"I doubt any guy could chase you."

"He hurt me."

"How?"

"You're dingy as a woman sometimes." Peg sighed. "He took me when I wouldn't permit it. Okay?"

"Who?" Pork asked her.

"Raymond Charles."

"Like the singer? Ray Charles."

"Yes."

"He black?"

"Oh, for Christ's sake."

Peg spoke no more of Ray Charles, but a week later, he left a note for his parents that he'd gone bear hunting. That night, he arrived at Wenatchee's high school. His driver's license failed to trip the door bolts, disillusioning him with TV spies. He jimmied a classroom window and wedged his legs through the opening, but the bulk of him flopped outside like a fish on a stringer. He finally abandoned subtlety and smashed a bathroom window with a construction block. Lurching through, he tore his forehead.

In the building, he carved Peg's name into anything that took a blade then ripped a blanket from his trunk into bandages and stitched himself with fishing line. Morning, he registered for classes using Elston Howard as a moniker. For parents, he penciled none and when queried informed the secretary they'd been assassinated by thieves mad on reefer. The secretary offered him a cookie.

Wenatchee's school could hold ten of Pork's. A few boys snickered at him; one hummed "Yankee Doodle." Pork shoved him into a locker. Peg's name was in the girls' bathrooms, too, and passing time, a dozen assembled and fussed over a beauty named Sharon.

"If she was coming back, she'd cut your name into the wall, not hers," one of them said. "Then you'd be in trouble."

"She doesn't make sense," Sharon said. "That's not how she does it." Even agitated, part of the girl's face looked as placid as a glass pane.

Pissing the first afternoon, Pork asked a towheaded boy about the hoo-ha. Some girl, he said. The next day, Pork learned Peg had lived south where the houses gave up to double-wides. Her grades were Cs. She refused homework and relied on test scores to pass.

Afternoon, the principal, a gaunt man with pinched eyes and a patchy goatee, summoned him inside a windowless room. He shoved Pork into a chair and stood over him.

"How'd you acquire your injury?" he asked.

Pork recounted his murder story, adding his assailants had creased him, but he'd managed to chase them off with a samurai sword his father had stolen from his captors while in a Japanese prison camp.

The principal swooped his face into Pork's. "They didn't allow Indians in World War II. Not in the Pacific."

"You not heard of Drunken Ira Hayes?"

"I have not."

"You don't listen to Johnny Cash?"

"No."

Pork resolved to say no more, believing a man who shirked country music couldn't hold much moral authority in his community.

That night, Pork eased his car to an empty park and let the radio play. Sleeping on the seat crooked his back and the single blanket was all he owned for warmth. He saw no clear end to his chore, indeed had no notion whether he'd initiated anything other than a criminal record and a bent for prevarication. But the other half of his head argued with slivered moans and cries and images of Peg's fear-contorted face like victims' black-and-white photographs in detective magazines. Envy quickened Pork's heart though he realized it shouldn't because where he stirred most was south of there.

He discovered Ray Charles the next day. In the locker room, Charles traced the carved letters under the mirror.

"You cut that?" Pork asked.

Ray Charles tried to scoff but sounded only like he was losing air.

Afternoon, the principal met Pork in the cafeteria. "I've notified the police. They're looking into you."

Pork followed Ray Charles throughout the day. He played baseball and, judging from practice, was neither star nor bucket hauler. He'd enrolled in the hard math classes and squinted at his notebook's polynomials, writing and erasing equal time. In the hall, he strode as if firm of conviction. Students parted for him, but it had nothing to do with fear. The girl, Sharon, appeared and vanished at his side, looking puzzled.

With a phone book, it was simple enough to find Sharon's house. The Chevy drew attention, so he parked several blocks away. Her street neighbored a park. There, Pork scaled a substantial basalt rock beyond the swing sets and monkey bars. Through the kitchen window, he could observe Sharon spray and dust a kitchen table. She set no plates and, when her parents arrived ten minutes later, then dressed for the evening and exited, she loaded cereal into a bowl, added a little milk, and carefully spooned it into her mouth. Half an hour later, Ray Charles cut across three house lawns to her door packing an armload of books.

They appeared again in her bedroom window, which was open despite the cold. Pork heard them check each other's answers. The bandage tightened; Pork felt himself feverish. He considered hunting some aspirin then heard them again. It began as roughhousing, but soon Sharon was crying. Pork scrambled the rock for a cleaner look.

Both were naked. Charles reclined against the bed's headboard, legs extended, face tipped back; Sharon, cross-legged over him, coaxed his lifeless organ. Without clothes, she looked milky and thin and fragile.

Charles halted her hands with his own. He patted hers gently. Her sobs didn't cease and didn't turn hysterical, just continued.

The next day, a cop met Pork at his homeroom. "You Elston Howard?" he asked.

"You listen to Johnny Cash?" Pork replied.

"Every day," the cop said.

"Name's just something I saw in a baseball mitt."

The cop wore a heavy mustache that disguised his smile. "Going to give me your real one?"

"I better not," Pork said.

"You got until that last bell to be gone or come clean," the policeman replied.

"Yes, sir," Pork told him.

The next period, Pork slipped off with a bathroom pass and stationed himself in front of Sharon's locker until the bell. A green ribbon held her blond hair. Her eyes hit his, then one dropped and one did not.

"You put her name all over the place," she said.

"Your eye?" Pork nodded. "Peg did that?"

"Yes."

Sharon patted the books in her crossed arms.

"With a hammer," she said. "The claw side. In English we were reading *Oedipus*."

Pork didn't speak.

"Are you in love with her?" she asked.

"Yes," he said.

She blew out a breath. "You all are."

The rest he ascertained from straight-out inquiry. Ray Charles and Sharon Brouilette dated since grammar-school play days. Peg turned Charles's head. He'd promised to wean Sharon from him, but the pace didn't suit Peg. She'd come at them both on some lover's lane and would be in the juvenile hall except Ray Charles refused to point her out from the witness box.

Baseball practice, Charles took extra cuts. He was the last to leave, which simplified matters. Pork hemmed him against the gym wall with a bat.

"Give me that jacket," Pork said.

"What do you want with it?"

"Evidence," Pork said.

"Of what?"

"You know."

"No," Charles said. "I don't know."

"Well, me neither, but she wants a pound of flesh and seems inclined to get her way."

"It cost me seventy dollars."

"I could beat seventy dollars from you and take the jacket anyhow," Pork said.

Charles removed the coat. Pork tucked it under his arm. He scanned the empty gym.

"Just say I stole it," Pork told him.

That night, Pork opened his own arm with a pocketknife and bloodied the coat. The next day he drove to Peg's uncle's and knocked.

"Here, goddamnit." He threw the jacket at her.

She stood openmouthed then touched the blood. "You pig," she cried. "You stupid pig."

Later that day he checked himself into the emergency clinic where they treated his infected forehead wound for staph. When his parents inquired, he informed them he'd gashed his head on barbed wire. No one argued and he decided he enjoyed lying and resolved to embrace it whenever the truth became burdensome.

Two weeks later, reclined beneath his Chevy, he greased the universal joint and wheel bearings until the shop door banged and Peg entered. He recognized her through the engine well but determined to complete his grimy task. Then her blouse and bra and pants and her balled-up underpants settled on the cement floor. He crawled from beneath the chassis and, together, they took the wrong turn that was each other.

After, he stared at her hymen blood dotting them.

"It felt like rape," she said. "It felt like it."

3

EXODUS

August 1991

The bear had food enough in his belly to hope for more. Andre lifted the rope end and pulled. The ham twisted like a needlefish lure in a current. The bear followed. At the truck, Andre scrambled into the cab and accepted the rope from Smoker through the sliding back window. Coming out, Smoker met the bear full-on. For a moment they eyed each other, but the ham was inside the camper and the bear lowered his head and shuffled up the tailgate.

"Well now we got a bear to trade," Andre said.

Smoker halted the truck at a deli up the hill where they purchased a pound of salami then hit the liquor store and a grocery. In the parking lot, they combined Quaker Oats, milk, and bourbon in a mop bucket then added Alka-Seltzer, worried over the animal's humor with a hangover.

Soon after, they discovered the block and address provided by the biker. No one answered their knock. The houses that lined the street were small but well cared for, flowers bracketing the foundations and aloe plants and doodads on the windowsills. Smoker pissed behind a shrub. The bear rifled the cabinets and grunted.

"Think we ought to get him another ham?" Andre asked.

"He'll just eat it."

"That'd be the point."

"No it's not," Smoker said. "We need something that'll occupy him. Any of these yards got a dog or cat?"

"I doubt he requires a pet."

"Something he'd have to kill," Smoker said. "Then there's tearing skin and pulling meat from bone. Hell, it'd keep him till morning sucking the marrow loose."

In the camper the bucket clanged.

"We're not doing that," Andre said.

"What'd you figure he'd do on his own?"

"He isn't on his own."

"Goddamnit, how'd you come to be straw boss on this excursion?"

"I ain't bossing."

"What do you call it, then?"

"Saying no."

Smoker kicked at a rosebush. Leaves and petals scattered. He stormed toward the truck. "You think rescuing this bear makes you better than me?"

"No," Andre said.

"You think it will help find Bird?" Smoker shouted.

"Will killing it?"

"No," Smoker said.

"Did going off to chase it?"

Andre began for the truck himself then stopped. "What if we got it wrong," he said. "What if it was a boulevard or place or court? We just hunted street."

Smoker shoved his hand through his hair. Bump appeared capable of that kind of error, he admitted.

Andre asked the Albertsons meat department to slice five pounds of salami thin then package it in plastic then brown paper then white. He purchased duct tape and kite string and encased the package as thoroughly as a mummy. At the camper, Smoker cracked the door and flung the bundle inside. They listened while the bear licked and sucked and whined and bit the wrapping. Having no luck, the animal lifted and dropped the package on the floor. Andre peeked through the window. The bear looked stumped.

Smoker drove them past North Market Street into blocks where just dirt and chain-link fences separated the lots. One porch, an old man sat in a refrigerator plugged into a porch outlet. Clouds lifted around him in the afternoon heat. Dogs serious with intent yapped and scuffed the hardpan. Smoker stuffed his Luger in his belt and Andre packed a sawed-short two-by-four behind his leg to the stoop of one house then another until a lady fatter than the doorway pointed them to a neighbor with the windows painted shut.

Andre put himself out of sight behind the door, while Smoker knocked. A barefoot woman in a dress that looked like a sack answered.

"I heard you all are running a dope business," Smoker said.

The woman hurried off and a man limped to the door. He wore pants and a Raiders cap but no shirt. His short torso was roped with the muscle cons acquired lifting iron.

The man said, "I'll bet you're drunk. I never seen a sober Indian."

Smoker smiled. "And I'll bargain you ain't enjoyed real sex since you quit dating them brothers in the hoosegow."

The con punched Smoker over the eye. The blow backed him from the steps. Smoker touched his brow and recognized blood just in time to get cracked in the mouth. Andre whacked the con mid-back with his board. The man howled and Andre dropped the board hard onto his collarbone twice. The air left his chest. Andre thumped the con's kidneys then wrestled him full nelson to the ground. Smoker lifted the board and walloped the con across the kneecaps twice, the third he clobbered Andre, who wailed for him to stop and Smoker did.

The woman with the con shouted from the porch and threw an open Pepsi can at him.

"Shut up," the man told her. "The law'll come for sure." He panted. Andre cinched his wrestling hold tighter. Smoker's lip had fattened and his teeth smeared with blood. He stood, shaking. He looked from the man to Andre then back. The man had quit struggling but Andre pressed his face into the grass, worried it was a ruse.

"You wouldn't let a brother stand awhile, would you?" the man asked.

"Nope."

The con slanted his eyes so he could see Smoker. "Don't say much, does he?" the convict said.

"Didn't bring him for conversation," Smoker told him.

The man said his name was Calvin. He extended what he could of a hand. Moles starred his arms and tattoos spelled something across his knuckles. "No hard feelings?"

Smoker took it. "My child's missing," he told him.

"And his wife," Andre added.

"She a looker?"

Andre jerked Calvin's arm toward the sky. Calvin sucked a breath through his teeth.

"I admit she don't act too wifely most of the time," Smoker said.

"I'm in no position to comment here."

"He lets you up, you tell me how to find them?" Smoker asked.

Calvin nodded. Andre stood and allowed him to do the same. Calvin gave Andre a hard look. "Damn, my legs are going to ache."

"Fifty enough to soothe you?" Smoker asked.

"Be a start," Calvin said. He stretched the bill between his thumbs.

"Where are they?"

"The child is on the mountain with my pop. The reverend. Harold. He's God-fearing but not right since Mom died."

"Which mountain?"

"One in Idaho. Bonners is the closest town. He won't come down for love nor money."

"What about Dede?" Andre asked.

Calvin shrugged. "I run dry of what kept her entertained," he said.

"She lit out without Bird?" Andre asked.

"No," Calvin said. "She wanted the girl with Harold. Thinks he's saintly, I guess."

"You got directions to this Harold's place?" Smoker asked.

Calvin nodded. "I can write you a map."

Smoker pointed toward the camper. "Paper and pencil in the back. Cold beer there, too. Help yourself."

Calvin strode to the truck. When he opened the door, the bear stared at him and grunted.

"He gets out you're putting him back," Smoker hollered.

Calvin slammed the door. "You boys ain't run-of-the-mill crazy, are you?"

He disappeared inside his house and returned with an address and a paper and sketched a map.

"That Bump said you came looking for Peg."

"Bump Rasker's dumber than a twenty-year-old fourth grader."

"Special needs," Andre said.

"Needing ain't special."

"What did you want with Peg?" Smoker asked.

Calvin looked at his scarred, off-kilter ankle. "Old score," he said.

"Well she's got more of that kind of debt than Mexico," Smoker told him. "And she's too broke to pay attention."

"Besides that, she's passed," Andre said.

"I heard," Calvin said. "Happy hunting ground and all."

Smoker shook his head. "I doubt she's happy and I know she ain't hunting."

Calvin glanced at Smoker. "Lip hurt?"

"Be something wrong with me if it didn't," Smoker said.

"I ain't been out but two months," Calvin replied. "Still a little jumpy."

Neither Smoker nor Andre spoke.

"I'll give you your fifty back and two hundred cash for the animal," Calvin said. "I could turn a bill or two matching him with these dogs."

"No, sir," Smoker said. "That bear's particular. He won't eat nothing that doesn't come from the butcher and my brother here doesn't permit him to indulge in violence."

LAMENTATIONS

February–March 1984

The judge sentenced Smoker to time served and restitution for the tires, which Andre bartered to five hundred dollars then squared. In exchange, Smoker conceded to deliver Pork to the Yakima alcohol center. Andre phoned Pork and ordered him to pack. Pork refused. Andre advocated loading the truck despite Pork's obstinance; Smoker agreed, with the caveat they drink Pork through the weekend out of sympathy. Overruled, Andre accompanied them. They closed Crazy Eddie's both nights, Andre sipping Pepsi and settling bills. Smoke, caffeine, bad food, and sleep deprivation finally wrenched his stomach, and Sunday morning he languished in bed, hungover from a sober bender, which seemed a mean joke.

Drunk he could at least have avoided philosophy and dread and instead focused on simplicities like showering and arriving at school before the second bell clanged. Sober, he was forced to gaze into the chipped ceiling and stare at the faces in swirling panels' wood grain expecting them any moment to scold him. He saw no sleep for him past death, which, if the retrieval of his pistol from the pickup didn't require such effort, he would have seriously considered.

Three times, he heard raps against the cheap front door. He answered none. Gravel clicked the window glass and he finally mustered his energy and lifted the window.

Claire hollered from the street below, "Are you all right in there?"

Andre waved her into the building then opened his door.

"Are you hungover?" Claire asked.

Andre rubbed his temples. "I didn't get drunk."

"You smell like you did," she said.

"We got to detox the old man," Andre said. "Smoker thought he needed a runner to get it out of his system first."

"You agreed."

"I bankrolled it and chauffeured them so they wouldn't put a crease in anyone."

Andre tipped himself through the open window into the weather. Rain soaked the roof and rapped the concrete below. Claire leaned into him and rested her face against his back. Her profile blued in the window reflection. She hitched her arm around him and snaked it under his shirt. She circled her palm over where his heart was.

"Me and Smoker have to usher him to rehab."

"You didn't drink?"

Andre shook his head. "I never realized how dull a tavern was."

Claire directed Andre to sit and he did. She rifled his dresser for fresh socks then twisted them onto his feet. His tennis shoes were under the bed. Claire untied the laces and shod him, then secured them with double knots. She collected her jacket, then his. He looked at her quizzically.

"It's raining," Claire said. "You want pneumonia?"

Andre drove. Claire, squeezed between him and Smoker, sensed her isolation. Smoker and Andre and even Pork and, on occasion, her students, too, had recounted odd stories about Coyote, or, in Salish, the local native language, Sinkalip. She loved the name: It tickled her though she couldn't say why.

Winter, Sinkalip must starve until his stories are told. Sinkalip's acts must be spoken, not only committed to paper; words written and divided from a tongue allow neither Sinkalip's absence or his presence because words turn liquid and spill from the page. When the people speak or the wolf bays or the elk bugles, Sinkalip doesn't consider order or chaos. He only seeks its distance and direction so he can deceive Mole and copulate with his cousins or defeat Dog Monster. He forgets the stones are the bones of his mother and, instead, employs them to construct huts that hide himself when he masturbates. If perplexed, he calls his turd sisters to cramp his belly and he shits them into scat for their advice. If they offend him, he threatens to piss them into oblivion.

Sinkalip taught the people how to trap the salmon and what roots to eat and how to make a good lodge. He told everyone he was a great warrior, but he was not. Who knows why the Animal People chose to step across his carcass the appropriate number of times and resurrect him. Perhaps it was rebellion, rescuing their last contradiction and returning it to flesh and blood and bone.

Or perhaps it is simply Coyote's boldness that redeemed him. Or maybe he was just too entertaining to do without.

Claire was not certain why people would pick such a hero, but, she realized, she was uncertain, too, why she was drawn to Andre and through him Smoker and the rest of them. Yet she remained apart. Race was not the cause; Smoker and Andre, half white and half Indian, seemed unable to see or uninterested in the border in themselves where those two met. They were halves of all things and wholes of none, but it was not race or a culture that divided each, she understood. It was what they were not, not what they were.

"My whole life we ate on paper plates with plastic forks and knives," Andre said.

"Why's that?" Claire asked.

"Because the folks kept breaking the good ones on each other. And us on occasion."

"They hit you with plates?" she asked.

"Only if you lacked the sense to duck," Smoker replied. "It wasn't personal, like calisthenics in PE. Sometimes the person next to you kicks you or whacks. Just part of being in PE."

"I hated PE," Claire said.

"One thing about growing up in my house," Andre said, "I learned how to take a punch from a man and a woman."

"How about Smoker?"

"They were scared of him. He didn't fight fair. Once he stabbed Pork with scissors then drove them into Peg's thigh to mix the blood. He figured their poison would counteract each other." Andre chuckled.

"This is funny?"

Smoker shrugged.

"I hated PE, too," Andre said.

They were quiet awhile.

Andre tapped a finger to his temple. "I remember something made me feel weird," Andre said. "High school sometimes I bunked with classmates in town. You know. Two away games on Friday and Saturday. Hardly time to drive home before it was time to drive back. What amazed me was breakfast. I'd wake up and the first thing I smelled was food. One by one everyone in the house would stumble into the kitchen. Except the mom or pop who would be flipping eggs and hotcakes and sausages or bacon or ham in separate skillets. And pretty soon, the kids would assume pancake duty or the eggs and another would line dishes and silverware on the table. And then they would pile plateloads of food and set them in the table's center where the group would trade the dishes, and split the morning paper into sections, swapping until they'd examined the whole of the thing. I was almost afraid to eat."

"Why's that?" Claire asked.

"It was not my country. Unless I'd busted an egg or something I didn't know the language."

"And now you cook breakfast for us on the weekends."

Andre shrugged. "I like to eat."

At the lip of the coulee, a fenced yard corralled hive-like cable insulators bigger than rooms. Others, attached to the hundred-foot towers, shuttled electricity from the dam generators beneath. Between them, swooping power lines spanned the coulee wall then dipped several hundred feet below to the powerhouses.

Claire said to Andre, "I remember the first time I came out here. You showed me how to milk the cows."

"To the rest of us that was a chore," Smoker said.

"Well, for me it wasn't," Claire told him.

Andre veered left on the road named for his family. Gray snow remained in the shaded depressions; the rest was drab and tawny dirt and dormant flora. Andre's first kill was not a quarter mile from here. Pork and he had gutted and dragged a two-point along a cattle trail to the barn where Andre sawed the hooves below the shin and permitted the dogs their share while Pork separated hide from meat and fat with his knife blade. The deer skinned, they cut the bullet from its ribs. The impact on bone flattened the lead. Pork drilled a hole in it and threaded a rawhide strap through, then draped it around Andre's neck. The next morning, at dawn, up to feed cattle, Andre gazed at the barbed-wire fences and the first tinge of green wheat and half a dozen deer scattered against the horizon light, indicting him for their loss.

Ten miles of washboarded gravel and they met the driveway gate: three boxed logs with the family brand burned into a flat piece of driftwood that dangled from the center pole. A bird trilled. A lark of some kind, Andre guessed though he wasn't sure. Smoker spent most autumns at the place getting his venison and a freezer full of birds to feed him and Dede through winter. Andre, though, visited the place only holidays. His father was more stubborn than most men, but he wasn't a god. Pork would die and the place would fall to Andre and Smoker and they would lease the ground to a bigger rancher who would farm it and leave the house to collapse on its concrete foundation. Someone would scrounge the good in it—the stove, some clean timber—then set a fire. Springs, the grass would renew itself and the locusts would green up and the foundation would turn one more concrete crypt visited by crows and wandering cattle. Outside, the bird spoke again and Andre listened. Separating a lark's song from a sparrow's cheep was something he might have managed once. Though he'd never been taught the difference, he should have had it in him to know.

King, Pork's ancient malamute, limped down the house steps and coughed out a couple of short barks. Behind him, Pork perched on the porch swing he'd built for Smoker and Andre years before. Andre bent and rubbed the dog's ears.

"You're supposed to keep out the riffraff," Pork hollered at the dog.

"Coffee inside?" Andre asked.

Pork nodded.

"It poisoned?" Smoker asked him.

"I considered it," Pork admitted. He smelled gamey as an elk and his breath made an awful racket. Smoker offered him a cigarette and lit it. In the kitchen, Andre topped Pork's cup with coffee and filled three others for Smoker and Claire and himself and delivered them to the porch.

"How's your mother?" Pork asked.

"Meaner than a rattlesnake on fire," Smoker said.

Pork stared at them from the swing then let out a sigh. He gazed into his coffee cup like the black liquid there that was supposed to rescue him had failed. Then he dumped it on the porch floor. The gaps between slats drained the puddle.

"Jail'd be kinder than the dry house," he said.

"Cheaper, too," Smoker told him.

"Save your goddamn money, then."

"You ought to talk nicer to them trying to keep you with the living," Smoker replied.

"You ain't got no say," Pork told Smoker; then he turned to Andre, "And you're too much like your mother."

"Hush, you old bastard," Andre said.

"Why do you speak to him that way?" Claire whispered.

"Because there isn't any other way to," Andre said.

Pork wheezed. "You're a pitiful pair. Motherfucked, both of you." He stopped. "I apologize. I forgot the lady."

"Listen to me," Smoker told him. "You're going to dry out or I will shoot you in the ass sure as I am standing upright breathing air."

Pork said, "You ain't got it in you."

Smoker stormed to his truck and withdrew his pistol from under the driver's seat then put a round between Pork's feet.

"Told you," Pork said.

They all stood on the ancient porch. King limped to the old man and Pork patted his haunches.

"He'll need fed."

Andre nodded. "We aren't going to watch a friend starve."

Smoker packed Pork's suitcase with fresh underwear and jeans and the plaid shirts he favored then lugged it from the house to the driveway. Pork, though, had found a gas can in the shop. He soaked the suitcase then dropped his cigarette and the clothes went up quick as tinder. He unbuttoned his Western shirt and added it, then stepped out of his pants and skivvies and tossed them to the blaze, which left him naked aside from wool socks. Pork glanced up at Claire but didn't cover himself. She didn't know where to put her eyes and finally turned her back altogether. Andre covered him with a bedspread, then pressed him into the passenger side of his trap wagon.

Smoker climbed under the wheel.

"Watch him," Andre said. "He might pull loose the wires just to get you pulled over and he's hard enough to explain dressed."

Andre and Claire watched them go then left, too. The pickup ascended the canyon above the ranch until Andre spied an open gate. He slowed to shut it then recognized tire tracks in the wet dirt.

"Somebody's drove up on top."

"A neighbor person?" Claire asked.

"A lot shorter ways here from their places."

Andre reached under the seat for his pistol and examined the cylinder. He left the hammer over the empty chamber then eased past the gate and halted and hooked it behind him. The truck slid in the mud until its tires found the old feed ruts. It crawled through the dips and they lost the tracks, but Andre knew even a four-wheel drive would have to keep to this fence line.

He discovered the Chevy pickup on a ridge that straddled the ranch and the neighbor's, Broke Hole. In the truck's rear window, a gun rack held two rifles. Two high-school boys hooded themselves in sweatshirts against the rear quarter panel. Andre wedged his truck perpendicular to the front bumper and switched the ignition off. They stashed their beer cans beneath the back tires.

Andre cranked his window open.

One of the boys laughed nervously. They both stood.

"You're a teacher," one said.

"Not today," Andre replied. "You left the gate open down the canyon."

The taller one spoke. "We weren't going to be but an hour or so."

"Don't take that long for a cow to wander."

"We didn't see any cows."

The other one nodded.

Andre fished for a sawed-off baseball bat behind the seat. He tapped it on his palm.

"I built that goddamn fence," he said.

Claire patted his arm. "They're just kids."

"They are where they hadn't ought to be."

Andre stepped from the cab. "Stay where I can see you," he warned the boys. On the dash he found their ammunition boxes then unbolted their rifles and ejected the shells. "Empty your pockets." The boys did. Andre threw the lot over the bluff's edge. He listened to them clink in the rocks.

"You hightail it," Andre told them. "I don't see you aimed east on the pavement in three minutes, you won't need to look for me. And close the goddamned gate behind you."

The truck disappeared then bobbed below in the draw. The clouds feathered a gray, low ceiling over the river. Long bars of sunlight shone in the breaks. Most of the hole below dropped into the shadows. The boys paused for the gate then sped Black Lake Road toward town. Andre dropped the bat. Claire hit him with it. The blow caught his hip clean and something electrical fluttered his leg. Before she could swing again, Andre stepped close and covered her arms. She spun away but remained in his embrace.

"You can't do that," she told him.

"I know it," Andre said. "I do."

They were quiet a long while. Andre surveyed the country below. As a more hopeful child, he'd looked in the encyclopedia at sextants and constructed one with staples and scrap wood from behind the shop, believing if he could get the lay of that great country above, he might pilot himself through his days on earth like the sailors of old navigated the oceans.

Examining the country with Claire beside him, he recalled the last time he and Smoker ran away as children. Out a basement window the two of them escaped. They trekked a dry creek bed. Smoker discovered where a deer had bedded and rolled himself in the hair and matted grass, then, beneath an owl's roost, busted up the pellets and dug loose mice bones.

Andre wandered, eventually encountering day-old deer tracks, lazy steps, not the four boxed hooves of a hurried bounce. Later, a coyote broke brush at the draw's bottom, head up, tongue lolling out of his mouth. The scent of burned and disked fields rested over him.

At the river, he lay over a flat rock. He held his breath and dropped his head between his arms. Blood-sound beat through his ears and quieted his thoughts. He opened his eyes. The river's current, hurried by the dam's generators, pulled tiny sticks across the rocky bottom. He splashed his cheeks and his chest and bowled out more with his hands and soaked himself. The sun burned high and the shadows of the coulee commenced their slow incline eastward.

Any knack for the manly arts related to nature had fallen to Smoker. Andre envied his brother's ease in all things and its seed seemed to have sprouted from the certainty of instinct. Andre understood his lack was some of his own doing. He had little interest in the workings of a weapon or the habits of deer.

He did, however, have an affinity for the river. As a child, he liked to swim and wade and throw rocks or float bark barges. Older, he loved boats and skiing or riding an inner tube. Returning from college, he only felt home when he broke past the rocky wall separating the farm country from the coulee and spied the river. He read in Classics that Heraclitus claimed you could never step into the same river twice, but Andre thought of it differently. When you put yourself in a river you were everywhere the river was, and the thought of such constancy and permanence comforted him.

Downriver, a hundred yards or so, Andre discovered a lightning-shattered tamarack. It drooped from a ten-foot ledge that delineated the historic flood line. The lightning left half the meat intact. A termite wandered from beneath the torn bark, then another. In the draw above the bank, Andre found two rocks he could barely lift. With the first, he labored onto the tree until the termite's nest was below him and let it loose. The boulder bounced. Shattered pine and bark peppered the beach and the panicked termites scattered.

The second stone weighed more. Andre could barely waddle it the length of the log. He grunted and shoved the stone higher. His arms quaked and swelled. The rock hovered over his head a moment then crashed down. The tree folded and straightened, then swung past straight, popping the last veins that strung it together. The rock slid off and so did Andre, dropping on all fours in the gravel.

Andre rolled the log to the river. The work slashed his hands with slivers. Balled sap clung to his skin. He doctored himself in the water. The current tugged at the tree. This part of the river, the dams spun the water into a maze of eddies and whirlpools impossible to guess with. Andre shoved the log into the main current. He floated with it. Rocks and trees dotted the banks, shapes so large they dwarfed him. Birds circled. He grasped a branch stub and shouldered himself onto the log. His feet dangled below;

they seemed numb ghosts that belonged to someone else. He lifted them and they ached with the cold of the river, but he felt inside as if he'd swallowed knotted string but undone the worst tangle. Soon Smoker whistled from a hilltop and beckoned and Andre kicked for the shore.

Evening, Pork appeared aboard his old bay. Smoker and Andre prepared for a whipping. The old man, though, undid his bedroll and put it between theirs. He stirred the fire, complimenting the good coals. He unwrapped a deer liver and set it on the grass and sliced it into three pieces, then cut some sticks.

Smoker and Pork and Andre cooked and listened to the coyotes yip.

"I'd hoped to be good-looking," Pork said. "And rich." He nodded to himself. "We got what we got, boys. Though roasting a hunk of good venison over a good fire ain't all thorns and briars, even if I am compelled to share with a couple of criminals."

They watched the meat sear in the pink light. Grease and blood spat and blackened against the coals.

Suddenly Andre recalled a time before the drinking too, Peg pampering bilious rosebushes and daffodils with peat. He and Smoker, little boys, trailed her to grade dirt and harvest dandelion hair. Evenings, Pork, still in his work clothes, would saunter across the cool grass, lift them by the ankles and hose the garden from their legs while their mother gathered her implements. Often those nights, they ate on a picnic table while the shadows stretched and the crickets sawed at the cool night.

The detox orderlies collected Pork and told Smoker to wait.

"Name?" the desk nurse asked.

"Pork White."

The nurse nodded. "Name of patient?"

"That is his name," Smoker said.

Her white-capped head popped up and her mouth tightened.

Smoker finished the form himself. Eventually a doctor, not much older than Smoker, called him into his office. He motioned to a battered leather sofa.

"Your father put up quite a fight," the doctor said. "We had to sedate him."

"He hurt anyone?" Smoker asked.

"No, but the orderlies got some exercise." The doctor tried to laugh, then, looking at Smoker, gave up. "We had to restrain him. He'll have some bruises." The doctor passed Smoker several pamphlets.

"Can I see him?"

"Just remember, he's sedated. Don't let that scare you."

"I think I seen him sedated before," Smoker said.

Smoker followed the doctor into a darker room. Noisy breath clacked in the chest of each man they passed and a bitter odor haunted them. In another bunk row, a thin man in fatigues slept in a fetal ball. Below him a fat Mexican rested, his open eyes staring into the board that held the bed above him. Pork was in the last section, near the nurse's station, strapped down.

Smoker leaned over the old man. Pork's long black hair sprawled around his head, broadening his face and showing his smooth temple. Smoker stroked the wrinkles in his father's forehead then placed his open palm on his father's bare chest, feeling his heart at work.

At his apartment, Andre excused himself to shower, something he hadn't done in four days. The spray beat his scalp and the water's hush surrounded him. He twisted the knob hotter and huddled underneath. He didn't hear Claire enter the room and drop out of her clothes. She stepped into the shower with him. She was hot and damp as breath. Claire turned her body and let the shower spray hit him full-on. It ached but he let it beat him. She steered his back to the water so it could thaw him, then began with soap and a washrag. The room clouded with steam. Andre studied the squarish outline of Claire's feet and knew he would never see another woman this way.

GENESIS
Autumn 1958

According to the Catholics, Andre came into existence several weeks before Pork found himself in his Chevy studying a medical clinic's glass door. Suddenly Peg's shape grew in the entry, her face dark with thought until the glass pane flattened it. Stunned, she stepped away and swore then pulled instead of pushed and successfully exited the building.

"You laughing at me?" she asked, inside the car.

Pork shook his head. "Funny story on the radio."

"Do I have a black eye?"

Pork lifted her chin. "You'll play piano again," he said.

Peg blew a sigh into the windshield. "Well it'll be a nursery tune."

"So I guess we should marry," Pork said.

"You sure this baby is yours? I've screwed most of the football team and might be with child from the defense. I'm not sure which player. Their plumbing all looked the same after I got to the linebackers."

"They well put together?" he asked.

"Like bulls."

"I suppose you'll be wanting to marry one of them instead. He'll support you well. Just needs people to tackle all his life and someone to pay him for it."

Peg slapped his forehead like in the Three Stooges. "You really believe I'd open my legs to those barbarians."

"Nothing here but barbarians. You included."

She laughed. "I'm the worst."

"I ain't one to argue."

She patted his thigh. "That's because you like it. Doesn't mean you're the one made this baby."

"Seems to me you're making it. Farmer don't grow the wheat."

"Just plants the seed and moves on," Peg said.

"Not if it's his farm. You got to weed and fertilize and worry about weather. Then maybe you'll have a crop."

"You think I'm a field to sow."

"I expect you'll be harder to put a fence around than forty acres or four thousand and I don't figure a ring and a notarized paper will do the trick any better than barbed wire."

"How will you tell what's yours, then?" Peg asked.

"I figure I'll brand you."

She laughed. "Like hell, you will."

"Only hurt awhile. You seen. Those steers get right back to their business."

"What would you put on me?"

"Probably a devil with a pointy tail."

"Where?" She held his hand when he offered it.

"Inside of your thigh or your belly button. Somewhere near a rustler's intent."

"And where would I mark you?" she asked.

"You already did," Pork said.

Peg kissed his cheek. "You're sweet. In the city, though, they got doctors that can erase this."

"They tear you up like a chainsaw, what I hear."

"That would make farming tough," Peg replied. "Well, I'm not deciding this minute."

"If I'd expected a direct answer I would have brought a pistol and shot you till you agreed."

Pork arrived at her uncle's the next morning to gather Peg for school, but the door didn't open and the lights didn't flicker as was their code when Peg took ill. The next morning the same occurred, so he parked and knocked. "She's not here," the uncle told him. "And I don't know where she's gone." He laced his work boots. "We been calling hospitals and listening to the police scanner for her."

Peg retraced a path to an old cave in the reservation country where Pork had brought her to hunt and make love. She organized a green-wood fire to clear out the porcupine that resided there. The place was gamey but open to the east and the sun's rise. Morning light painted the country below her and shimmered on the dark water and Peg was, for the first time she could recall, calm. The sensation felt like she had imagined penetration might as a young girl, a sort of painful, weeping pleasure. In the cave's mouth, she pondered why anyone chose house living. She stirred the fire and for hours watched it wrinkle the air and light.

She'd packed fishing gear and a gun, but her appetite had vanished. The first day her bowels and bladder protested, but the second they calmed themselves into near retirement. Her blood thinned but her head felt alert. The work to exist seemed too much like prayer, stupid diligence.

It was not Pork twisting inside her, she understood; it was a thing her own. She at first feared she had too little to nurture Pork or the infant, but upon more consideration, her apprehension became the opposite, that she would overwhelm them with the tornado that was herself. As she drifted through her starved, liquid consciousness, she waited for her guilt to rise and pass judgment and, finally, the relief of penance. That ritual, however, wasn't in her; she felt nothing akin to sad or culpable. Pork would do what he ought, but he was not seasoned enough to determine if it was what he wanted or the costs. He'd require from her more than even a child might.

The fourth morning, she heard clattering in the rocks above. She fired a shot toward the sound.

"It's me, goddamnit," Pork shouted.

"I wouldn't be shooting at nobody else," she hollered.

He ducked behind a rise. She studied the place recognizing full well he'd turn up somewhere she couldn't guess and by then he'd be too close to shoot without seeing his face. Twenty minutes later, he tapped her with a stick from behind. She had placed the gun between her feet and made no attempt for it. Instead, she trailed him to the fire pit at the cave's maw, where he stirred her fire until the coals awoke then added a length from a nearby deadfall. When that snuffled and burned, he fetched two more. Soon a blaze lit the darkening evening and the cave's deeper portions. Once it ebbed, Pork formed a spit with rocks and a green stick and roasted two pheasants he'd killed on the walk in. He coaxed Peg to eat a drumstick, then a thigh, and then to sip the cold broth in his canteen.

Full night, Pork stared at the moon and stars like words misspelled. He pored over them to find a vowel he'd heard wrong or a tricky letter like the *f* sound *ph* made. Peg was a word he'd write and write and misplace letters all the while, never learning them, let alone what the sounds added up meant.

Peg recognized an abrasion dried between Pork's knuckles. Likely he had clobbered a rock hiking in. She bent and attached her mouth to the wound. Her tongue wavered like a bee hunting pollen and she tasted his metallic blood. Pork's head quieted then filled with other sounds: birds calling and insects crawling and plants growing and flowers opening and hoofed animals browsing and the clawed killing for their meat.

They went to sleep, Peg with her head upon Pork's stomach, listening to his insides work.

The next morning he told her, "I'll find some work. I'm a good hand."

4

EXODUS
August 1991

At the Chewelah city park, Andre and Smoker hooked the bear's leash with a fishing pole and led him from the camper for a walk. The bear remained docile even when Andre hosed it off with a sprinkler. That evening they rented an RV spot at a gambling hall and restaurant housed in a long metal structure resembling a warehouse. Behind it loggers had thinned the forest and developers were shaping a golf course. Smoker purchased half a dozen chicken sandwiches in the restaurant.

In the truck cab, Andre unwrapped one. "I should've let Calvin beat on you a few more minutes."

"Tide'd turned quick enough."

Andre laughed. "You were finished from the first blow."

"Why's that?"

Andre took a bite and chewed. "Because he landed the second."

Smoker opened a soft drink.

"You don't ever calculate past talk," Andre told him. "That's what you're good at. Well, Calvin's good at hitting."

"We got along in the end."

"How many times I whack him with that board?"

"Three or four."

"Six. And he was still froggy. Most would be finished with the first. Calvin, he was just loose enough for conversation. That ought to tell you something about him."

"Tells me good thing we whipped him," Smoker said.

Andre finished a sandwich. The bear fussed and Smoker opened the slider and tossed it the last one, paper and all.

"You're just looking at it how you want it to be," Andre told him.

"How else is there?"

Smoker would persevere because the endeavor involved Bird, but he would rely as always on foolishness with style, which passed for bravery and good sense under a beer light.

"You don't have any idea what you're up to, do you?" Andre asked.

"Nope."

"That's likely to become a damned problem," he told his brother.

They slept late and treated themselves to a country breakfast and delivered their scraps to the bear. The luxury meant they were late on the highway, though Smoker seemed neither in a rush to arrive nor in the mood to travel the most efficient direction. Andre examined the county map and Calvin's hen scratch. Smoker had abandoned the route. Andre inquired and Smoker informed him there were lots of ways to get to a place and only the narrow-minded relied on maps.

The highway paralleled the Pend Oreille River's wide valley into the gap between granite cliffs. Metaline Falls, the town, was crammed between. The falls itself was drowned by Boundary Dam.

Higher, Smoker angled onto a dirt road bisected by others that wound through meadows or between twilight-draped fir and pine, country occasionally dotted with trailer houses with rusted carports or hand-built plywood-sided hovels. The truck traversed a grassy meadow and rounded a knoll to a double-wide that overlooked a grassy creek bed. Dede's car was next to the front steps.

The bear lurched into the camper wall when Smoker halted the truck. Andre waited while Smoker walked stiffly to the door and knocked. Dede answered. It appeared he and Dede were flirting until Dede frowned and spat a word at him. Smoker appeared to disarm her and she smiled. But soon another cloud darkened her face and before Smoker could manage more sweet talk she slammed the trailer door on his hand.

Smoker yowled and hopped and thrust his left hand back and forth. His pinkie finger, clearly broken, dangled beneath the others, but he hooked a cigarette from his pocket and struck a match one-handed like a broken finger was nothing new to him.

He waved Andre from the truck.

"Getting dark," Smoker said. "We might as well bunk indoors. I doubt that bear will share his abode."

"Might be safer with him than her," Andre said.

"She's spit her venom," Smoker said.

Inside the trailer, Dede emerged from the bathroom along with the smell of lavender soap and hair spray, her black jeans and cowboy shirt arced by her hips and breasts, turquoise stitched across the latter. Her dark hair parted in the middle and crescented around both sides of her face allowed her almond eyes and delicate nose an audience.

She tipped her whiskey glass at him. Andre waved his hand.

"Again?" Dede asked.

"Again," Andre said.

Dede rattled the fridge for an orange. She drove her thumb into the peel and sheared it like pencil shavings then divided the sections. She flicked one in Andre's mouth. When he finished, she fed him another.

"Go on and tell him," she coaxed Smoker. "Explain it like you told me."

"You're not being polite," Smoker replied.

"I'm past courtesy." Dede tipped her head and drank her whiskey, graceful as a bird.

"Long time past." Smoker held up his useless left hand. "How's it going to look getting this broke in a door?"

"Just say you were drunk and fell," Dede told him.

"Nobody ever seen me fall drunk. They aren't likely to believe I started just now."

"Suit yourself," Dede said.

"You left my child on a mountain with strangers."

"Might not be yours," Dede told him.

One look at Bird and Smoker left little doubt about her bloodline, but Smoker stalked the room and lowered his face to Dede's.

"Fuck you," he said.

Dede rose to her tiptoes and kissed Smoker's nose. "Not for a while."

"I'm not liable to wait."

"Me neither," Dede told him. "Let your brother here take the baby and we'll fuck the whole country, you and me. Everyone except each other. See who holds out longest."

Smoker blew some smoke into the ceiling.

"Maybe you best go on and bunk in your truck," she said to him.

"You want to treat us that cold?"

"Just you," she said. "Your brother can have the couch."

Smoker lifted his cap from the chair back, eased it over his head with his good hand. He disappeared out the door.

Dede poured herself more whiskey then banged ice from a tray. The soda was outside with the beer and she retrieved a cola and filled a glass with it.

"You're not off caffeine, I hope."

Andre shook his head.

Dede delivered him a soda.

"On the mountain they're batshit crazy, but Harold, he reads to Bird every night. He has building blocks and spirographs and a workbook where she does long division. Her math is better than an accountant's. And she reads the Bible. King James with the thous and thees," Dede said. "I love her." She nodded toward the door and truck outside. "I love her as much as that rat bastard." She drank. "I just don't have much to teach her." She perched next to Andre like a ball, as if she wanted to keep small. "The only time I got with her was the time he'd gone off. Otherwise, it's always him and me or him and her."

Dede picked at a cuticle then lifted her hand to her mouth and chewed the dangling skin.

"I gave her a locket from my grandmother," she said. "You know what your brother did? He stuck a picture of himself in it. You think I'd leave her with him?"

Dede drank then stared at the whiskey bottle; her empty glass shifted in her hand. "I wish I could quit like you," she said.

"Drinking?"

"Everything."

"Smoker?"

She nodded.

"You two went that way before."

"You quit liquor a time or two, didn't you?" Dede closed her eyes and a muscle in her jaw tightened. She sucked air between her teeth. "He's a rat bastard," she said.

"He's my brother," Andre told her.

"And you know best."

Neither spoke for a long while.

"You hear from Claire?" she asked him finally.

Andre closed his eyes. Growing up, he had prided himself on distance. It was all he possessed Smoker didn't, but he was not any more able to hear or speak to a person's heart than rock was to keep seed.

"Mentioning her was mean of me," Dede said. Andre rubbed at the ache in his neck. When he looked up, Dede had undone her shirt. He peered at the white bra that kept her in and smelled again the hair spray and the liquor and lavender on her. She undid her jeans and, in her skivvies, kissed him as if she were trying to inject her sour tongue into him or, maybe, suck the poison in him out.

"You're after revenge is all," Andre said.

"Don't you think he needs getting back at?" she asked. All the boldness was off her. He said nothing and after what must have seemed long enough for him to answer, she undid his pants and helped him from them.

LAMENTATIONS

March–June 1984

Andre and Claire didn't speak of Pork or his troubles. Conversation between them concerned mostly schoolwork and students and grocery lists and recipes and ingredients as together they concocted their meals and school lunches. She aided Andre with Carl's essays. He applied to local schools: Eastern, Western, and Central Washington Universities, low-profile but less than a day's drive. Together Claire and Andre determined Carl should discuss the effect of his illness on his grade point. Andre did the same in his recommendation, adding that the boy's mother was single and on disability.

Smoker visited a week into Pork's rehab stint, and he and Andre addressed a pornographic card to Pork, care of the clinic. A week later Andre received a return letter protesting the cafeteria's hamburger gravy and processed potatoes. From the newspaper circular Andre snipped a coupon for rib eye and Smoker attached a Post-it note: "Stick it out, you picky bastard." Pork's next correspondence was the yellow-stained ad and no words at all.

A week or so later, a neophyte orderly informed Pork he was voluntary and Pork beat feet for the door. He panhandled bus fare and the next day arrived at Corrigan Auto Body Repair, which doubled as Grand Coulee's depot. There, he phoned Andre who transported him to the ranch without argument. If the old man remained sharp enough to jailbreak the hospital, alcohol had not completely undone him.

The next evening, though, Andre and Smoker brought him iced tea, a box of fried chicken, and a Hawaiian pizza along with four boxes of groceries. They devoured a meal together, with no drink other than soda pop, then hiked into the poplars behind the corral to hunt a coyote harassing Pork's calves. They got off no shots but heard the criminal yipping up the canyon.

Eventually Andre abandoned Claire twice a week to tend Pork. Late those nights, he entered their bedroom reeking of cigarette smoke and men. She suspected he was drinking; Andre knew but he was unsure how to soothe her. The truth seemed inadequate.

They chose the Melody Café because none of Pork's cronies frequented the place. Entering town, they took the back road past the Methodist Church. Smoker pointed at a Pinto in front of them. A woman's blouse fluttered from the window along with her socks and bra. They passed and through the rear window, they saw her wrestling off her jeans. The male driver shifted to kiss her. She appeared to laugh and finished with her drawers. The car stopped entirely. Smoker passed then circled back and found the Pinto's door open and the naked woman dancing on the pavement. She had black hair and beige nipples. Mostly, though, she was an abundance of pale skin.

Smoker blasted the horn. The woman glanced at her pubic hair then loped into a vacant lot. Rocks and thistles reduced her to hopping. The driver rifled his trunk for a blanket then hurried into the field and wrapped the woman tightly.

"I remember naked women," Pork said. "I forgot I liked them."

Smoker stopped at the bar after he had returned Andre to Claire's. Eddie toweled dry glasses and a few construction workers shot pool in the back.

"Seen a naked woman today, Eddie," Smoker said.

"You looked at your share, I hear."

"This one was in the middle of the road and in plain day."

Eddie halted his towel and examined Smoker. He appeared skeptical.

"Pork will testify and he's sober," Smoker told him.

"Till he remembers what he was drinking for," Peg said.

At the end of the bar, she sat in the shadow of the television: Smoker's mother, Pork's wife. Her eyes remained an animal's—portals through which to observe the world. In them was not the spark of charm or even passion but the lunacy of an arsonist's torch. Peg was not a modern beauty: She didn't possess Botoxed lips or a starved, boney face; no pointed chin nor straight-angled jaw, the kind of look a geometry teacher or perhaps child molester might appreciate. Neither anorexia nor bulimia, nor silicone nor saline contorted her figure into some cartoon you wanted to fuck.

She turned and her face pulsed in a blinking beer sign. It was full, without flaw, like Ingrid Bergman when the cameras shot close. Her butterscotch hair could hold together in a breeze, but parted and mussed stylishly when she raked her hand through it, and she was well put together, tall enough to have the pins of a dancer but curved more like the Vargas girls in *Esquire* or *Playboy* in their salad days. In her countenance resided a siren on a perch that coaxed men to smash themselves against her rocky shores.

"Where's your brother?" she asked.

"He's domesticated and good for him."

Peg had taken Andre's most recent run at sobriety as a hard

slap. She did not care for Claire and complained she thought college put herself above them. When Smoker pointed out Andre had earned his sheepskin, too, it did no good, as she suspected the same of Andre.

"You're happy here. I'm happy here," Peg said. "Eddie, you're happy, aren't you?"

Eddie shrugged. "If you say so, my dear. I'd say we don't want much. Doesn't strike me as the same thing." He passed his gritty hands across his apron, leaving streaks.

"Andre aspires to more than us," Peg said.

Smoker shook his head. "Different is all. He wants different."

"Still an insult," Peg said. She sipped her beer.

"If you're set on pouting, do it quietly," Smoker told her. "I'm trying to tell a story here." He turned to Eddie.

"Was this naked woman on her own?" Eddie asked.

"Pour me a cold one and I'll tell you," Smoker replied.

Eddie did.

"Some bald guy chased her out of his car. That's how we happened upon her. They were stopped in the car in front of us," Smoker replied. "None of us knew him from Adam. Peculiar, too, because he's not the kind strikes you as forgettable. Dressed like a cowboy going to the high-school prom. Bolo tie with a silver dollar hasp. Turquoise buttons on his shirt. No hat, though."

"Big ears and John Lennon glasses?" Peg asked.

Smoker nodded.

"The Reverend Harold Mansell."

"Preacher ought to be in uniform," Smoker said. "He didn't wear a frock or a collar."

"I believe his religion is inclined toward the casual," Peg said.

BRUCE HOLBERT

Smoker shrugged. He encountered few faces he didn't recognize in the coulee, but it was possible Peg was ahead of him on
this Harold. Peg was famous throughout the county for both her
beauty and her antics, and she met all sorts in her preferred line
of work. No friend to hourly wages, which interfered with her
self-destruction, she rarely kept jobs longer than it took for her employers to file W-2s. After, she would politely resign. Her employers
could rely on her stint doubling the male patronage so they
endured her intermittent leaves without complaint.

In the hiatus between legal jobs, Peg earned the income that
fueled her vices under the table.

Eddie refilled both their schooner glasses.

"How'd you meet up with a man of the cloth?" Smoker asked
Peg.

Peg grinned and drank and refused to answer.

"Well, I doubt it was church," Smoker told her.

That evening, Andre returned to Claire perched on the kitchen
table in her terry cloth robe. In front of her was a bottle of whiskey and two glasses.

Andre eyed the bottle hard.

"Don't mistake mean looks for strength and don't think I do,"
Claire said.

"You see it like that?"

"That's all those boys you harassed know of you."

"One instance all it takes to make it the rule?"

Claire intertwined her fingers and put them in her lap. Andre
switched off the radio.

"No," she said finally.

"Then the argument you're in is with someone else, not me."

Claire opened the bottle and filled two tumblers.

"Those are hefty shots," Andre told her.

She lifted a glass, drank, grimaced, then drank again and ordered Andre to do the same.

"I'm on the wagon."

Claire drank again and swallowed, her face a clenched fist.

"Your inexperience is showing," Andre said.

"I used to drink before you," she told him.

"Didn't have you pegged for a lush."

"I had a glass of wine every other day and both days on the weekends," Claire said. "Now drink up."

Andre declined.

"You don't want to drink with me?"

"It was mean of you to bring it into the house," Andre said.

"I want to understand," Claire told him.

"Understand what?"

"Everything."

"Well ask, goddamnit."

"You won't tell me."

"That's only because I don't know either."

She stared into Andre's face.

"What?" he said.

"I believe you," she said. "You don't lie."

Andre emptied the second glass into the sink.

"What's it feel like? To drink, I mean for you?" Claire asked.

"Giving up. Losing."

"How about when you stop?"

He considered the question. "The same," he said.

"How about scaring those boys?"

"The same. Like I got beat by something."

"Everything feels that way to you, doesn't it?"

"Mostly," Andre said. "Except you."

She touched her glass with her finger and circled its rim, then she smiled. Andre placed the bourbon bottle in the high cabinet. "Maybe give that to the Senior Citizens Center. They're due to stir things up."

Claire said, "I'm going to feel terrible tomorrow, aren't I?"

"I'd bet your paycheck on it," Andre replied.

It turned out Reverend Harold had owned a patchwork of alfalfa fields quilted in the flats between the rock and forests of the Selkirk Mountains. He fed most to his beeves to augment their summer grazing and sold the rest to neighbors with less ground or more cattle. Three years earlier a hoof-and-mouth outbreak had scared the FDA off Midwest stock and prices doubled. Cash happy, the reverend bought a fancy wheel tractor for which he could no longer manage payments. Selling was out of the question, as it would leave him upside down on the loan.

He approached Peg at a barter fair in Tonasket, a homemade wooden cross looped around his neck.

He poked Peg's inoculation scar.

"You're marked," he said.

The Christians in the woods didn't care for shots, or for science in general. It posed problems they already possessed the solution to, and when the scientists' answers differed from theirs, they determined someone somewhere had pulled a fast one and these

Christians loathed fast ones more than they did science, government, modern poetry, and abstract art put together.

Peg had to admit they didn't completely lack sense. The oxymoronic concept that to avoid biological scourges doctors ought to isolate the disease in a petri dish and then inject it into the public's bloodstream through schoolchildren seemed strange magic even to her.

Peg withdrew a pint of bourbon from her basket of possibles. She studied the brown liquid in the afternoon and drank, then tipped the bottle at Harold.

"I'm guessing you don't imbibe."

"No," Harold said. "Thank you. You have kids?"

Peg nodded.

"You look after them and they still go off the rails."

She laughed. "They would debate that."

"Which?"

"That I looked after them."

"Mothers can't help but look after their kids, can they?" the reverend asked. "I mean, it's nature and it's in the Bible."

"Now you're a goddamned philosopher. You don't know my life or my children's. You don't know how I wounded them."

"Did they wound you?"

"Only by existing." She paused. "You're a retard and I think our business is done."

Harold laughed. "They're right. You're perfect for this work."

The rocking-horse economy pitched from bear to bull, but money in the country had divorced itself from actual labor years ago. In the mountains, tapped-out loggers and long-haul truckers abandoned their rigs, lifts, or skidders on remote forest service roads rather than surrender them to the banks in town. The banks preferred equipment on paper, and rather than retrieve their assets, they simply printed another ledger with red numbers instead of black.

So Peg hired crews and parted out the rigs to shade-tree mechanics or fly-by-night boneyards. In this endeavor, she was unlike herself, cautious enough never to hire the same person twice, and she refused to recruit anyone she couldn't ruin with a phone call.

"How's that?"

He pointed at her scar once more. "Inoculated, like I said."

"It doesn't cure everything."

Harold laughed. He recounted his predicament and they made medicine easily enough. The reverend's son soon appeared and Peg insisted he drink with her to seal the contract. He was not as reluctant as Harold would have preferred.

Peg hunted a crew that evening at the Elkhorn Saloon: hippies, but sociable, and strong enough to lift what she could not. The work took two days and another to deliver, but the money was better than she had expected, and she and Harold both took enough from the endeavor to feel like good fortune may be attached to the other, though Peg would later curse herself for her optimism.

Spring settled them all. Peg was occupied with business, which forced her into low gear. At the ranch, Pork planted and tended his small cattle herd. One weekend, Smoker and Andre helped him nut his steers.

"I just read Marty Robbins is dead," Pork said.

"Passed several years back," Andre told him.

"Well why in hell didn't you tell me."

"I figured it would go hard on you."

He paused. "You figured right."

"At least we still got George," Andre said.

George Jones's voice was past even art, it seemed to Andre.

"I heard he stopped drinking," Andre said.

"He's taking a sabbatical is all," Pork replied. "Like me."

They continued: Pork heated the brand and Andre and Smoker tossed calves and steers. Pork cut the males and they all sang "Streets of Laredo" and "Cool Water." The work went quickly. Labor and a month clean left Pork ropy with sinew. His stamina had rebounded and so did his preference for solitude. As the three washed up, he thanked them for looking after him and told them now they could knock it off.

Released from duty, Smoker took work logging near Loomis. Andre applied his attention to Claire and closing the school year. One afternoon not long after the weather broke, the high-school principal visited Andre's classroom. Claire allowed him in. He remained in the doorway in a three hundred dollar suit.

The man said to her, "You should hear this, too."

"I suppose she'll do as she pleases," Andre said.

Claire sat in a desk at the rear of the room.

"That boy has gifts," the principal said.

Andre nodded. "He's got a name, too."

"Well, he could be at Stanford or Cal," the man said.

"His mother has emphysema, can't work. The father left for Alaska ten years ago. Her kin is all in Wisconsin."

"He worries about his mother and it will hold him back. I talked to her. She understands," the principal replied.

"No, you bullied her," Andre said. "He told me. If you go there again I'll help him file a restraining order and deliver the paper to the school board myself with the family in tow."

The man glanced at Claire. "Living in sin can besmirch a teacher's reputation."

"You ought to address yourself to me if you want this to remain civil," Andre said. "How long you been in this place?"

The man shrugged. "Nine months."

"Well, I'd suggest you inquire around." Andre laughed. "One of them school board members humps his secretaries and another bumps uglies with his wife's cousin. Both are barely secret."

The man straightened his tie like that could prop up his argument.

"You're trying to put the boy into a big-time school," Andre said. "He wants one he'll finish. He's got too much in him to abandon a sick mother six months at a time. He goes to California, he'll be back here bagging groceries at Safeway before Halloween. In-state, he can visit when he gets the notion and his mother can ride the bus to get to him. Corrigan at the garage, he operates the Trailways bus desk. He's got my credit card. She calls him. He sends a boy to chauffer her to the store and she hops the bus. The boy, I got him another card for her hotel."

"And you pay?" the principal asked.

"It won't cost much."

"What's this to you?"

"I had the boy in class, seventh grade. Once he raked my yard without me even asking. Wouldn't take a dollar for his troubles. His mother—when I was a pup and she was well—patched me after a bicycle wreck and drove me to the nurse."

The principal was silent.

"You aren't likely to pick that kind of news up in nine months," Andre said.

The principal glanced at Claire. "I shouldn't have been personal."

Claire nodded.

"Is there anything I can do? Other than keep out of the way, I mean."

Andre laughed.

"Maybe could help him transfer to someplace later, if it suits him," Claire suggested.

"That's country you know better than the rest of us," Andre added.

"Be happy to." The principal bowed.

Andre rose and shook his hand. "Was all you wanted some public relations on him?" Andre said.

"Well, it started out that way, I admit."

The Reverend Harold's son, Calvin, was in the deep end without a paddle.

"He didn't appear a chip off the old block?" Peg said.

Harold shook his head.

"Takes after his mother, I assume."

"She was a saint."

"Was?"

"She passed."

Peg's contract required her to retrieve Calvin when he crossed the Mexican border and transport him to the Idaho mountains. Harold slid an envelope across a booth in the tavern. "It's five thousand dollars, all I have, so don't bother bargaining."

"He wanted?"

"In Mexico."

"The law?"

"There's worse things than a Mexican cop, I'm coming to learn."

"I've heard," Peg said.

"He's in Riverside. You won't have to cross the border."

"But his friends, they have no compunctions about coming this direction. Otherwise why spend your money."

"Now you know as much as I do," Harold said.

"That doesn't comfort me much."

"Nor me," he said. "But there it is."

"Will you bless me?"

"Of course," the reverend replied.

She crossed herself then laughed at him. Ticking away in every life was anarchy and she enjoyed seeing others unraveling.

"I want a beef to boot," Peg said finally. "Butchered and wrapped."

"I'll see to it," Harold said.

Driving, Peg drummed the steering wheel, tapping a rhythm that outran anything on the radio. Occasionally she halted the beat and flattened her hand like she might to divert someone attempting to refill her coffee.

She could rationalize the crime easily enough, and in her conscience she remained acquitted and reminded herself how right and wrong, good and evil, and moral compunction were beyond her concern, and though she saw them twinkle in others' skies, they were light with no warmth for her. Which did not mean she was without an ethic. Hers was, in fact, shared with every life, plant or animal: self-preservation. Such motive was not shocking; its lack of adornment was the scandal.

She enjoyed travel, though only alone. A highway encouraged one's thinking to unravel in loops and knots where you could unsnarl it like fishing line. Late nights, she listened to the radio stations. The generation preceding Peg played Lefty Frizzell or George Jones and drove drunk into telephone poles and tried to recall a train whistle's moan. Peg's era, the young scorned such music, though, in muscle cars and four-by-fours, their cassette and eight-track decks reincarnated such music and their fiddles and steel slides in rock and roll. Peg and her peers whispered the lyrics like prayers and drove in circles and drank beer and shot road signs and thought they were plowing new ground, which was, in fact, dirt that had played out long ago.

Midnight, Peg maneuvered the Impala behind a cluster of long-haulers at a California truck stop. The clattering diesel engines soothed her thoughts and she snoozed until disturbed by an ambulance whine. It turned out a fat trucker's bladder had determined to pass a kidney stone. The trucker's pain drove him to the bathroom's tile floor, which broke his hip, and he screamed like an Indian until the EMTs hit him with Demerol. Peg's eyes shut until dawn's light yellowed the flat horizon and Mount Shasta loomed over the reservoir. She turned the ignition key and the motor knocked until the spark fired the cylinders and the pistons chugged into their ordered rhythm.

Fourteen hours later, Peg bought a liter of Pepsi and cigarettes at a Circle K to make change then dialed the numbers Harold had scribbled on a grocery bag.

"Five minutes," she said.

Peg circled the block in her Impala, and on the second pass, Calvin stood at the curb in front of the run-down ranch-style house. Peg slowed, shoved open the door, and he and his knapsack dropped into the seat next to her. He was a bony kid with stick arms in a white T-shirt, no muscle or gut punctuating the cotton. He appeared as if he were made of angles pointing several directions at once. His face was similar, a narrow chin with a square above it that was his cheeks and forehead. Only his nose varied from the pattern, slightly misdirected from a past mishap, Peg assumed.

He closed his eyes and allowed his head to sink into the rest and was asleep before they left the city. He had no beard, which meant he had not encountered steady pussy. Religion and awkwardness likely were culprits. He imagined he'd escaped, Peg figured, and all he had left was a long ride. He was a child and, like a child, thought running would unloose him from a hornet's nest he'd bumbled into when likely it would just hurry him into the next until hornets were all he knew. Still, she let him sleep.

Andre moved in with Claire on the first weekend in April. Two pickup loads—one for furniture, another for boxes—were all the chore required. Carl helped pack. He had decided on Western Washington University. He was curious about the ocean. The math department offered him the works and Safeway agreed to transfer his job.

In Claire's house, Andre was at first uncomfortable. She cooked the first three nights and did the dishes and he felt of no use. She recognized this the fourth evening and arrived with supermarket chicken and coleslaw she knew he'd grown accustomed to. Andre shoved the coffee table back from the couch and he and Claire propped their heads with the same cushion and their legs with another and bent in the middle to leave room for their meal. They watched the news, then part of a basketball game, then a half-hour comedy. She felt for the first time like she imagined her parents, married thirty-two years, might have.

What Claire thought refreshing about Andre was that he refused to speak drivel. In fact, he rarely talked aside from responding to her questions or posing one if necessary. But he was in attendance with others more than anyone she knew. When he corrected homework problems, he drummed a green pen against his temple, which pocked his skin. If he glanced up from his work and recognized Claire's attention, a shadow rolled from beneath his eyes and surfaced as if waking, and he smiled a smile that nearly drew her tears.

GENESIS
Autumn 1964

Pork supported his family two years working at the seed plant in town. Wendell, their second son, who would be called Smoker because he melted his candy cigarettes with a lighter, soon shared the second bedroom with Andre. Eighteen months older, Andre tended his brother like a shepherd. The two jabbered steadily. The older comprehended the younger's gibberish well before Pork or Peg. Too young yet for grudges and running feuds, they hollered at each other one minute then turned partners the next, plotting havoc against the cat or dog or arranging soldiers on the coffee table.

When Pork's father, weakened by a congested heart, accepted a move to the Senior Citizens Center, Pork planted his family into the much-neglected ranch house. Throughout fall, he remodeled the bathroom for Peg and jerry-rigged two bed frames into the boys' bunk bed, while his father swallowed handfuls of nitroglycerine that did little good. He passed in November. Several signatures and a thousand dollars to a shyster and Pork owned the place.

Some evenings, he and Peg would prepare an early dinner, hire a girl for the boys, then travel to the town taverns. There, the locals gossiped against one another or complained over jobs or a lack of them. A couple of hours of this closed Pork's days nicely, as he felt above such gripes, but its monotony agitated Peg to the point she lit firecrackers and flicked them under the pool tables for excitement or threw ice at the juke when she found the music objectionable. One day a week satisfied Pork's inclination to socialize, but Peg champed at the bit for more people and neon. Eventually Pork wearied of town and Peg's pyrotechnics and surrendered town to drink beer on the porch, fortified with more whiskey than he admitted. This did not deter Peg, who trundled the feed truck to the tavern four nights a week and found no trouble attracting company.

Some nights Pork awoke in the morning dark clammy, heart whomping, arms numb, thoughts hurtling so fast words couldn't match the pace. In his head a hiss leaked the seconds away like air exiting a tire. The town doctor pronounced him fit, but Pork told Peg he felt smothered in bed and moved to the couch.

Peg remained absent three days to spite him. The fourth,

Pork awoke to her stroking his forehead like a feverish child. She unbuttoned her shirt and loosened the sweat pants he wore, then dragged his rigging to ready and slipped over him. He heard her heave at the air while she threw herself against his pelvis. Together they made a clopping sound. The muscles in her face squeezed against one another as if she was in great concentration or attempting to read a faraway sign. She did not cry out, as was her wont, or speak or pull at his muscled chest and back. Instead, when she reached her place, she clamped her legs and hips onto him then blew out a long broken breath. After, she kneeled beside the couch, her breathing slackened and her eyes shut. With one finger, she tracked through his hair, over his forehead and then his nose. Her nail tapped his front teeth, clicking. She drew the C shape of his jaw over and over. The TV light flowed across the both of them like they were pebbles scattered by the same stream.

She returned to their bed alone. On the television the morning cartoons soon flickered. Pork fried an egg and a length of German sausage, then showered and dressed in jeans and a fresh T-shirt. At the ranch tank, he topped off the pickup and aimed it for town where he withdrew seventeen hundred dollars from the savings, then at the liquor store bought a pint of bourbon. At the hardware, he added a rose starter, the roots in a plastic bag along with a shovel full of peat moss, a farewell for his oldest son, who favored flowers, a fact that might cause some fathers trauma, though Pork recognized the boy was just stricken with growing things.

By the time he exited town, cars had switched on headlights. A steady rain rattled the cab; Pork's worn wipers streaked the window. Dry months the whole country prayed for this weather:

honest-to-God-get-down-on-your-knees-and-call-Christ-by-his-first-name prayers. Rain was more than good luck; it was payment for being in the right life.

As Pork neared a county-mile marker white light flooded cock-eyed into the sky. A wadded Pontiac lay in the ditch bank against a broken road sign. In silhouette, a boy labored through the driver-side window. His left forearm changed course between his elbow and wrist. Rain pasted his hair to his head and his soaked shirt hung like hound skin. Behind, another set of headlights approached and halted. A man hurried past, his hair combed backward and his sideburns cut wide: folks called him Elvis.

"You call an ambulance?" Elvis asked him.

"I just got here," Pork said.

"My sister's in there," the boy told them.

Elvis directed Pork to press a handful of rags from his trunk to a nasty leg wound. Pork felt the girl shift under his hands. The boy looked in through the open window. He was praying. Her eyes fluttered and she sighed deeply, a death rattle, Pork worried.

Elvis rushed to a nearby ranch house and back. Not long after, an ambulance strobed the sky. Two EMTs hoisted the girl from the wreck and belted her to a gurney. A cop joined them. Pork and Elvis watched the boy climb in with the EMTs and the ambulance door shut. They listened as the siren whirred. Red lights beat against the low sky.

"We saved her," Elvis said.

Pork stared into the pavement. "I don't know."

"We did," Elvis said. "We saved her."

"Okay," Pork replied. "We saved her."

His house, Pork navigated the darkness to his bedroom. At the dresser, he unsnapped a suitcase and began to fill it. Andre startled him in the doorway. Three feet tall, the boy shifted from one leg to the other and peered at Pork. He tugged a dresser drawer and unpacked what Pork had packed, neatly stacking underwear, socks, and the rest. When one drawer was filled, he pulled loose the next, certain and full of the grace that accompanied good work. Pork's coat pocket was heavy with his emptied savings, but all his son knew about it was that clothes belonged in drawers.

On top of the dresser was a small wicker basket that held a pocket watch and a silver dollar, a gift from Pork's father when he graduated high school. Pork raised the dollar and contemplated its weight. His son wrestled up the mattress and buried himself next to Peg. Pork had no past before Peg and the children. He'd existed instead in the blissful blank of the present. Peg had not delivered him into calamity; he went willingly, full steam.

Pork undressed and dipped beneath the sheets. Andre shivered against Pork's cold skin, then dug into him. Peg shifted toward Pork. She put her palm against his chest.

"So, you're staying?" she whispered.

"Yes," he said.

After the divorce, the boys resided on Pork's ranch summers and vacations. The school year, Peg dragged them to various addresses and took on men like middle schoolers adopt insects, to ignore or torture them. Andre and Smoker cottoned to few, though their opinions were of little matter. Those who played cards with the boys or invited them to shoot bottles at the dump Peg soon lost affection for. The bad ones who busted up the house when she talked back stuck.

Andre responded by squandering hours shooting a basketball. Often, Smoker tagged along. Sometimes he rebounded for his brother, but mostly he roamed with children in similar straits, smoking cigarettes and stealing soda pop from the grocery. Andre, though, remained engrossed in the backboard's thump when it directed the ball through the rim—bank shooters didn't require touch, just geometry. The lack of elegance turned the shot strangely his own and the breach in the world he would later identify as self widened enough to consume not just him but his surroundings. Smoker, meanwhile, graduated to wrestling the drawers from the prettiest middle-school girls in a nearby thicket.

Andre may have disappeared into himself entirely if he had not broken his ankle on a court's concrete edge. The incident eventually trapped him in his mother's house with her most persistent suitor, Merlin Archer, who not long after clouted Andre's ear with a liter of Pepsi. Rather than bolt, Andre drove his head into the man's nuts then pounded his kidneys with his fists. Meanwhile, Smoker found an X-ACTO knife and attacked the man's hair like he meant to take the scalp.

Peg, suddenly out of the bathroom, laughed. "Merlin, get your ass out of this house before the children butcher you."

He scrambled through the back door.

"Boys," she said, "I'm going to Eddie's to get you a bucket of chicken. You're better than mean dogs."

They moved to Pork's for good. Like most ranchers, Pork maintained a barnload of cats to kill rats but he had no patience for them. He kicked any within the reach of his legs and in return they ambushed him from the barn trusses or under the wagon seats, biting fingers and thumbs to the bone. Pork mocked Andre, who treated the cats to fresh milk and tripe when they cut up a beef.

One day, out of the blue, Andre planted a cur-colored yellow kitten onto the table and let it lick the gravy boat. Pork nearly spilled his meal when he bolted up. Smoker worried he'd clobber them both. But he knew Andre was born with blood in him and a death wish, too, and Smoker's brother looked at the old man in a manner that halted Pork like nothing Smoker had seen stop the man, and Pork argued no more.

That cat—Andre refused to name him—turned into Andre's shadow. It commandeered his saddle horn when they worked cattle and hunted the field's edge while they plowed, supplying Andre a portion of any kill. The barn cats once tore his ball sack for his housecat standing, but Andre didn't consider dehorning the animal like a steer or gelding. Instead, he cajoled Smoker from his bed. They knocked the cat out with horse dope, then sawed a chunk from Andre's own arm with a skinning knife and sewed it into a tent over the cat's rigging. The next morning, Pork woke to Smoker asleep on the floor and Andre bandaged and patched in the armchair, the cat next to him.

5

EXODUS
August 1991

Andre escaped through the back door of Dede's trailer afterward to get his head right. In the grassless yard, an orange cigarette ember went red and lit Smoker's face. He hunkered on a cedar chopping block. Andre could hear a nearby creek hurry through the dark landscape.

"It's cooling off," Smoker said. "I'll start a fire."

Finding no suitable fuel, he unloosened the wooden steps with a crowbar. He hauled a portion to the crude fire pit and splashed it with gasoline from the shed. When he struck the match, the blast shriveled his eyebrows and consumed his arm hair altogether. The sheepskin coat took a spark. Andre whacked it.

Smoker wheeled, fists doubled. "I'm out already!"

A wedge of light from the trailer blanched them. Dede stepped over the porch's ruins. She wore a long duster and a hunter-orange stocking cap and rubbed her bare legs together like a cricket.

"What're you going to do?" Smoker asked her.

"Take a shower. Go to the tavern in town."

"Then what?"

She scratched at her hair underneath the hat. "Stay drunk awhile."

"You leave Bird to me then. I'm not putting lunatics in charge of my child."

"Lunatics have been doing the job all her life."

"Well at least I'm a crazy she is familiar with."

Dede glanced at Andre. "Maybe your brother would do better than them or me or you."

"I'd be the last person he'd let tend his child," Andre told her.

Dede smiled at him. "You aren't so bad," she said. "Not near as awful as you're worrying." She aimed her chin at Smoker. "He's no victim."

Smoker added a long two-by-six to the blaze. The dry wood caught and burned hard. The heat backed them into the darkness.

"You best get on if you're going," Smoker said.

"How about your hand?" Dede lifted an aspirin bottle from her pocket and began counting them out.

"Don't pile your car up worrying over it."

"Don't make this about me," Dede said.

Smoker squinted and cocked his head.

"What?" Dede said.

"I'm looking for stretch marks on your arm from being twisted," he told her.

"You're a rat bastard," she said quietly.

Andre found a woodpile on the other side of the shed and toted an armload of tamarack to the fire pit. Smoker put the chopping block on to burn. The fire roared. Andre glanced up into an empty window. He and Smoker had pressed their faces in similar instances keeping vigil for Peg or Pork, two days absent, winter, on ice-slick roads, sure one or the other or both were dead and they were just waiting the night through to hike to the neighbors.

Andre glanced at Dede.

"You broke his hand. You never broke bones before," Andre said. "What were you wound up over?"

"I don't remember," Dede said.

"He put you up to it," Andre said. He turned and glared at Smoker. "This don't make us square, goddamnit."

Andre hurried past Dede inside to take a piss. A puny .410 rested in the mudroom corner for nuisance crows. He collected it, cleared the bolt, then pressed a round into the chamber. Outside, he fired a load of bird shot into Smoker's ass.

Smoker collapsed to all fours, groaned, then scurried for the dark.

Dede, beside Andre, shouted, "I hope he creases you again, you rat bastard."

The pickup door opened. The 30.06 Smoker stowed beneath the seat put out the porch light. Andre heard the bear batting the camper's paneling.

"Knock it off, goddamnit," Dede shouted.

A bullet snapped her flapping duster below the knee. With a wounded hand, he would need a rest for such shots, but Andre could see no rock outcropping or deadhead pine. Dede hissed

126

and rounded the front of the house. Andre heard her car's ignition turn and the tires bust the gravel.

"You thought I had it so good," Smoker shouted. "Jesus. Well, I guess now you know."

"I don't know nothing of the kind," Andre yelled back.

Andre set the .410 on the steps and stared into the dying fire. He considered adding more fuel though it would make him a target in the light. He sat. A minute later, he heard a rifle safety click in the doorway behind him.

"You going to shoot me anymore?" Smoker asked.

Andre shook his head.

Blood blackened Smoker's jeans pocket. It followed the seam's path then ticked on the linoleum.

"All right, then," Smoker said.

He hobbled in the truck's direction. His broken finger dangled on his left side and his shot-up buttock forced a limp from his right. Andre followed. Smoker had taken the passenger side so Andre hit the ignition and let the motor warm. The fire glowed in the rear mirrors and cast its light up the hill.

Andre and Smoker found an open grocery in town where Andre purchased all the gauze and medical tape he could carry along with a bottle of rubbing alcohol and another ham for the bear. Outside of town, they hunted a turnout. There, Smoker bent over the tailgate while Andre determined how to doctor him. The shot peppered his skin but had not got to muscle or bone. Still, digging it out seemed past Andre's knowledge and Smoker's patience.

"Ain't all that bad," Andre told him.

"You know what would be better?" Smoker asked.

"What?"

"Not being shot in the ass."

"Maybe that will learn you."

"Learn me what?"

"If you don't know, I guess I'll have to shoot you again."

Smoker eyed him.

Andre found his buck knife and prodded a lump and extracted a BB and then several more.

A pickup slowed. Its headlights floated over them then remained. A man opened the door. He wore a graying beard that hung to his chest and carried a shotgun in one hand and a flashlight in the other.

He waved the flashlight at Smoker. "He hurting you?"

Smoker nor Andre replied.

"I ain't inclined to intrude into others' personal business," the man said. "Just don't believe anyone ought to force themselves on the other."

"He's my brother," Andre said.

"Well, that's against everything I know. Maybe you boys ought to think it over."

"He shot me in the ass," Smoker said.

"That's true," Andre replied. "I'm just trying to patch him."

"It an accident?" the man asked.

"Nope," Andre said. "He deserved it."

"You say," Smoker replied.

The man extended his hand. Andre shook it. "I am Rufus R. Jones and I have a brother I wish I'd shot in the ass a hundred times. It's a pleasure to meet a man who followed through."

"What about me?" Smoker asked.

"Seems to me you're lucky he is taking the time to fix you."

He returned to his pickup and delivered a whiskey pint to Smoker.

Smoker drank. "You don't even know the story."

Rufus took a pull from the bottle. "Story's as old as the Bible," he said. He returned the bottle to Smoker and left them in the darkness. Smoker aimed a flashlight at his ass. Andre dug some more.

"There's one deeper," he said.

"Go on," Smoker told him.

Andre poured the last of the old man's whiskey over the knife blade. He lit a match and slid the steel over the flame. It flickered blue. He thrust the knife in Smoker's glute. Smoker roared. Andre rotated the blade then felt the shot come undone. Andre held it in the light.

"Not as big as a jujube," Smoker said.

LAMENTATIONS

June 1984

Peg scanned rest areas and emergency turnouts for nondescript cars or trucks carrying two or more men and scratched the details on a notepad beneath her seat. A seedy-looking pickup sauntered onto the highway in front of them. Four men lay in back under a canopy, but four exits later they departed into thirty square miles of strawberries.

Peg paused to top off the radiator and add an equal amount of antifreeze then filled the gas tank. Another pickup pulled through the pump beside her, but its noisy occupants ended up only being high-school boys loading up on beer and ice. Peg retrieved her floppy hat from the trunk and donned sunglasses then strolled inside for mustard and bread and lunch meat.

The boy awoke. Distance or boredom along with a Big Gulp coffee loosened his tongue and he began a makeshift biography. He hailed from the north country, Stevens County. He had attended community college, toiled at a discount clothing store, and served senior citizens dinners on trays at a local buffet. Recently, he had seen the tiger smile, he said, and watched a man's last breath leave him.

Peg said nothing. The boy was ridiculous but amusing.

"Scientists, they pluck the first flower of spring, just to see how it works," he said. "Science. Space and time, spinning planets orbiting stars. Big words to make whoppers against Providence when we are just thoughts bobbing and sinking in God's mind." He paused. "It ruins the flowers," he said, finally.

Evening, she stopped for gas again and used the restroom, then let the boy have his turn. He vanished into the 7-Eleven and reappeared with a grin on his face and a long-stemmed yellow rose in cellophane. He extended it to her. They traveled on. The flower between them rocked on the seat. He'd paid likely ten times its worth.

Midnight, they parked in an abandoned gravel quarry Peg had scouted on the trip down. Together they built sandwiches and ate, then drank bottled water. Peg swallowed a sleeping pill, but the boy didn't require one.

Morning, they continued, pausing occasionally for coffee and gasoline or a dozen donuts. Then he began a homily against words. He put no stock in them or their symbols. Lying was as old as Adam. If it was a miracle for near-apes to separate their grunts into chains that made sense beyond onomatopoeia then it was just as significant a miracle to undo such matters and close the circle. The pages of every book were only white space and ink scratches and, though the marks had multiplied into a torrent that made Noah's deluge appear a summer squall, their slashes and dots and intersecting lines could not construct the truth.

He broke from his monologue to build them each another sandwich. Peg watched him devour his and the other half of hers. She had forgotten how much she enjoyed watching men eat. Women let each bite teeter on their forks, balancing the pleasure of taste and a sated appetite against the monster in the mirror they would encounter afterward. Men had no such compunctions. They ate like children, as if there were nothing but joy in it.

The boy picked up his one-sided conversation. Everyone gave too much credence to the story in their heads, Peg knew. The physical world and those who peopled it often reduced themselves to little more than dull television characters, and that included the artists and craftspeople at barter fairs hawking their work, clear-eyed, too sedate to be fully present and the rest, persecuted by their furies, scarcely capable of harnessing themselves and their tempers.

Most managed to discount their poisonous narratives with work or drink. Others countered with their own tune and argued themselves into school detention as youths or got two-checked at work. The doctors diagnosed them and pharmacists filled the appropriate prescriptions and the poor souls swallowed the medicine according to the directions, but it did little to soothe their angst. And the few who heard nothing owned it all.

"Who knew once upon a time could be so much trouble?" Peg replied.

"Don't make fun of me," Calvin said.

"I guess I'll laugh at what I want to," Peg replied.

The boy turned sullen. She ignored him and drove on.

She obeyed the speed limits and double-stopped at every sign indicating even a yield. Traveling the highways rather than the interstates checked their progress, but time was outside her concern. She noted more makes and models and license plates and scanned for repeats but recognized none. She encountered three police cruisers from differing counties and tucked herself behind semi rigs to govern her speed and avoid the overcautious behavior that appeared as guilty as driving a hundred.

Calvin said, "You have children, my father says."

Peg nodded.

"They must hate you," Calvin said.

"There's a good chance of that."

"That would mean they love you, too, then."

"I doubt the latter."

"You can't feel one without the other," Calvin responded.

"Mine would say different."

Calvin drank from his soda. "What would you say?"

"I just told you."

Peg drove two miles without speaking.

"I mean about love and hate."

"I know what you mean," Peg said.

"Then why aren't you answering?"

"Fuck you. That's my answer."

"Fuck you, too," Calvin said.

"Good," Peg said. "Now we understand each other."

In the Sierras, thunderheads fixed on the sheer peaks, white ethereal columns miles high. Pasty, glowing light sifted through them except where their underbellies blackened and hot air collided with cold to sculpt dramatic ridges and troughs pregnant with storm. Beneath, cloud tendrils drooped through gaps and passes and darkened the ground with squalls.

Evening, the dying sun threw the mountains' shadows across the valleys and sprayed the horizon orange and pink. Peg found an unused state gravel pit and changed license plates before entering the desert. In the few small towns streetlights and mini-mart neon played on the windshield like blurry old cartoons, yellows, watery blues and reds, and plain light.

The music stations thinned to static, and she hit buttons but found only talk programs or news or sports. It reminded her of a time during summer vacations when she and Pork had put Andre, Smoker, and Penny in back of an Oldsmobile station wagon with sandwiches, potato chips, and a mattress. Jim Bohannon and Larry King came through the speakers now like a couple of stoned intellectuals, interested in fingernail cuticles if that was what mattered to callers.

The next morning, they trekked through Oregon, swam on a green-black gloom of cedar and fir and spruce, vanished in shadows between mountain troughs and rose in the sunlit meadows. They avoided Portland with a bypass that spilled them into the Columbia Gorge, then, at the Hood River, crossed a bridge for Washington State, the river's less-traveled side, though the two-lane highway hurt their time. The road swept up the dry canyons into irrigated farms that dotted the flat above in the concentric arcs the rotating sprinkler pipes necessitated.

She slowed the Impala in the manner one might pull a hill under cruise control. Behind her, lights closed in the rearview mirror then disappeared, then appeared next to her across the center line. The car was gray or silver with a male driver and another on the passenger side. It passed. The red taillights bobbed the pavement ahead. Another car approached, dissimilar to the last. The light fixtures sat higher, orange fog lights beneath them. It did not close in on her, which led her to believe it had come from the ranches. She determined to allow it to follow rather than slow and force it to pass.

She alternated speeds for fifty miles and encountered nothing unordinary. Still, her neck ached even after she stretched and popped the vertebra. She watched Calvin's cigarette rest on a soda can spiraling smoke toward the roof. The ash grew until it tipped filter and all into the can's opening.

On a highway, twenty miles from Goldendale, the pavement banked for a hard curve through the rock, then straightened, then bent the opposite direction. Between was a dirt road that led past a knoll big enough to hide the Impala. She exited and switched off the lights.

Stopped, she cranked down her window after the dust passed, then unlatched her car door and stepped out to breathe the early-morning air. East, the horizon purpled. Birds prattled at the dawn. Another car passed and slipped off. Peg closed her eyes and rubbed at the burning lids. A deer rustled in a field or a coyote hunting late. No coursing wind traveled from the river channel this far from the gorge. Instead a hospitable morning breeze raked the grass and rock like a broad, gentle hand. You could hear it in the trees and draws and thickets.

And then a dull, thick pain in the back of her skull halted the pastoral with a sound so loud and close and intimate that she would recall it later almost tenderly. When she regathered herself, Calvin had torn her shirtfront and cut the elastic in her bra with a pocketknife. Presently, he attempted to drag her pants below her knees. He had not yet considered her panties.

"Hey," she said. "Let's go back to the car."

He halted.

"It's softer," Peg said. "We might as well be comfortable."

"Okay," Calvin said.

Peg squirmed herself to all fours, then pulled her pants over her shoes and stood and stepped out of her panties. The flashlight that Calvin employed to clout her lay in the gravel. He'd discovered it in the glove box, she guessed. Nude, she aimed herself to the Impala. Still woozy, she staggered then caught herself. By the car door she had her bearings. She lay on her back on the benched front seat, lifting one leg over the steering wheel and hooking the other on the driver's-side headrest.

Calvin undressed hesitantly. When he'd finished, he tipped himself over her like a falling tree. She allowed him forty-five degrees, then smiled and grabbed his cock and balls savagely with one hand and meanwhile unloosed the .45 stashed between the seats with the other. She drove the barrel into his chest.

The boy was wild-eyed. Peg twisted his genitals like she was cranking sausage. Calvin's face turned ashen. She let go and let him vomit on the gravel. He glanced up, the sandwich remnants and silver drool puddled beneath him. She busted him in the mouth with the gun barrel and he lay useless in the sand.

She checked the pistol cylinder, then cocked the hammer and allowed the chamber to roll onto a live round. She put the barrel to his Achilles tendon and then tugged the trigger. Calvin screamed and bled and writhed like a worm. In the trunk, Peg found her bungee cords and a tire iron and twisted them into tourniquets.

Peg ordered him to crawl into the passenger seat, where she tied his wrists behind him with nylon rope then tethered him to the door handle. She used the last bungee cord to anchor him to his seat, then wrapped it under the seat mounts to his ruined ankle, so if he moved, it would cost him. She dressed herself and threw a wool blanket across him.

Finished, she engaged the ignition and aimed them toward his father and Selkirk county, but stopped instead at Metaline Falls where the Pend Oreille county sheriff operated an office. It was past dark. She dragged Calvin from his seat and chained him to the police cruiser with a logging chain and a padlock then fired a shot into the night and sped away.

GENESIS

July 1984

Peg remembered Penny on the floor in front of her bed, cross-legged with a coloring book and a blue crayon, scribbling the entire page. The picture tore then tore again, until finally it was a few blue streaks hanging from the stapled binding. The other books on her shelf had been wrecked the same way, even the ones meant just for reading. When she grew excited or frightened, her coloring left the pages and she rubbed the hard floor with the crayon, which turned it into shards of paper and wax. The boys coddled her like a puppy. Pork, too. He insisted on delivering her lollipops once a week that were bigger than her head. No matter their squabbles and arguments and plain disgust with each other, they agreed on Penny.

Already capable of steering the men in her life to surrender candy or juice or crackers at her whim, she now pouted or giggled and examined their responses to employ the information later if the necessity arose. Occasionally in such instances, her eyes found Peg's and her face turned sober and uncertain. Her separateness from the boys and her father left them at her mercy and herself alone. It was Peg she looked to for reassurance, and in those glances passed that silent and vital woman's code for which men have no equal.

For a year after Penny's death, Peg stuffed her house with candles and painted the walls soft colors. She learned calligraphy and wrote inspirational verses and scripture on art paper and taped them to the appliances.

Smoker rose from the lake with Penny in his arms instead of the block. Pork joined the boys breathing into her mouth and pressing her chest, but Peg knew better. The police and ambulance raced toward the dock, their lights painting the water. The boys shivered in their wet shorts. Peg still recalled the hard look she put on them and the bruised one they returned.

"Ain't their fault," Pork said.

She put her face into his. "You," she howled. "You!"

In the vacation cabin's kitchen, Peg had boiled potatoes for the only salad the boys would eat. The radio played a sentimental country song that Pork favored. She glanced at him and winked, then bent for a decent-size bowl. He put himself behind her. She stretched her arm backward. He was near ready. Outside, the boys splashed beneath the dock. Penny, on the wood decking, watched them. Peg blinked and coupled herself to Pork.

Finished, she could see through the window Smoker and Andre alternate dives from a rowboat anchored with a mason's block.

"Where's the baby?" Peg asked.

Smoker would recall Penny on the dock, a few minutes earlier. "Lucky Penny," he coaxed. "Come in the water. You can ride my stomach and I'll be your boat."

She shook her head.

"Why not?"

"I'm too little," she said.

"I'll carry you," Smoker said.

Again, she shook her head. "That water is deep," she said. "I hate it."

Twelve months to the day from Penny's death, Peg bought a fifth of the best bourbon in the jar store and forced Pork to wolf it down with her, then they undressed and quit quitting.

6

EXODUS
August 1991

Andre bought the bear a pair of chickens at the last grocery, but the bear groused in the camper for more. Smoker took a turn at the wheel. Andre rolled down his window while they drove and allowed in the cooling night. A hundred miles north, the stars spattered the sky and blued the high ridges and treetops. The moon was halved, the dark hemisphere remained, a shadow of the other. Andre tipped his cap bill over his eyes. They drove into the mountains until pavement surrendered to gravel, which turned to sloppy dirt logging tracks and passed gutted rigs, rusted in the long winters, and solitary houses built from whatever the denizens could muster. Deer and elk dotted clearings. Smoker drank his coffee.

"How come you know so much about animals?" Andre asked him.

"Listened when folks talked and read the old man's *Field & Stream* till the staples came out."

"I didn't see no girl magazines in the house."

"They were under the bed."

"I don't recall them containing directions."

They slept in the truck cab. The next morning the roads coiled and unraveled through the Selkirk Mountains and on to the Kettle River Range. The miles were slow; the air cooled. The pickup descended onto a stretch of fresh pavement and entered a town of a hundred. A beer light flashed over the only restaurant. Next to it, a metal corral held a shaggy bison humped at a water trough. Smoker limped into the tavern to inquire about fuel. The bartender directed him to a pump on the corner, then took his twenty and followed to watch the dial.

Next to the bar, Andre found a rickety phone booth.

"Are you in jail?" Claire asked.

"No."

"What do you want?"

"I'm lonely."

"Me, too."

Andre studied the locals gawking from the tavern window.

"I ought to just come back."

Claire blew out a sigh.

"Well if it suits you."

"That just sounds like something you'd say to make me feel better or worse."

"It does," she said. "I'm sorry."

Andre nodded though she couldn't see him. "I got to go," he told her.

"You really don't need anything?"

"Just to come home," Andre said.

"Well, do."

"I can't."

"You sure do a lot of things you don't want to," she said.

He listened to her hang up and, afterward, cradled the phone.

LAMENTATIONS

June 1984

Outside Smoker's house, Bird shot baskets in the driveway. Andre had lowered the rim to five feet to keep her from learning bad habits. It was bent from her use. He found a wrench and pliers in his truck's toolbox. The backboard bolts were rusted, but when he twisted them the rim tightened.

Bird dribbled the ball on the hard-packed dirt. It got loose from her and Andre passed it back. Bird lifted the ball like a pumpkin over her head then threw it back to Andre. Andre shot from twenty feet. The ball fell through the bottom of the net.

"Wow, that was lucky," Bird said.

"You think so?"

"I bet you a pop you can't do it again," Bird said.

Andre did. The bet went double or nothing up to sixty-four cans of Coke before he missed.

Bird tried a shot from her chest. The ball clattered the backboard hard.

"Easier. Shoot it, don't throw it."

Andre cupped the girl's hands then set the ball in them. She held it a second then banged a shot against the rim front.

"Here, let me show you." Andre manipulated her wrists so she could balance the ball with her left hand and push with her right. "Just use one hand to shoot; the other steers," Andre told her. The shot dropped through.

"Now pretend your hand is reaching inside the basket."

Bird tried again.

"Better," Andre told her. "When you finish, your arm and hand should look like a gooseneck."

Her next shot fell. She ran for the ball and set herself. The tip of her tongue circled her upper lip. "Gooseneck," Andre whispered.

He glanced up to find Dede on the porch in a worn blue bathrobe. When the ball rolled her direction, she kicked it Bird's direction.

"Thanks, Mom," Bird said.

Andre looked to her. "We wake you up?"

She nodded and put her hand into her hair. "Why are you playing with her?"

"Because I like Bird and I like basketball."

"I'd rather you didn't."

"Why's that?"

"Because she'll get used to it."

Smoker appeared from behind. "Maybe some of him will erase some of you."

"Fuck you," Dede told Smoker. She turned inside. Andre collected his tools. Bird looked at him, then the doorway that had held her mother a minute ago. Her face was smooth and as indifferent as the pavement.

Andre wagged his chin at Smoker's truck. "Kennel up, Birdy. We'll fetch the horses."

Andre delivered them to a mountain turnout almost to Twisp. He assisted Smoker unloading the trailer, then saddled and fitted Bird's horse for travel. She watched him seriously so she could repeat the chore on her own when she and her father made camp. Smoker withdrew a map from his pocket that identified where he intended to be each night. Attached were emergency numbers and the weather service so Andre could organize a search if events turned sideways somehow.

Andre put his cap on Bird's head as she had forgotten one and returned the truck and trailer to the ranch. In a week, he'd collect them at the first camping area you could get a vehicle to.

Saddled and bridled, the horses packed Bird and Smoker onto the broad trail that meandered into pine and birch. For Bird, Smoker had selected steady, congenial Ike, a gelding mature enough he didn't feel compelled to prove himself, and for his own mount, Cassandra, who had a hellish bent but could run for miles without rest if they met difficulty.

The day cooled and the sky cleared and the air thinned. Red Indian paintbrush claimed several fields, bluebells another. Purple coned lupine dotted it all. Mottled snow resisted summer in the shadowy canyons and tree wells. Mule deer browsed the meadows.

Cassie walked him into a low limb. A yellow pollen fog clouded him. Bird laughed. She was going to be pretty. In the old myths, beauty was often a curse; maybe those heathens had it right. It made Peg a desert: cactus, sand, cold nights, seething days. Pork, once there, could find no path out, and it would leave him just bleached bones.

The first night, Smoker shot a grouse with his twelve-gauge

and skewered it on a green stick and let it bake. They ate then opened their mummy bags and stared into the sky.

"Mom didn't want to come?" Bird asked.

"Just didn't work out," Smoker told her.

Dede had hoped to join them, but Smoker wouldn't permit it. Bird fell silent. Smoker roughed her hair. His mind did not ordinarily weigh such matters, but he found himself studying his hand and Bird's hair and the scalp it sprang from. He wondered how his hands spoke through all that and what they might say to her and if it was what he intended. And then he wondered what, indeed, he did intend.

The next morning, they stewed coffee and cobbled breakfast from dinner's scraps then set out. The dense forest abated, replaced with low grass and rock. Most anything else alive was sheltered beneath thin jackstraw. Soon ridges and sheer granite-faced mountains stacked their path, too steep to hold vegetation, just hard lines against the sky. The trail ahead narrowed to a switchbacked ribbon. Ike snorted then warily went on. A mile past, several blind creeks had gouged the path and the horses stepped gingerly through the mud.

Smoker and Bird halted at Bing Creek to drop a line. In the clear water, they could see brook trout study the baited hooks. Finally, an eighteen-incher rushed one. Smoker landed the fish. Bird reeled another to the bank. Smoker stowed them in a burlap sack.

The trail squeezed into a defile. Smoker took the lead. They crested a granite fin. On the other side, a long, ramparted ridge feathered the blue sky. Shale shingles roofed the inclines. At their foot, a bowl a thousand feet deep looked like a moonscape: nothing green except lichen and moss in the shadows.

"What happened?" Bird asked.

"Big ice," Smoker replied.

They backtracked to a dirt hollow protected by three enormous root wads, the remnants of two-hundred-year-old fir trees. A good deal of light remained. Smoker hunted a sharp rock then set out toward the sound of rushing water. Bird followed. Smoker halted at a long stalked plant with tiny yellow flowers. He dug the tubers beneath and deposited them in the gunnysack. "Kouse," he said. "We'll have it for breakfast."

They came upon a huckleberry bush past the bloom. Huckleberries meant bears, so they hurried on. A couple hundred yards later, Smoker dug a balsamroot, then plucked miner's lettuce, and found mushrooms he determined healthy. He warned Bird that plants with colored spines or thorns or fine hair meant poison, same for three-leaf bunches and stalks that bleed white and anything inside a pod.

They ate the fish and Bird fell asleep. Smoker recalled Pork hauling the boys to the July Fourth Circle Celebration. Andre and Smoker tepee-creeped for unattended whiskey bottles and cigarettes while the drums took up. Eventually the boys, like the rest, headed toward the dancers. In a rotating circle, the participants chanted in high, children's voices. The drums, hidden from the light, beat fast, first thunder, then later, rattling rain. The dancers leapt and landed, painted feathers and buckskin turning deer and elk alive.

Later, they found Pork at the stick games. In the firelight, the old man's face turned gold, round and ripe for creases, his large nose bent from some unrecalled scrape. It could've been a hundred years ago. He could've been weathered by battle. The gambling songs bluffed and called. Neither Smoker nor Andre understood the words, but the song, skinned of meaning, was like seeing inside an animal, the bones and all that moves it through a place.

A few threw money on the blankets. Pork's eyes were wild. The elders nodded toward him, waiting on his portion of the song. Pork tried his voice, but all it could croak was a sound no one had heard before. When Pork opened his mouth again, just breath followed. He unclenched his fists and let the sticks loose.

The next morning, Smoker awoke to an inch of snow mantling the country outside the tent. He removed the tubers from beneath last night's cook fire, piled them on pie plates, and slathered maple syrup over them. He added huckleberries and inside the tent stirred them into a tasty mess that Bird approved of. The morning sunlight made short work of the snow. Single file, they rounded through the rubble and scree. A turquoise cirque reflected like a gem in the sun. Smoker put a ball cap on his head and Andre's hat on Bird's.

At the cirque, the horses drank, but Bird and Smoker took no lunch. In the open rubble a storm would blast their tent to confetti and Smoker worried the morning snow augured more weather. The trail paralleled a rock-flour creek the color of old snow. A mile later they settled on a pine copse to stake their tent and ate a cold dinner of jerked deer and raw carrots and drank water from the canteen. Wind and rain and hail and then more snow hammered the tent. Bedtime, Bird scooted her bag next to Smoker's.

"Could we call Mom?" she asked.

"No phone."

"When we get to where there's one can we?"

"We'll see," Smoker said.

"Can I write her a letter?"

"If we had paper and pencil, maybe, but then we'd need a mailbox."

Bird closed her eyes to sleep, but Smoker heard her whimper and opened his mummy sack. He arranged hers inside his and made a nest where she could comfort herself. Despite Dede's suspicions, he didn't compete for Bird's affection. He enjoyed Bird and was inclined to partake in what he enjoyed. He knew it cut into her mother's plans but it was of little concern to him. It divided Bird, too, and that he found disconcerting.

"You won't die for a long time, right?" Bird asked.

"Not in my plans, baby girl."

"Will you ever just go away?"

"No," Smoker said. "I'm staying. Except if you're going somewhere, then I'll be right behind."

"Okay," she said.

"Okay," Smoker replied. He listened to her settle then her breaths whistle as she dropped to sleep.

Morning, they topped Canuck Ridge. Smoker directed Bird's attention to the braided streams that broke at the canyon rim and collapsed into a misty horsetail falls. The water doesn't know where it's going yet, he told her. Bird asked questions and he described where each creek divided or circled the humps and buttes and crags, ending on one that divided Storm King Mountain.

"Agnes Gorge," Smoker said. "The water comes so hard off the glacier it gouges solid rock. A hundred foot deep, sometimes straight down. You got to walk in the creek the whole of it. Daylight can't even find you."

"Are we going that way?" Bird asked.

Smoker shook his head. "Nothing there but water and rock and trees."

"But you did?"

"Someone told me I couldn't," Smoker said. "All I got was wet and tired." He looked at her. "That's why I brung you. To keep me out of trouble."

She smiled a wry smile that belonged to neither Smoker nor Dede. Smoker clucked the horses and they descended. Twilight, they camped at High Bridge where Bridge Creek met the Stehekin River at a dead-ended Forest Service road.

A turkey flock had spread itself across a ferny hillock. Smoker and Bird stalked them with the shotgun. Smoker fired and the flock gobbled and tottered off. Some took flight and managed a few feet before their weight grounded them. Smoker hoisted the dead bird and the two walked back to camp.

Bird and Smoker plucked and cut the bird then he fried the drumsticks in the skillet.

"This kind of food is best if you ask me, Bird."

"How come?"

"Because we killed it."

Bird stared into the fire. The turkey's grease hissed over the cooking coals.

"The Bible says not to kill, but it don't mean animals," Smoker told her. "How else would those Jews get their corn beef?"

"Maybe at the store," Bird said.

"Somebody killed the cow. You eat a McDonald's hamburger it's something someone killed."

Smoker cut into a drumstick. Still too pink, he raised the spit to finish the bird slower.

"You get all your food at Safeway and pretty soon you forget a steak was a cow and the cow was alive and it walked around and chewed its cud and considered what it could of the pasture. There ought to be a little guilt in eating. Not like dollars at the store. Not to pay and square the bill. Killing is too big a bill to square, let alone eating."

"What will we leave for the turkey?" Bird asked.

Smoker considered a minute then unpocketed his cigarettes. With a rawhide strap from his saddle, he tied feathers to the box then hid it under a rock.

"Turkeys don't smoke," Bird said.

"No," Smoker replied. "But they can trade them with the buffalo."

"Buffalos like cigarettes?"

"Yep. It's why most all of them died. They learned though. You hardly ever see a buffalo with a cigarette nowadays."

The next morning rose bright and clear. The road tracking the river's berm turned gentle, diverting only when the water's course hurried into a falls or series of cascades. An hour after lunch, Cassie's ears pricked. She reared, but Smoker soothed her back to all fours. Smoker retrieved the shotgun and a box of shells from his scabbard along with his 30.06. He handed the shotgun to Bird.

Bird shook her head. "I don't want it," she said.

"It's no time for a debate," he said, but Bird appeared adamant, so he scabbarded the weapon then slung his 30.06 onto his shoulder. He swung into his saddle and put Bird and Ike behind him. A hundred yards and Cassie halted them. A cougar and two cubs padded onto the path. The big cat growled. Her haunches rose. Cassie whinnied and backstepped. Smoker bit her ear enough to draw blood. She settled. He hoisted the rifle to his shoulder. One kitten chased the other across the packed dirt; both rolled into the bar ditch. The mother's tail switched. Her glare alternated from the horses back to the kittens. Smoker eased the safety off.

"Go away!" Bird shouted.

The startled cat looked at her and blinked.

"Shoo," Bird hollered. She waved her arms.

"Yeah," Smoker growled. "Shoo. And sock. And pants and a hat."

The cat turned leisurely toward her kittens. She butted each with her forehead and they trailed her up a game path into a copse of quaking aspen.

Smoker glanced at Bird. She looked back, stoic.

"That'll work, too," he said.

Beside them, the river was blue and clear. They could see its bottom shift and bugs struggle in the current and others, dragonflies and gnats, hovering the banks. Finally they arrived at Stehekin, a small town only ferries could reach. Smoker bought hay for the horses and rented a cabin with a shower. Cleaned up, the two ate a restaurant dinner with the tourists and slept like stones in the earth until well after light, when they took another restaurant meal and coffee for breakfast. Bird inquired about a phone, but the place possessed only an old military receiver the proprietors used to contact police or the Park Service for emergencies.

The horses bore them onto a bench between the mountains and the lake. One more day and they wandered into abandoned logging treks and slash piles and discovered a rusted skidder the coyotes seemed to have converted to a den. Deer and cattle took turns at a salt lick. Ranch houses appeared at the orchards' edges. Occasionally propellered contraptions loomed above the stunted fruit trees. They were designed to stir the air when the temperature neared freezing.

"What if the wind is already blowing?" Bird asked.

"Then they eat a lot of applesauce."

A mile later they followed a gradual path to the lake and allowed the horses to drink. Bird dismounted and pulled her pants up past her knees then waded.

"It's freezing," she said.

"It comes from all them streams we saw. Might have been ice a month ago."

"I like it," she said. "It feels awake."

Bird returned to the bank. On the gravel beach, water beaded and slid from her calves. Smoker tossed her a sweatshirt and she dried herself.

"Do you think Mom's sad?" she asked.

"Why?"

"Because she's not here."

"I doubt she's too put out."

"We left her."

"Well, we're on our way back now."

"She told me you didn't want her to come."

"That's right, I didn't."

They passed another orchard and, later, an enormous plantation house and matching outbuildings that served it.

"She will come next time," Smoker said.

"No, she won't."

"Why's that?" Smoker said.

"Because you don't do things you don't want to do."

They were quiet for a while.

"Why didn't you shoot it?"

"I didn't have to."

"It might have ate me."

"But it didn't. I thought you decided against guns."

"Me shooting. I like when you do it. It's fun."

"Okay," he said.

"Are you mad?"

"No," Smoker said. "I just couldn't figure why."

Bird grinned suddenly. "I don't do what I don't want to either."

Another hour and they arrived at a parking lot, where Andre enjoyed the end of a drive-in hamburger in the truck and trailer that would cart them home.

GENESIS

May 1971

In general, Andre remained an agreeable child until he reached twelve. Soon after his birthday that year, he discovered himself pitted against a cloudy fury behind his eyes. The doctors pronounced him twenty-twenty, but he squinted at objects far and near and the muscle below his jaw cramped like iron. He unloosed it by battering Smoker. He'd had some reason. Though two grades behind, his brother whipped him regularly in footraces, which got him elected captain and quarterback during recesses. Smoker picked Andre first and let him hike, but one day Andre centered the ball into Smoker's throat, which collapsed his brother to all fours. Andre arrived not long after the ball. He bent and boxed his brother's ears then headed to foursquare with the girls, right where Smoker had put him. Soon he folded his hands to fists and blindsided even kindergartners to hear them wail. Violence was new math—a logic he'd acquired with no place to apply it. The school expelled him the final three weeks, hoping summer would provide a difference. However, Peg wasn't waiting on a season. She directed Pork to the pickup and dragged Andre behind him by the ear and ordered Pork not to come back with a goddamned criminal. The two loaded the pickup, Smoker watched, disappointed because he was stuck with school and Peg's whims.

The War Bonnet Tavern was their first stop. Pork hoisted an ice chest from the truck bed and hauled it inside. The sun dragged the clouds out of the sky and beat through the windshield. A new one-ton, freshly washed, parked in the space beside Pork's rig. A man barely past high school locked and windowed the rig. Inside, a boy, maybe three years old, fooled with a windup toy.

Through the rearview mirror Andre could see across the street. There Francis Timens had tucked himself inside a wrecked Chrysler. He lobbed bottles over his head while his older brothers blasted shotguns at them. Bird shot and tinkling glass rained onto the Chrysler. Francis deflected it with a garbage-can lid. Andre had attacked the boy twice in the last month.

By noon, the sun swallowed the tavern's shadow. In the one-ton truck, the boy cried and pinked. Andre climbed from Pork's pickup to rescue the boy. When Francis Timens recognized him, he howled and balled himself under the Chrysler's dash. His brothers approached the pickup, still armed. Andre fetched Pork's .357 from the glove box and put a round over their heads and they hightailed back to the yard.

Meanwhile, the boy in the cab gasped and cried behind the

closed windows. Andre rapped the glass and pointed to the door latch. The boy did not understand. Andre considered the windowless tavern door. Entering meant a beating.

Across the gravel, the Timenses' father, Red Archie, in his underwear lumbered through the yard onto the pavement, twirling a walking stick for an equalizer. When he was within a few feet, Andre lifted the pistol and fired past the man's ear. Archie halted. Andre pressed forward and put the gun into Archie's belly; his skin swirled like a cyclone beneath the barrel. Archie elevated his hands with great caution. Behind them, Andre heard the tavern empty of men drunk before lunch. The new truck's owner hurried to his rig and retrieved the boy who sucked the cool air and shuddered and sobbed. Andre felt holier than the church choir. If Archie'd twitched, Andre would have tugged the trigger and become altogether saint.

"I got my packages, son," Pork said quietly. Andre retreated to the pickup then lowered the pistol. The rest of the regulars retired into the cool tavern. In the hauling mirrors, Andre watched Archie lope for his house. His children gathered under him at the gate like slaughterhouse chicks to a hen.

Pork paused at the grocery and fished a twenty-dollar bill from his billfold. He ordered Andre to go in and get what he wanted. Andre bought steak and eggs and lettuce, bread, a carton of milk, and cans of Campbell Soup and pears and peaches: enough to fill two bags. Looks like what an old lady would get, Pork told him. Take it back. The second time through Andre loaded twelve bucks' worth of penny candy into a basket and a *Playboy* magazine. He packed it to the truck and dumped the bag on the seat.

"That don't look like enough candy to me," Pork said.

Andre put the magazine under the seat. Pork uncapped the

whiskey and had a snort, looked both ways at a stop sign, then drank again to congratulate himself on a clear highway. He aimed them west toward the river, then north, then west again until Andre had no notion where they might end up and doubted the old man did, either. Pork's talk wandered with their travels. Without whiskey, he was vague. With it, everything turned obvious, but only to him. It don't matter what kills you if it makes you strong, he would say, or, heaven's hard to get to and hell ain't nothing but a long hangover.

Three hours later, they happened upon Lake Roosevelt, the stopped-up Columbia River. Forty miles later, where the Spokane River fed the reservoir was a cavalry fort and an enormous picnic area and campground that brimmed with campers on ten-by-twenty-foot grass rectangles. A table and firebox chained to fir trees accompanied each. Pork had to talk fast to get one. He arranged two lawn chairs around a concrete fire pit and hunted the cooler for another beer. In the other camps, radios played, few agreeing on a station.

"Get yourself a beer," Pork said.

Andre shook his head. Pork waved a hand to dismiss him and proceeded to nap in his lounge chair. Andre snuck a cigarette and smoked it. He wandered the park until he encountered a trail that wound alongside the Spokane River's western bank on a dusty ridge that overlooked the water. One or two pleasure boats had anchored near the bank in the first mile, but after that heat and trees and sagebrush seemed to own the place.

The trail thinned to a slim game track that forked and forked again as the deer diverged near the water. Ticking insects that as a younger child Andre mistook for rattlesnakes tittered the air. Ahead, the bluff bent hard where the river met a seasonal creek.

Under its lip a mud bank shot with swallow nests fell off to a sandy spit below. At his approach the birds retreated into the tiny pocks or set their wings and darted for gnats.

On the opposite shore was a canoe on a cutbank beach. Three small children pursued one another around the boat. Their parents rested in a drooping pine's shade. The kids switched to slinging wet sand until the youngest bawled and the father hollered and they emptied their hands. The mother—brunette, thin, and pretty as far as Andre could make out—hurried to the crying child and cupped her hands to bathe his face with water.

The sun dropped behind the rocky horizon; the air cooled. The father pitched a plastic football in arcing passes while the boys streaked along the water's edge under it. Before dark, he shoveled a hole with a folding military spade and the children scurried for what would burn. Over their fire the children browned franks on green sticks then marshmallows. Their shadows grew in the fluid light, exaggerating the length of a chin or brow like totem heads. After a time, the woman coerced the little one into pajamas and ordered the other two to do for themselves. The father secured the canoe's bowline with the anchor then bent the boat seats into beds. The wife spread a wide blanket on the beach and mummy bags for herself and her husband. The moon had ascended the sky before they quit hushing their children. The couple talked awhile, then cooed, and finally discarded their clothes at the edge of the firelight. Their skin flittered in the coals' pink light while they whispered and sang out.

After, they slept spooned. Their neglected fire waned. Andre hunted a path to the water. He halted at its edge and studied the tiny camp, then stepped in and ducked quietly under. He held his breath and swam the distance between underwater. He rose behind the boat. He touched its gunwale; the canoe tipped like a cradle. Inside, the girl had burrowed beneath her brother's shoulder.

On the beach, a picnic basket lay near the dying coals. Andre lifted the lid and ate half a sandwich, which tasted so good he ate the rest. The husband dozed heavily. He had swung one leg over the other to free it from the sleeping bag, which uncovered his wife's breasts and legs. One of the children muttered. Andre turned and when he glanced back, the woman was in front of him, naked. She walloped him in the side with a shovel.

Andre teetered and regained his balance. She stared into his face. Her eyes held thoughts he didn't recognize, like the faces of paintings in library art books. She swung again and caught him on the chin. His skin opened and he felt blood drip from the wound. Two steps and he was under the water again.

"There," the woman cried out. "He's out there!"

At their camp, Pork fried boloney on a stick and struggled to eat it without burning his hands. The emptied whiskey bottle lay on its side in the grass.

"Have you a beer, goddamnit," he said.

When Andre didn't reply, Pork threw a half-full can into his chest, then, spent, went back to his cooking.

"Get me another," Pork said after a while.

Andre fished the last can from the ice and set it on the picnic table. The tab broke, so he whacked the lip with a hammer. The blow exploded the can. Beer foamed and soaked them both and puddled on the table and ground beneath.

Pork lumbered up. "You ruined my beer."

Andre hurled the hammer and it caught Pork in the chest and

backed him into his lawn chair. The toolbox remained on the picnic table. Andre dug into it and threw a crescent wrench and the wire snippers at Pork. Pork protected his face so Andre took a ratchet to his belly, then pelted him with sockets. The remaining tools were smaller, so he threw them in handfuls. Pork grunted. The toolbox emptied, Andre flung gravel and wood and empty beer cans, then the box itself, which opened a gash on Pork's arm. Pork sucked for wind and gasped.

"Uncle," he whispered. "Uncle, goddamnit."

Andre hid in the truck cab and locked both doors and slept. Dawn, he woke and climbed into his swim shorts then wandered to the boat launch. Fishermen unloaded for the morning bite. Their boats' oily smoke draped the outboard motors and the water reflected the sound of the chugging engines. The lake split for the hulls, easy as a bird cut wind.

Andre waded into the water. It was colder than he recalled. He didn't take off his shirt and the material felt like loose skin that he could shed. He bent and washed the gash beneath his chin. He wondered about the woman: if he had haunted her like bad medicine or if her husband convinced her Andre had been nothing but a nightmare in a wild place.

Water splashed behind him where Pork, on the sand, was attempting to skip pebbles. Scabbed blood blocked one of his nostrils. He put his finger over the other and snorted it clear, then got on all fours and washed himself. Pork pressed as far as his rolled-up pants would allow, then went deeper, soaking his clothes. Andre's hand trailed in the water and Pork's passed it like a fish, then plucked it up awkwardly. The skin was callused, a man's.

"I'm sorry," Pork said. "I shouldn't have left you in the truck. Most of the time, I don't know what I'm doing."

7

EXODUS
August 1991

The road rose again through a string of switchbacks. The speed-ometer needle barely cleared zero. This deep into the woods the loggers had quit; the path was little more than a pair of ruts evened by a four-wheel drive pushing a blade. From each loop, Andre could gaze into the canyons, empty of people and light.

Andre stopped the truck to change Smoker's bandages and adjust the finger splint they had fashioned from a cotter pin and electrical tape.

"You remember the first time you saw Pork's dick?"

Smoker laughed.

"Do you?" Andre asked.

"Well, I saw it, but I don't recall the date or place."

"I walked into the bathroom and he was pissing. He had one of those morning hard-ons."

Smoker nodded. "Those are my favorites."

"It scared the shit out of me."

"You seen your own hadn't you?"

Andre nodded. "And I'd seen yours, too. Little tiny thing, I recall. Like someone cut off a pinkie at the first knuckle."

"Yours wasn't much either at that age."

"No, likely not. But the old man, I remember it like it hung to his knees."

"I seen Peg's bush once," Smoker said. "It was just a blank though."

Andre nodded. "I seen that, too, and thought the same thing. It scared me, too."

"Why's that."

"I didn't know what was under there."

"And with Pork you did, but it scared you, too."

Andre nodded. "I guess so."

"I never thought about it," Smoker said. "I'm inclined to not want to know. Thanks for bringing it up."

They drove awhile longer.

"Pork's dick isn't any bigger than normal, anyway," Andre said. "I pissed next to him in Eddie's plenty of times."

"What's your obsession with all this talk of uglies?"

"They were normal," Andre said.

"Well normal is damned strange, then."

Andre shook his head. "What if we made them up?"

As night came on, the ground below gathered in the shadows and lost its form, until all that held them up was darkness and all that was in front of them was more of it except what the lights could cut and those shapes appeared and disappeared so quick they felt dreamt. Above, the sky was scattered with lights so that it seemed they were on some planet closer to it. Andre worked through the gears. The engine wound and relaxed with the degree of grade.

Smoker turned off the radio; no stations reached this high. He stared at himself in the glass and then he began to laugh, at first a chuckle, then whole hog.

"What?" Andre asked him.

"I'm shot in the ass," Smoker said.

"It doesn't hurt?"

"Hell yes, it hurts. It's the situation that's funny. Not the hurting."

"I doubt I'd find bird shot in my butt so amusing."

"That's because nothing amuses you."

"I laugh."

"Name a time."

Andre drove for a mile then another.

"You can't," Smoker said.

"I laugh all the time."

"No, you pretend to laugh. Like a dog, you bark at the mail truck when it passes, but you don't know why."

"Maybe I'm polite."

"You shot me in the ass, Miss Manners."

Andre nodded. "I did, that's true. On that we agree."

"Yet I'm the one laughing."

"Maybe funny to you isn't to me."

"You think that old man coming up on you cutting my ass wasn't worth a laugh?"

"I felt bad for him. He thought something and it wasn't so.

Not his fault. He's trying to help and it turns him the butt of a joke."

"Hell, he'll tell the story till the day he dies," Smoker said.

"I don't make sport of others. It's one-sided," Andre said.

"You got brains to graduate from college. You got a woman who only strayed once and for someone so like you he was kin. You got good fortune. Now you're going to fuck that up because you don't have a sense of humor. Good God, you're a worse sinner than me."

LAMENTATIONS
July 1984

Throughout spring, Claire hoarded their change. Early summer, she booked a vacation cabin on Lake Chelan, an hour into the mountains. Andre resisted, but she promised he would not have to be a tourist. They read two poems a day and occasionally dined in the restaurants lining the water. Mostly, though, they slow-cooked ribs or bratwurst or brisket and constructed coleslaw according to a recipe book left in the cabin's tiny library. Evenings, too dark to gawk at scenery or meander the shops, they gambled small stakes in the Indian casino with retirees and later commandeered the resort's hot tub and whispered into the morning hours.

Andre recounted high school when he calculated others' needs and responded, never considering his own. He appeared unselfish but such a demeanor swapped honest selfishness for a dishonest brand. Andre manufactured a self others found amicable by winnowing out most everything in him that wasn't. It made tolerating him easy and knowing him impossible. He'd left no room to love or hate him. His generosity was never as natural as Smoker's self-interest and he appeared disingenuous at best.

On the last afternoon of their holiday, Claire and Andre entered an ancient hotel to peruse its antique silver collection. Inside, the place smelled like laundry and closed windows. A man Andre's age dealt canasta to a gray-haired woman who tallied scores on a napkin. Claire slowed. The man's eyes peeked from beneath his brow. Claire's hips shifted as if accepting his weight.

"Of all the gin joints in all the towns," he said. The two hugged. Claire introduced him as Marlon. He shuffled the cards then plopped the deck on the table and excused himself and led them to the bar. Behind it, he filled a plastic cup for Claire—tonic and lime—without asking.

"You?" he asked Andre.

"Bourbon," Andre replied.

Claire crossed her eyes at him. Andre ignored her. He gentled the glass to his mouth and sipped the top, then reached into his pocket and deposited a ten on the bar.

"Your money's no good here," the man replied.

"How's your mother?" Claire asked. "I'd heard she died."

"I've been playing cards with a ghost, then."

Claire laughed. "I don't know how some news gets to be."

"Well, I'm glad it got to you before me." Marlon patted her hand on the bar. "I'm pleased you stopped."

He glanced at Andre. "The both of you. It's nice to know what became of her."

"We're teachers in the same high school," Claire said.

"Didn't we play you in softball one time?" Marlon asked.

"No," Andre replied.

163

More whiskey and Andre could hit him. He unpocketed his wallet and deposited a twenty on the bar.

"I said I got it," Marlon told him.

Andre let the bill lie. Marlon shrugged then filled Andre's shot glass. Andre drank it and signaled for another.

"How many you plan on putting down?"

"Many as you fill," Andre said.

Marlon lined four glasses and poured. The bourbon was piss-colored. It lacked bite and the good going-gold that follows the genuine article. It would leave him only weary and dejected. Tequila tasted so harsh even a teetotaler would note it was thinned. Andre made short work of the line and ordered Two Fingers. Marlon poured him two.

"He forgot how to count," Andre said to Claire. On one end of the bar was a stack of plastic Solo cups. Andre poured the shots into one. "Excuse me," he said.

At their cabin, he switched clothes and sank into the hot tub. He sipped the tequila. The sky purpled and the clouds cleared and the night rose, a black blanket salted with light. Steamy threads lifted from the water, looking vague. He did not know how long afterward he opened his eyes and recognized Claire idling next to him in her red one-piece. The material shimmered on the clear water. Her black hair clung to her neck in tendrils.

He laughed. "Goddamnit."

She floated next to him and touched a spot on his chest. "If I met your old flame, I might do the same."

"You wouldn't."

"You don't know that."

"You tell me you'd drink over me like that."

"That doesn't mean what you think it does."

"Did you sleep with him?"

Claire nodded.

"When?"

"At night."

Andre didn't laugh.

"We'd dated for three weeks, I think. I was a virgin then."

"Did he know?"

Claire glanced up. "He told me before that he thought I was."

"That must've tickled him."

"I'd like to think what tickled him was me."

Andre gazed into the night above. Claire extended her hand to his face and traced the shape of his jaw.

"It was three months for us," he said.

Claire's finger tapped at his Adam's apple. "I can stop this talk right here, if I just press."

"How did you know him?"

"We had a class together. One day he inquired about the time, though there was a clock above the professor's lectern. Past that, I spoke to him at a dorm mixer. We danced a couple of times, then stood by the door where it was cool and we could hear each other. He asked if I'd go to a movie with him."

"You worked with me," Andre said. "We had conversations."

"That was a good thing."

"It took you a long while to cozy up to me."

"Maybe if you had asked earlier, this argument wouldn't be necessary."

"Maybe I might've if I'd been better convinced."

"Darling, you require more persuasion than most men."

"I require more whiskey than them, too."

Claire closed her eyes and massaged them with her wet hands. The muscles of her face clenched then let go.

"Who are most men?" Andre asked.

"I have a male harem. I abandoned them all for you. They castrated themselves with rusty knives out of frustration."

Andre slapped the water. A wave flooded the other side of the tub. He watched it break and return to his chest, then calm until the surface was broken only by the pumps. He ducked his head under and listened to their hum until his lungs ached. He surfaced.

"Did he come inside you?"

"You're feeling awfully holy aren't you?" she said.

"Did he?"

"I don't think that's any of your business."

"Probably not."

"You really want me to answer?"

"I asked."

"Yes, you asked. Do you want me to answer?"

"No," he said. "Did you come?"

"Achieve orgasm. Sexual bliss. Did he find my G-spot?"

"Yes," Andre replied. "No," he said then. "I don't want to know."

Claire tipped backward and floated until all he could see of her face was the point of her chin and her eyelashes if she blinked. Her voice turned flat. "Not at first."

"I said no," Andre told her.

"I got pills," she said.

"For him?" Andre asked. He ducked under the water.

She spoke again when he emerged. "Because, it quit hurting."

"He hurt you?"

"It hurt me."

"Then it didn't?"

"I got wetter," she explained.

"Salt for my wounds."

"Your wounds?" she asked.

Andre tapped on the empty cup's rim. Tequila often blacked him out, but he thought that unlikely; in his experience, God was not that generous.

"You liked him better after a while, then?"

"Yes. And it."

"Better than me."

"Than us, you mean," she said.

"Than us." Andre laughed. He lifted himself out of the tub and sat on its rim. Steam clouded him.

"It was just sex," Claire said. "Not religion. Just something that happened." She swam to him and set a hand on each thigh.

"Never happened to me. Till you, I mean." He looked at her wet hair and damp skin. She had started to cry.

"That for him?" Andre asked.

Claire shook her head. "Maybe you could marry me," she said. "You'd be the only one that ever did that."

8

EXODUS

August 1991

The fork that wound them toward the house was half a mile. A dog bayed and then two more. Their long bodies paled in the woods as they tracked the rig. The nervous bear lumbered from window to window in the camper. Light from a fixture halfway up a bull pine bounced off the hard dirt driveway like day. Farther, gas generators clattered and a bald man appeared in the light. He lifted his hand and the dogs halted.

"They'll let you alone," he shouted to the truck. Closer, Andre recognized Calvin next to him, carrying a gas lantern.

Smoker extended his uninjured hand to open the truck door and labored out of the cab on his good leg then dragged the other behind it. He limped toward them. Andre followed. The reverend wasn't all bald, just his crown. He looked intelligent and odd, like a professor. He grinned an avuncular grin and directed them toward the cabin.

"You hurt bad?" Harold asked.

Smoker lifted his bent finger and glanced at his bloody jeans. "Which time?"

Harold shrugged. "Either?"

"I don't want to discuss it."

Inside was a fire and Calvin posted the lantern above it, then struck a match and lit one more and after that, half a dozen candles. The room turned orange and friendly, even the shadows. A Bible filled with marks lay open on a threadbare couch. Another sat on the kitchen table. Above the fireplace was a watercolor of Christ and next to it an elk rack bearing two rifles. Harold lugged several home-brew quarts from a root cellar.

"Dede warned me you'd come," Harold said.

"Well, she's a prophetess," Smoker replied.

Harold settled into his chair. "You here for business or pleasure?"

"My daughter," Smoker said. "And she's neither."

"That's not true. She's a good girl. Makes herself handy."

Smoker nodded. "She's a help, I agree." He unholstered his pistol and placed it between them on the table. Calvin rose and Andre with him, but Harold motioned for them to stand down.

"You don't need to educate me on my own child," Smoker said.

"You were right," Harold nodded to Calvin, "they're not subtle."

Smoker pointed to the Bible. "What part encourages kidnapping?"

"Her mother left her willingly. She was reckless. That's a bad trait in a parent."

"Judgment is supposed to be a sin in your line of work."

"Render unto Caesar what is Caesar's and unto the Lord what is the Lord's."

"Well, render unto me what is mine," Smoker said.

Harold stared at the gun. "That little girl has two parents."

"Then say it's my turn on custody."

"That's for the law to decide."

"I got me a lawyer named Reynolds," Smoker said. "He packs a shotgun in one hand and a summons in the other."

"That costs money," Harold said. "And you don't look like a member of the high-income bracket."

"Cop's cheaper," Andre said. The others looked at him. "We give the county you and that girl's got nowhere to go but my brother."

"He does talk," Calvin said.

"Thinks, too," Smoker replied. "I'd just as soon pay you straight out and get it done. Cops take a while." Smoker looked to Harold. "A thousand dollars is what I got. Firm. Take it or don't."

"Where'd an Indian get a thousand dollars?" Calvin asked him.

"You got a problem with definition, white boy. I'm no more Indian than I am white. You look to be divided by twelve and I bet you don't know half your DNA," Smoker said. He turned to Harold. "What about it? She's coming one way or another."

Calvin said, "Not if you ain't leaving."

"I wrote directions and give a time to my wife," Andre said. "She doesn't see me in the flesh day after tomorrow, she gives them to the first cop she finds."

"Cash?" Harold asked.

Smoker nodded.

"Calvin will have to run down the hill. She's playing with the neighbor children."

"I didn't see no other lights coming in."

"They shutter the windows. Separatists. Afraid of the government. You're lucky you didn't land there. They'd shoot you."

"Why's that?"

"You come from heathens. Mud people. I don't hold with that."

"Glad to hear it," Smoker said.

LAMENTATIONS

December 1984

The day before his brother's wedding, Smoker's first whiff of trouble was Pork sitting on his pickup's tailgate in insulated coveralls and an orange hunting cap, half a case of Olympia Beer under one arm. Smoker eased into Crazy Eddie's gravel parking lot and dismounted his truck cab. He waved a hand toward his father. The old man nodded then fished a second can from the box. Smoker told him he wouldn't drink elk piss and sauntered into Crazy Eddie's for a quart of Lucky Lager, which Eddie was short of even in the cans. Flummoxed, Smoker helped himself to the house whiskey bottle. The new barmaid, Myrna, winked at him.

Outside, Pork commandeered the whiskey and measured it in the remaining sunlight.

"Apt to be short if we're to give your brother the send-off," Pork said.

"He doesn't want any stag party," Smoker replied. "I asked him."

"Not up to him to want. Up to us to give."

Pork insisted they drive his rig. At the package store, the old man purchased a half gallon of Canadian whiskey and a pint of peppermint schnapps. He no longer cared for whiskey plain, but found soda too thin a cut. Back under the wheel, he uncapped both jugs. His brow pinched over his eyes, leaving him all forehead in the stretching shadows.

"We could get double-drunk and run you down some split-tail," Smoker said. "Just let Andre be." Whiskey would shut Pork like a door to a black room. This was the last opportunity for reason.

"I'll grant he'd prefer that."

"Let him be, then."

"He's holing up at the one place we're sure to find him," Pork said.

"Because he's expecting us. Not because he enjoys the prospect."

Pork blinked at the streetlights oranging. "We're obligated. So's he."

Pork's driving was none too good sober, but drunk he grew mindful and Smoker abandoned hope they might be arrested before they could do harm. The truck exited the pavement for a gravel road. The federal government had surrendered damages to the Colville tribes for what they lost to the dam and the reservoir; it was no mean sum; Smoker had attended the meeting. They'd have put a teacher like Andre into a fine home, interest thin as a communion wafer, but Andre wanted only the rooms in which Claire had lived.

Andre answered Smoker's knock and glanced past him at Pork's idling truck.

"He was set to come with or without me," Smoker told him.

Andre allowed Smoker inside. Pork, they knew, would not leave the truck.

"Where is the bride off to?" Smoker asked.

"Somewhere and won't come back till I leave. She says you're not to see your wife on the wedding day until the vows."

"I know a few who make a habit of not seeing them after," Smoker said.

"Not me," Andre said.

"No, not you," Smoker agreed. "You can bunk with me."

"I'm set up already," Andre told him. "Though I'll spruce at your place in the morning if you don't care."

Smoker nodded.

"How's Bird?"

"At the hairdresser with Dede. She's taking this ring-bearer job as serious as rent."

"Sounds like you all got civilized," Andre said.

Smoker had kept near a season of steady work and hadn't provoked Dede in six weeks. His best-man tuxedo, for which he paid cash rent, hung in the trailer-house closet with new shoes under it, a worthy accounting until he'd surrendered whiskey to the orneriest drunk within a hundred miles and picked as poor a day as there was to do it.

"You think we could stall old Porkchop till the jar store closes?" Andre asked.

"He's been. Anyways he'd only drag us to a cocktail lounge."

"We could run him out of money there."

"Us, too," Smoker said. "And he'd just write bad checks."

Smoker retrieved a soda from the fridge. Photographs checkered the appliance's door. Bird's school picture occupied the

173

highest point, pinned with a drugstore magnet. Claire and Andre populated the bulk of those below. They had managed a thorough record. Summer, the couple vacationed on a lake and buried each other in the sand; a month or so after, Andre stood downtown in front of the new grocery for a photo; in another Claire read or weeded a garden. Occasionally a photo of Smoker made the door for a week or so before it was replaced by more of themselves.

Pork chauffeured them through Grand Coulee, then Electric City. The frozen lake was as white as the ground, though flatter. Yellow fires dappled the surface where the Russians had sawed holes to fish.

Andre sipped a Pepsi. Smoker drank from the whiskey bottle. Alcohol greased a zerk for Smoker, just proper maintenance. He'd nurse a beer all day and not feel shorted or down eight and want only a nap. Likely as not he'd choose lemonade. For Smoker, the comfort in drinking was the solace that kept the army manned— you enlist by yourself, you come out the same as the others. Andre, though, alcohol stranded. Even clean, anticipating liquor sawed him off from others. Claire seemed the only way he could tolerate sobriety.

"You think married's easy?" Pork asked Andre.

"Easier," Andre said.

"Than what?"

"Calculus."

Smoker laughed.

"One drink and you're goofy as women," Pork said.

"You been married," Smoker told him. "You do hard math?"

"Jesus."

"Anybody you know do it?" Smoker asked.

"This ain't about adding and subtracting."

"No, there's division and geometry. What's 472 divided by 128?"

"You don't know, neither," Pork said.

"Ain't me giving advice. You got to be qualified."

Pork thumped his chest with his thumb. "I'm married," he said. "Was, at least." Pork surrendered the wheel to Smoker then bent across him to Andre. "You got a heart, goddamnit," Pork said. "That'll work against you."

"Turn," Smoker said.

Pork raised himself to permit the wheel to spin. "I had me a heart once," he said.

"You don't know heart from kidneys," Smoker told him.

"I know enough to figure I ain't the only one ever felt something," Pork replied. Pork fisted Andre's coat lapels and shook him. "You might not like it, but I got things to tell you."

Andre leaned on the window and closed his eyes. "You don't listen no better than you ever did," Pork said. Pork retook the wheel and the whiskey. They progressed beyond the town's glow, where the high coulee walls blackened both sides of the water and the moon shone like a blister on the ice.

"Maybe I'm considering the source," Andre said.

"You got no right to say that to me," Pork muttered.

"No?" Andre asked.

"Well, maybe you do," Pork admitted. "But it isn't kind." Pork extended the bottle across Smoker to Andre, several months dry. Andre undid the cap and swallowed until Smoker wrenched the jug from him.

"Let him be," Pork told Smoker.

"Seems like I said the same thing an hour ago, you goofy bastard," Smoker replied.

"Well that was then and you were wrong and this is now and I am correct. You don't know half of what you do and none of what you think you do."

"You saying you do?" Smoker said.

Pork shook his head. "I'm saying I don't. But I know I don't."

Andre laughed. "You come damned late to philosophy."

"Least it ain't religion," Pork said.

They drove a mile in silence.

"Say," Smoker asked the old man. "How you figure I'd do married?"

"Not good," Pork answered.

"I make them stick, sometimes two or three at once."

"Many are easier to manage than one."

"Dede," he said. "We been steady awhile."

"I doubt you'd give up fishing just because you landed a keeper."

"Andre did."

"He was being skunked."

Pork wheeled through a turnout and looped the truck back toward town. "Switch up the heat," he said.

"I'm too hot already," Smoker told him. Sitting in the middle left Smoker accountable for the fan.

"You ain't the only sheep in the herd."

"But I'm the only one that can reach the heater."

Pork bent for the button and twisted it. The truck swerved then hot air swam into Smoker's lap. The old man grinned a toothy grin. It wasn't a minute later the engine wheezed. Pork tapped the dash gauges like they might correct themselves.

"Should've kept the fan off," Smoker told him.

"Heater don't use gas," Pork said.

They limped the pickup to the road shoulder. From under the seat, Pork ferreted a plastic jug, the top sawed to the handle. He marched toward town and the filling station without a word, clouds of breath steaming behind him.

Smoker and Andre let him go and huddled in the cab to keep from the wind. The fan blew cold air and Smoker clicked off the ignition to keep the battery fresh. Soon the window glass frosted and Andre drew a bear print then a peace sign in the white rime. Just a hen's track in a circle, Pork had told them growing up. Andre hunted the whiskey then opened the truck door and set off toward the highway.

"It don't take but one for the gas," Smoker shouted.

Andre ignored him. Smoker caught up at a half run. Andre drank like he had a bet on it. Cars passed, none carrying Pork nor anyone generous enough to offer them rescue from the weather. Andre and Smoker labored half an hour then encountered the grade to Claire's street. Together they circled the duplex through an alley. Andre halted beneath a tall spruce and indicated Smoker to do the same. The dense tree stunk like gin. Under it the ground was frozen and bare. Andre shoved his arm through the canopy of branches until a long lawn chair and mummy bag fell from inside.

"You're going to be frosty by morning," Smoker told him.

"That's a fact," Andre said. From this vantage, they could observe the apartment without being seen. Smoker recognized

Claire in the big front window, bent as she hemmed a bridesmaid gown at her machine. Andre pulled from the bottle and Smoker had another turn himself to back up the chill. After a while, Claire stood and ambled to the window and stretched her arms. She raised one hand and one foot like a setter on point if the bird were straight up. Her hip thrust forward suddenly and the other back and she spun. Her circles slowed and her hand fell from above her head like slow water, and when it met the other she let them both spread about her waist as if they were pooling. On her face was an expression Smoker had only seen in children.

Then Dede rose from the couch, which faced away from the window. She lay her own dress down. Smoker had no idea she would be there, though it seemed natural enough. He watched her laugh and try to whirl, too. She could muster only half a revolution. Dede was as pretty as a wildcat and about as hard to get along with. Her snug jeans and tightly tucked shirt directed a person's attention to where it ought to be, but she seemed wanting as she labored to make a circle until Claire cupped her elbow and steered her into a wobbly spiral.

"Claire's the only girl I've ever seen naked," Andre said.

Smoker shook his head. "That yell leader I brought back to your dorm room. She was naked."

"That was because you grabbed her blanket and made her chase you."

"I was sharing," Smoker said.

Andre drank again. "You were lording it over me."

Smoker guffawed. "You really never seen another woman undressed?" he asked. The purpled sky had surrendered to black. Smoker gathered a handful of pebbles and lobbed them into the gray snow, which swallowed each without a sound. Andre inhaled a breath and kept it until he hacked from his own exhaust, then took another and did the same. His face swelled and eyes emptied. In the park, as children, he and Smoker had entertained each other by hyperventilating into blackouts and now Smoker recognized Andre's thoughts were swirling.

"She's worried I want someone enough to take anyone," he said.

"That so?"

"It's her worry. She's putting it on me to get a good look," Andre said.

"You don't know that."

"You're right," Andre said. "It's an uneducated guess. I don't have much practice with love."

"Hell, you're the only one of us with any training at all," Smoker told him. "You got all the goddamn feelings."

"And you got all the stabbings."

"They're overrated."

"Many a night I'd liked to have found out."

"How about we trade?" Smoker replied.

Andre shook his head. "Not now."

He drank again, sighed, then choked down more alcohol. Smoker watched him coil on the chair and study the twisted tree root and decaying needles encircling it, as if he might bore all his attention onto the tiny strip of earth and shed drink like a drill's shavings.

"Why didn't you just gargle the bottle or take little sips. The old man'd never have known."

"You'd know," Andre said. His heavy brow hooded his eyes and he fell asleep. Smoker considered himself and his talent for undoing a woman. He possessed no bent for healing, though, and no appetite to acquire it. Tenderness irritated him and he allowed every woman he'd bedded to dress, then fester like an open sore until she forsook him for some other, believing the lacking resided in herself. He closed his eyes then tipped his head back and let them open. The sky was a starry liquid, blowing in waves above him as if he were a fish at the bottom of a lake studying the boundaries of his world.

An hour after, Smoker heard Pork's truck cough. The old man had guessed right. Smoker motioned him toward the alley to protect Andre's camp. Pork let the pickup idle and stepped out.

"That Myrna woman has a shine for you," Pork told him. "I figure you can parlay that into some goodwill for your brother. I bought her a couple of highballs to grease the skids. She's most of the way drunk already."

"So's the groom," Smoker replied.

"We'll stir him."

Together, they propped Andre against the dumpster. He slid off the metal onto the cold gravel.

Pork stood over him. "You hungry for a woman, son?"

Andre laughed and flapped his arms and legs. "Gravel angel," he said. They were quiet awhile. "Where's Claire?" Andre asked.

"She don't require you tonight," Pork told him.

"I got to piss," Andre said.

Smoker parted Andre's feet for balance and pulled his shoulders up the dumpster's white metal.

"Piss," Smoker told him.

Andre worked at his pants. He had no luck.

"Good Christ. He's going to piss himself," Pork said.

Smoker bent and unbuttoned Andre's jeans and dragged the

zipper and tugged on his brother's underwear until he freed him. A piss stream arced into the light and splattered the gravel.

Pork shook his head. "Fruits," he mumbled. "I raised me a couple of fruits."

Smoker broke a knuckle on Pork's bridgework. The old man collapsed to all fours. Smoker stood over him, rubbing his aching hand. Blood from Pork's mouth puddled the snow.

"You once told me whoever gets the first blow is likely to land the second," Smoker warned him.

"Only thing I taught you that stuck seems to me."

"Everything stuck, goddamnit."

Andre laughed and slid down the dumpster again, his penis dripping.

"You going to belt me again?" Pork asked.

"I might."

"I don't guess you'd hit a man down."

Pork crawled to Andre and lifted his chin in his hand. He tipped Andre's face toward him. Sleeping people were supposed to look pure as the young, but Andre appeared only himself. Pork brushed the hair out of Andre's eyes. Smoker saw the mess he'd made of the old man's face. Together they hauled Andre to the lawn chair and rolled him into his sleeping bag, then zipped and buttoned it, so only his face was exposed to the cold. Smoker found a halved tamarack round and propped Andre sideways like parents kept babies from choking on their stomachs.

"You know, you can get some strange whenever you please. Your brother isn't so lucky."

"Myrna medicine for that, is she?"

"I ain't saying it's a cure. Us being good to him is all."

"It's you and me making him a present of what we'd want."

"We? You standing there looking like a goddamn prince saying we!" Pork spat. Cold light sprang from the gravel.

Pork struck a match and lit a cigarette, then put another to the burning end and passed it to Smoker. They both smoked awhile. Smoker made for the car and heat. Pork opted to remain with Andre. In the pickup, Smoker warmed his hands until they didn't ache. A pair of cars whispered past then faded and Smoker understood he was a selfish man and a poor brother and was prepared to do little about either. He dropped the clutch and backed away. The truck light poured over Pork's back and head and Andre asleep, then slid off them. Smoker wondered if Dede would sleep at his place. Him there first would be a shock to her. He imagined her shutting the door and blinking at the lump in the bed. The room would be cool, and she would undress quickly then crawl under the sheets and trace his shape with hers to redraw him for the warmth of it. She'd sleep and he'd wake, alone, with nothing but her breaths and the wind's sighs and walls' creaks as if a casket lid were set to close over him.

The next day Claire and Andre married. Andre stood at an altar with Pork and Smoker, half drunk in their tuxedos. Nobody inquired about Pork's broken lip. Crazy Eddie's Tavern hosted the reception. For his gift, Eddie offered the wedding party a turkey dinner and ten dollars' worth of quarters for the jukebox. Andre and Claire clasped hands and punched their favorites. The light made them glow. When the disc dropped and the speakers hissed and a song began, Andre set his open hand in the small of Claire's back and his other met hers and they danced. Andre's mouth opened and closed and Smoker could see his breath stir her hair. He realized his brother was singing. She kissed him and he parted his lips and whispered small things neither would remember.

Dede tugged Smoker's hand and he followed her to the dance floor. Past the bar sat Pork and Peg at separate tables. Pork had unbuttoned his jacket and his damp shirt stuck to him where he'd sweated through it. Both their faces looked yellow and un-healthy. Peg nodded as if agreeing to some voice only she heard. Pork lifted his glass at Andre. Andre nodded. Dede breathed in, surprised when Smoker pulled her closer.

9

EXODUS

August 1991

Inside Harold's cabin, Andre stirred the fireplace embers. Those that hadn't surrendered to ash pulsed in the damper's draft. Kindling had been piled in a wooden apple crate at one end of the hearth. Another larger box cobbled together from plywood and lumber scraps held split and quartered rounds. Andre wasn't particularly cold, but he enjoyed the heated air pressing over him.

Harold and Smoker drank from their beers.

"I think I quit bleeding," Smoker said.

"Congratulations," Harold replied.

Calvin glared up from the tablecloth squares he appeared to be studying. "I fucked your mother," Calvin told them.

Smoker laughed. "Guess that puts you in the majority of men acquainted with her."

"That include you and your brother?"

"We are freethinkers but not nearly that liberated."

"You're a couple of ungrateful assholes," Calvin said. "That woman brung you into this world."

"And that's a favor?"

"You ever see a woman in labor?" Calvin asked.

"No," Smoker said.

"Seen plenty of cows calving though," Andre added from the fireplace.

"Now you're comparing your mother to cattle."

"No," Smoker said, "he's comparing birth to birth."

"You know how many women's cause of death is their kids?" Calvin asked.

"Maybe in Buttfuck, Egypt," Smoker said.

"No, in America. This country is fifth worst in making it past five years old. Check your goddamned library. Poland's ahead of here. So's Canada. You got better odds getting to kindergarten in the fucking Yukon than in Spokane, Washington. And your mother brought you two into this world anyway."

"I see you have read an article somewhere." Smoker chuckled. "But you're still nothing but a goddamned convict. You going to tell us how to treat our mother? You may have fucked her, but you didn't know her."

Calvin stared at his toes. "I didn't fuck her," he said. "I tried." He bent and lifted his pant leg. "She shot me right here."

"You got off light," Smoker told him. "You should see what she did to our father."

"I saw her Cesarean scar," Calvin said. "You got off light, too."

"Shut up, Calvin," Harold said. "Sex. Sex, sex, sex. Tearing and scars and blood and . . . You are a scourge."

"People," Calvin asked, "or me?"

"You."

"I'm just a human."

"You're an animal."

"That, too."

"You can't be both," Harold told him.

"You're wrong. I can't not be. Neither can you, Pop." Calvin's voice had turned plaintiff. The man had a stake in what he said.

"With this!" Harold lifted his Bible and slapped the cover. "I can."

"Hold up *Moby-Dick* or 'The Three Bears' and you might argue the same thing."

"You've never read either," Harold told him.

"Wrong," Calvin responded. "Wrong. Wrong. Wrong. Prison's got a library and books. I read all three and there's not a lick of difference between them."

"You are comparing God's word to man's?"

"Are you going to fuck their little girl?" Calvin asked.

"What are you talking about?"

"You heard me, Father."

"No."

"Never?"

"Never."

"Because of the money. What if there was no money? What if these dipshits never stumbled this way? What if they didn't give a shit, like you figured?"

Harold didn't reply.

"What about the Thompson girl she's playing dominoes with?"

"She's a child," Harold said.

"She won't always be."

"Well, then we can revisit this conversation."

"Do you want her to bleed first? What if she bleeds, then will you take her?"

Harold sighed. "We must procreate. Otherwise the sinners will outbreed us."

"No," Calvin said. "We must not. That's the greatest sin. Who needs more of us?"

"You would not be born?"

"That'd suit you, wouldn't it? Is that how you took mother? Just circle her like a buzzard waiting for blood?" Calvin shook his head. "I did the goddamned math. She was barely fifteen when I was born. Means she couldn't be past fourteen and a half when you bedded her, and that's only if the plumbing worked right the first time. You were what, thirty?"

"She's dead," Harold said.

"How?" Andre asked.

"Car wreck."

Calvin shook his head. "On a straight road. Midday. Right off Sherman Ridge. No brake marks. Car was traveling fast enough to almost clear the guardrail. I was six. She got all the way to twenty-one." He looked at his father.

"Look at your career, so far. You would have hardly profited her. Maybe she saw the future."

Calvin did not reply.

"And maybe I can do better with another womb," Harold added.

Calvin laughed. "Sorry my mother's was less than golden."

"I'm sorry, too," Harold said.

"She was a child, blood or not," Calvin told him.

"So was Mary. You are not God."

Smoker rose and Andre with him.

"Not with your girl," Harold told them. "We need the money." He nodded at Smoker's bag. "She hasn't been touched."

Calvin laughed. "And they locked me up?"

Andre tried to ignore them. He added to the fire and watched the fresh wood catch and smoke, then burn. The pitch popped and crackled and tossed sparks onto the hearth that he extinguished with his bootheel.

LAMENTATIONS
December 1984–March 1985

Five days before Christmas, Andre wed Claire. The church, dolled up with holiday trimmings, produced a fine affair and the poinsettias were free. Before the reception, Dede deposited Bird with Vera and the event soon escalated to a bender. Andre packed Claire, drunk past consciousness, fireman-style to Pork's four-by-four. Pork backed out. Claire's mouth and cheek were flattened against the window glass along with one unseeing eye.

Two days later, Smoker resigned from the pole plant, and in solidarity Peg abandoned her dime-store stint, leaving only Andre employed, but, as school had let out for the holidays, he was not required to follow suit. Without jobs, the family gave drink and revelry their undivided attention. Outside the tavern window, locals passed, hastened by wind and temperature, stocking caps screwed onto their heads. The icy streets shone like rubbed silver and the shoppers and ambling children minced steps to avoid calamity. Andre spotted three students from his homeroom, a boy and two girls. He wondered if they would recognize him bearing a year's worth of drink in a short week. He felt the man Claire married yielding to the one hobbled by the years before her. He contemplated calling but feared he'd become too undone for her to remember him and hearing his voice, she would recognize it.

By Christmas Eve, the wedding party had run tab enough Eddie cut them off, but when Andre opened the door to his marriage house, Claire had boxed her things and left. He had not drank since. In fact, he'd done little except teach school and watch TV and avoid Claire in the hallways.

A month or so after, Peg surprised most everyone by returning to Pork and the ranch, part-time at least. She curried the horses and meandered the property in a bumperless pickup. Pork coaxed her to fish with him evenings. Andre and Smoker straggled along occasionally with a bucket of grocery-store chicken. No one talked much, but Andre knew Peg had wandered onto some road strange to her. She lingered those cool days on the gravel banks and studied the current like it was sketching out pictures, though not the right ones.

March, Andre stood in the dark living room of Peg's trailer until Smoker's headlight beams sprayed him with light. He and Smoker were scheduled to deliver Peg and the last of her things to the ranch. The truck door slammed and Smoker's breath fog lifted in the night air outside. He pulled at the trailer door without knocking and felt for the switch.

"Don't," Andre said.

"Why?"

"She's dead."

Odds and ends cluttered the floor: her shot-glass collection, ancient encyclopedias, worn winter coats that leaked ticking, a few photographs and cards. She was near dead when Andre found her. She left no note. Explanations, like endearments, were riders she had thrown long ago.

Smoker paused in the window's light and lit a cigarette. "She never mentioned being ill."

"Wasn't."

"How then?"

"That old .22."

"Jesus. In the head?"

"Chest."

"Didn't want to go ugly, I imagine," Smoker said. "I hope she was drunk."

"Bottle's on the end table."

Smoker fumbled through the dark, then lifted the whiskey and drank. "Damn, this is her holiday jug."

The whiskey swirled against the bottle glass. Andre had just come to where he could enjoy sobriety. Smoker lit another cigarette. Peg lay on the sofa behind him. Her face appeared and vanished in the match flash.

"You call the old man?" Smoker asked.

"Phone's disconnected. Haven't even told the police."

Smoker drank again then rolled the whiskey across the floor to Andre. "You see this coming?"

Andre lifted the bottle by the neck and enjoyed the liquid weight. He uncapped it and smelled. Andre was the one their mother was most inclined to. Smoker figured it was because Andre was oldest, but Andre understood it differently. Smoker was sharp-featured and rakish; women tripped over one another to be his fool. He had a knack for appearing to have feelings and the prospect of excavating his heart kept them on. His mother, though, was drawn to ugly men. She embraced their mean spirits and bent teeth as if penance. Andre was her spiritual burden. He closed his eyes and drank the whiskey and the feeling of liquor was on him again, more certain than anything in his life. He asked Smoker for a cigarette. Smoker tapped the pack on his knuckle until one slid loose. The smoke lightened Andre's head. "You gonna call the cops or me?" Andre asked.

"Not calling any cops."

"We need a death certificate for the funeral."

"Funerals cost money and it'll take into next week. Besides, who'd show?"

"You and me."

"You and me don't need nothing but a shovel."

"It won't be legal," Andre said.

"That'll suit her fine."

Andre argued, but Smoker heard none of it, and when he switched the light and worked to cover Peg in an old Indian blanket, Andre hiked her legs and rolled her to be wrapped. Pooled blood blackened her sweatshirt. Andre brought a towel from the bathroom and mopped what was left, then helped Smoker fold the blanket.

She was awkward as a bar drunk to tote. They swung her over the porch railing and Smoker's truck's tailgate. Andre arranged a logging chain and a spare tire to make room and snubbed her with duct tape to secure the blanket.

Smoker backed from the driveway while Andre checked how

his mother bore the ride. Her graying hair twisted into her mouth. She'd ceased fighting it the past month, which left her appearing a senior citizen while behaving like a fourteen-year-old on a dare. To newcomers she appeared simply tapped out. Only the regulars understood how much she'd squandered and how gloriously she'd done it.

Pork answered the ranch-house door with a rifle leveled at their waists.

"It's late to be calling." He set the rifle inside.

"Got some bad news," Smoker said.

"Spill it."

"Mother's killed herself."

"Christ, I knew she didn't want me no more than before." He pulled his glasses from his face and rubbed the welts they left on each side of his nose. "Come on inside."

"She's in the truck," Smoker said. "We need a shovel and a good place."

"That truck?" Pork pointed.

Smoker nodded. "You going to lend us a hand?"

The driveway light illuminated Pork's face.

"I'll lend you some advice," he said. "Take her home. Let them that know how to handle it."

"Nobody should care where she's buried," Smoker replied.

Pork spat. "I don't want her here. You hear that? I don't want to be wondering what pile of rocks she's under, what goddamned tree is growing over her."

"She's dead," Smoker said. "We're finished being mad."

"I ain't done." Pork huffed. "You should be as mad as me," he shouted. "I won't spend one second grieving her. You understand me?" He jerked the rifle from behind the door and waved the gun above them and fired.

Smoker and Andre bolted for the truck. Andre crawled into the driver's side and twisted the key. When he and Smoker looked back, Pork peered through the scope at the sky left uncovered by his shattered gutter. He squeezed off another round. The shot cracked and the report shuddered down the river. The old man studied the night, waiting for a vanishing star or planet, or maybe a bead of blue day to drip from the night.

"He didn't hit nothing?" Smoker asked.

Andre shrugged. "Maybe that's what he aimed for."

They navigated the dirt roads an hour farther upriver, Andre at the wheel while Smoker directed him and unhooked barbed-wire gates that marked each ranch's boundaries. Cattle lowed and wandered toward the lights hoping for a feed truck. The country opened and turned rocky as they neared the river bottom. In a washboarded stretch, Andre listened to Peg bang the truck bed.

Andre halted the truck on a hill knob. Smoker lit a cigarette from his second pack. The headlights painted the high yellow ditch weeds. Below was a corral and a tiny house like those thrown up for hands working the winter pastures. Barking came from it. Andre cut the engine and the dog quieted. The moon shone on the river's black curve. Andre heard the water pass despite his closed window. He shivered and slapped his hands together to warm himself. When it was clear they weren't going to start the truck and the heater, he wrestled some gloves from the jockey box.

"See that window upstairs?" Smoker's hand tapped the dash

then wiped the windshield clouded with breath fog. "The light there is a miniature of them Disney dogs. Dalmatians. She's got a Disney-dog bedspread, too. Did you hear barking when we came up? That's the real thing, the dog-movie dog."

Andre cocked one eyebrow. "Bird?"

"And Dede. I rented it a month ago. I visit weekends. Otherwise, if I got a present or a load of groceries, I drop it in the car while Dede's working and Bird is at school."

Smoker stared into the flat below.

"You know why I got to bury her tonight?" Smoker asked. "I'm poison in large doses. I need new rules." He sighed. "It ain't ill will. I never wanted Peg dead. How can you not love your mother? It's against some law, isn't it?" Smoker's mouth pocketed with a wrinkle. It was the first age Andre recognized in him.

"Probably," Andre said, "but I doubt they looked enough ahead to see Peg."

Smoker pulled his cigarette ash bright until it lit his face. Smoke filled the cab then broke up. In the pickup bed, their mother wasn't much more than the blanket and wind-tossed hair. Alive no one could get her that small.

Smoker passed what was left of the whiskey.

When Andre reached the age of interest, he made a study of his mother's suitors. Late one night his eighth-grade year, he woke to a friend of his father's rocking against his mother, who was on all fours in the television light. The man flailed like a hooked fish; his work boots trapped his jeans at his ankles. His mother's bra had been jerked to her shoulders, and her breasts swung in the TV's flickering. When she finally peered away and blinked Andre into focus, her brow furrowed as if considering an important thought, and he waited for her to speak it, but she only shooed him with a hand before the man could see.

After the man departed and she lay sleeping, Andre entered her room. Her nipples poked her nightgown and made a static sound. His erection ached him. She woke and saw and he waited. She said nothing, just rolled over, leaving him the bones of her back, no heart, no lungs breathing, just hard shapes.

"What do you want me to say?" Andre asked.

"Uncle," he said.

"Why?"

"Because you can't find a way to take her part."

Smoker gazed at the sparkling lemony lights below. It was March, Andre realized, and there remained a chance of snow.

"Uncle," Andre said.

The road wound half a mile along the ridge then switchbacked for the house. Andre started them slowly straight down the bald hill. He shifted gears to manage the speed. They barreled past a cattle path. Smoker opened the window and fired his Luger into the sky. Andre's window was open, too, and the cold seared his face. His eyes teared and his teeth froze cold as rocks.

They passed the house and flattened the wood corral gate. The truck's headlights spilled onto the little barn, then left it. A few seconds and the truck's nose dipped then bucked, and they were midair. Smoker, green in the dash light, grinned, and above the cab, their mother rose like a pagan goddess.

The impact with the water shoved Andre out of the cab. He surfaced and found footing on the hood. He extended his arm toward his mother but could reach only the blanket's edge, and the current towed her away.

Next to him, Smoker tread water. A gash sliced one cheek. Andre tugged him to the truck hood.

"Miss the brake?" Smoker asked.

"Just forgot," Andre told him. He pointed out the drifting body.

"So long, Mother," Smoker said.

He ducked into the water and swam and Andre did, too. They clambered over the bank and emptied their boots. Andre had never been so cold. His clothes stuck to him. He watched Smoker strip to his skivvies and did the same. They raced to the house and the faint orange light in the window upstairs. There were other lights now and Dede silhouetted the porch. They were too numb to feel the rocks and thistles slashing their feet, too numb to feel the wind. They ran flat out, while the dog barked his warning.

There was another way to recall their mother, Andre knew. Winters, as boys, Andre and Smoker split wood and cleared driveways then hoarded their pay in a half-gallon whiskey jug. Peg added her tips and cut back on cigarettes, though she remained gaunt as a blade. Once a week, she stole home early, stopping at the market for whipping cream and powdered chocolate. Andre and Smoker dumped the change on the table and counted while she heated milk. Spring vacations, they spun a nail on a road map and headed where it pointed until the money ran out, then turned back and employed her charge card to return home.

10

EXODUS

August 1991

Andre sat in a chair across the room from Smoker. The fire remained in his head so that even when he shut his eyes its light still glowed on his closed lids.

He heard a scooter outside kick-start and the engine whir. He and Smoker said nothing. Harold returned. He informed them he'd sent Calvin to fetch Bird. Harold joined Smoker at the table and began a cribbage game. They asked Andre to take a hand, but he declined.

The room was poorly lit and the walls thin. Winters in the place would be a drafty affair. A generator hummed somewhere. Two oscillating fans were the only cooling outside of a forest full of shade.

Under one window was a long bookcase, one lamp flickering above it. Coloring books, a few books from the Boxcar Children series—stories of abandoned children living in a train car—a set of children's encyclopedia, *The Berenstain Bears*, and *The Cat in the Hat*. A cigar box filled with crayons served as a bookend. Several colored pictures torn from their books lay in a pile next to it. Andre rose and leafed through them: dinosaurs, panda bears, a wolf, the lobster from Disney's *The Little Mermaid* cartoon. He could not tell if they were the products of several children or one, and if one, whether Bird was the artist or not.

The hours of driving and, Andre guessed, the disruption of his life by love and its attendant demons teamed up to disconnect him. He felt like he'd smoked a pipeful of marijuana and the air was clearing, but the fog in his mind had only just started. Andre hated marijuana. It pressed him to turn over the rocks in his memory, hunting the lichen and grit for even the most miniscule evidence against himself.

He despised memory as well. Every generation has its nostalgic touchstones. TV shows, music, documentaries about decades that seem to have just entered his rearview mirror and he later discovered were twenty years past. Andre enjoyed the music, though had no use for the rest. They offered nothing he didn't already know, and they delivered it in a package that romanticized years that are far from romantic.

Still, as he aged some, he expected to revisit the past and share amusing stories with others at reunions or happenstance encounters. Andre participated in those dutifully enough, but felt nothing like nostalgia. His first and strongest response to the revelry was shame. He mostly recalled confusion, drunkenness, and behaving as if in a play, acting parts written for others, but ones he desperately needed to master. So almost before recollections entered his head, he shut the spigot. But in instances like these—long drives, tedium—his mind escaped him and he couldn't corral it quick enough.

Peg downing a drink suddenly entered his head and he was too stupefied to deflect it. Eddie collecting her glass and washing it and mopping the bar top to occupy himself. He glances at Peg and then at Andre and Smoker at the other end of the bar.

Eddie patted Peg's hand and pressed her money back at her. Later he turned to Andre and Smoker. "Your Ma and Pop. They've been good business to me for more years than you two have been alive. You don't treat them right."

Smoker nodded toward Peg. "There's some reason for that."

"I suppose," Eddie allowed.

He washed another glass. "I do recall several instances Pork in here prouder than a three-balled rooster about some feat one of you two managed."

"I doubt that's so lately."

"Might be reason for that, too," Eddie said.

Peg rose. She left her money on the bar. "They aren't wrong," she said and disappeared through the door.

Smoker drank. He figured Eddie would leave it.

"Your mother, too," Eddie went on. "One of you'd get sick, she'd fight the doctor until he gave you medicine. Boxed his ears once. Whatever it took."

Smoker told Eddie, "Spit or swallow."

Eddie lifted the good bourbon, fifty bucks a bottle, from under the cash register and filled himself half a tumbler. He admired the alcohol in the light. He offered the boys none.

"Well," Eddie said and then drank and paused. The air

escaped him, like a lover's might. "Those stories got me asking one question."

"Yeah," Andre said.

"How old does a person have to be before he's his own damned fault?"

In the cribbage game with Harold, Smoker yipped over a sixteen hand and pegged each at the annoying pace of a home-run hitter jogging the bases. The hoots roused Andre. He glanced toward the game. Behind the two hung more coloring-book art. Andre approached the wall. Smoker and Harold ignored him. These pictures had names written in a man's sketchy hand. A few bore Bird's birth name. Andre required a long moment to add the two up.

LAMENTATIONS
March 1985

The last morning of her life, Peg ordered two eggs scrambled with bacon, cut Kansas City. Wilma, the stand-in cook mornings when Eddie performed his errands, offered her the dice cup. Peg shook four deuces and won her coffee, though what Wilma deposited in the cup resembled thirty-weight motor oil, three thousand miles past the window sticker.

Peg drank then toothpicked the dregs from her front teeth. "Thought you preferred it strong, Peg," Wilma said.

"Just like my men," Peg told her. Peg had enlisted Wilma's husband to join her for the short drive to the reservoir some years back, when Wilma cooked nights and shorted Peg on fries. The gossip drummed on Wilma just as Peg had foreseen. Her husband suffered, but not so much that he considered confession, which would have been no solution anyway.

Peg left Wilma no doubt she was watching her eggs from the shells to the plate, and when Wilma shoved the dish in front of her with the ticket and salsa in a cup, Peg ate greedily.

"I'm not likely to get a better meal," Peg said when she finished. "I think I'll kill myself and save the disappointment."

"Good day for it," Wilma told her. "If you're satisfied with all us outliving you."

"Not with a cat's lives will you outlive me," Peg said.

Peg could put a year's living into a long weekend. But she'd grown tired of fucking. Since the trip south, she could not find that second pulse, the one between her legs that pressed at her since she was twelve. The few instances she'd attempted, her head had jammed with cotton and she felt as if she were screwing a one-boned hand. Amphetamines nor quaaludes nor drink nor smoke could hound the numbness from her. Food was sustenance, water slaked no thirst, and cigarettes made her cough. She enjoyed nothing. She had not anticipated the condition, but after a time it turned to relief; she'd have lived forever otherwise.

Peg rattled some change onto the bar then placed a couple of singles beside the coins.

"Cremation," Peg said. "Tell them I told you so."

Outside, the hard sunlight blinded her and she drove the stringed towns in the coulee bottom with the shade tipped. Half of Coulee Dam lay on the reservation and the tribe had thrown enough cinderblock together to house a couple hundred slot machines and a few blackjack tables. The casino twisted the government's tail but drew a crowd all hours. Peg circled the building until she recognized Smoker's pickup. Inside it, Peg unholstered his Luger beneath the driver's seat. She rotated the gun barrel toward her. The metal gleamed where it reflected light. She poked her little finger into the barrel then tucked the gun under her sweatshirt.

In the casino, Smoker slid quarters into a silver notch in the machine and hit some buttons then tapped the spinner. He broke even on credits.

"What kind of mess would this make up close?" Peg showed him the pistol.

"Jesus Christ, put that away," Smoker said. "They'll eighty-six me for good." He looked closer. "That mine?"

"It is."

"You aren't hawking it, I don't care what's your straits."

"I got money in the bank and more coming. They re-upped my unemployment."

Smoker's hand scooped his quarters then let them click into a cup, his long fingers almost tender with the coins.

"Who you going to murder?"

"Myself," she said.

"Well, that'll bore a tunnel through you."

"Ordinary person, you'd call 9-1-1," Peg said.

"Let me know when you turn ordinary and I'll find the phone." Smoker returned to his machine. "And put my gun back where you found it." She left and he ignored her as he had most of his life.

In the teacher's parking lot, Peg put her car next to Andre's pickup. His open classroom window darkened then lit when her son's heavy shape passed. She caught blades of his voice; it hummed like a radio played low. She crept beneath the window and listened. Laughter marked his conversation with his students as it did nowhere else. His wit, sharper than any in the family, slackened with his students and his mind went graceful with purpose. The students loved him; she heard talk of it everywhere. She hadn't the heart to come inside, and he carried a .357, which would make as awful a hole as the Luger.

Pork's ranch house was empty. The sideboards had surrendered their paint and the lee side was reduced to splinters. Winters, frost collected inside and Pork fired the stove without letup to maintain a tolerable temperature. Not eighty years ago, his grandfather had put the place in the creek bottom because that's where the county wanted the only road and his wife had tired of being far from people. The bottom flooded every thaw, as he'd foreseen, and the house might've been ruined if he had not put river gravel beneath the foundation along with metal culverts. Spring, the floor trembled while the runoff passed, but not a stick of the house got damp. Pork lacked such ingenuity. Neither he nor the boys could match his father, separate or together. In two generations, his blood had thinned to a trickle and she'd been the one to dilute it.

Peg passed the rocker Pork had purchased to ease the children's colic. He had paid an old woman to engrave the back rail with their names. You steered your children through the day safely for the peace of seeing them sleep, Pork had once said, and though she doubted the accuracy of the sentiment, she recognized Pork did not. She'd taken a job once at the grocery in town early in their marriage, but the hours returned her home late. In a week,

Pork's nerves broke and he told her to quit. When she wouldn't, he blacked her eye.

Peg traipsed the basement stairs and forced the gun-case door with a screwdriver. Pork's .22 revolver lay on its floor. Dust clung to the grip and leather holster, but when she unpinned the cylinder, it clicked and rolled nicely. She short-loaded the powder on a couple of rounds so her kin might remember the best of her. She had read of a beautiful poet who gassed herself in an oven, but Peg's appliances ran on electric. She'd considered piling her car into Rebecca Rock, too. The noise would be dramatic, but no one would hear it and the result might not finish her and she'd be in a worse fix than she was now.

Driving out from the ranch, she stopped and gazed back. Dormant larkspur, cheat grass, and Russian thistle on the bluff tipped forward to catch five minutes of sun they might lose had they sprouted straight. West, the creek fell from a wheat ditch, muddy and foamed with farm chemicals. She heard a horse clop, and soon Pork and his mare appeared on the road in front of her.

She said nothing. He didn't speak either, though he did dismount to be cordial. She'd spent two-thirds of her life on him, off and on though it was. Once, she could figure his thoughts with some accuracy. But now they stood together, each knowing nothing of the other.

"I got a roast in a pot, if you're hungry," Pork said.

When she didn't answer he mounted his horse and headed that direction, not knowing whether she would follow or not. Pork had once tracked her a week straight in his old blue trap wagon. By then she had taken up with the butcher. An air compressor and fertilizer barrels filled the flatbed along with a toolbox the size of a closet. He was hard to miss but had no interest in stealth anyway.

He had not desired Peg in the manner a man does a woman; he wanted her as some want to be devoured by their God. It is why she married him and why she divorced him, too.

Eddie hunkered at the tavern griddle and stirred his house delicacy, chicken and homemade noodles. The tavern clientele pooled for a pasta machine a Christmas before and Eddie thanked them but swapped the crank-ended machine for a blender at the hardware. He trusted his own methods.

"Hello, my dear," he said. He was alone the slow hours between breakfast and dinner, having never courted much of a lunch crowd, hoping to encourage his patrons to remain employed. "You getting an early start on the night or closing yesterday late?"

"Neither, Eddie," she said. He filled a schooner three-quarters and topped it with an open V8 can from the walk-in. Peg shook a bit of salt into the glass and drank. The locals did not comprehend that rising mornings to accept the yoke of debauchery required more energy from Peg than selling car parts or keeping books or operating machines did from ordinary souls, and for her efforts she could expect no pension, no weekends off, no paid vacation. Her life required a will as profound as an epic hero's. All she lacked was the purpose.

"Eddie, would you miss me if I was gone?" she asked.

"Well, you haven't ever been gone, my dear, so it's hard to tell. I'd grant I'd notice," he told her.

"A fair answer, fairly spoken."

"You're starting to sound poetic," he told her.

"And you're reminding me of a politician."

Eddie nodded. "Operating a business means kissing everyone's babies." He turned from his soup, his apron soiled with broth and grease from boning the chicken. Peg smoked a cigarette and watched Eddie through the cloud it made.

"Come here a minute," she told him. He crossed the tile to the hinged opening of the bar.

"Farther," she said. He flipped the gate and stepped through. Peg winked at him. She rose and locked the front door and pulled the shades, then bent and undid his fly and fished out his bean. His flaccid workings stirred, then did not. She tugged at them.

She bent and hooped her mouth over the cool flesh, swirling the end with her tongue as she had rock candy as a girl. She heard Eddie breathe, but nothing below stirred. She tugged her T-shirt over her head and rubbed her nipples against his skinny, bare legs, then slapped his rigging between her breasts. She glanced up. Eddie's face was wet with tears and he looked off like maybe this was a movie someone else was in.

"I don't hate them," she said, the bullet inside her aching like she swallowed an anvil.

"Who?" Andre asked.

"Any of them," Peg said. "But I don't like them much, either."

She was tired and closed her eyes. She felt she was watching herself from the ceiling, a goddamned cliché.

11

EXODUS
August 1991

Andre stared at the crude colored pictures on the wall. Smoker and Harold pegged and counted and exchanged cribbages. Andre pressed his finger against a picture. The crayon residue was slick and somewhat fragrant, though the smell had no relationship to the color.

He continued to drift. He recalled fishing as a child, line and lure slapping the water and fighting their slow drop. Smoker, six or so, cast a baited hook into a current strong enough to bend his fiberglass rod into a U. Ten minutes or so, Andre's pole jumped. Andre jerked and cranked the reel. An enormous trout leaped above the surface and attempted to spit the hook. Andre allowed it line enough to clear the snags and riffles then slowly retrieved what he'd given with a little less each run.

The exhausted fish surfaced a few yards beneath Andre's perch; the head and fin barely cut the water. Andre lifted the played-out fish from the deep water below to the rock edge toward him; the fish weighed eight pounds, easy. When he'd hauled it close, Andre leaned over the ledge and put his fingers into its gills, but the trout snapped itself against his arm. Andre lost his balance. The fish was still in his hand when they both hit the water.

The water and the fall stunned him. When he moved, his legs felt dead. He pushed his arms above the water, but they sank and he ducked under, thinking he was there a long time, a cloudy minute before his legs kicked him ahead again. He couldn't remember why he was in the water until the river threw the trout to the surface, still hooked to his lure. He grabbed the fish. Smoker scurried to the rod and began to reel them both, but the line snarled.

Andre paddled with his free arm, just attempting to move. The river towed him under once more, but he twisted and rose for a deep breath. His father stood on a jetty; Andre caught a look on his face. Pork's hair hung to one side of his head. His eyes skipped across the water, calm, measuring the distance. His skin was smooth. The water's reflection made it shine. Suddenly, a deeper pull towed Andre beneath the surface. He opened his eyes; it was dark and quiet. His heart crashed against his ribs, his lungs burned then breathed water. A small quiet welled like wet sky behind his forehead and a smell like old socks rushed in through his nose and mouth.

Then Pork's hand clamped Andre's limp neck. Andre hacked

out a lungful of water and sputtered and gasped until he was breathing. Andre's fist still held the fish's gills. He let loose and Smoker collected the fish as if it were his own.

Pork hustled Andre to the truck and blankets. He started the engine and set the heat on high then worked off his own wet clothes. The motor in the heater whined and the hot air enveloped Andre like the river before. He stretched his hands and toes, testing for their good, dull ache. He set his fingers on the dashboard, weighing his senses, relieved and disappointed the world felt the same. He guessed at how long it took a second to pass or a minute, counting a thousand one, a thousand two, weighing it against the time in the water.

After Peg's passing, Pork locked himself up on the ranch. He neither smoked nor drank. Smoker and Andre delivered him groceries and Louis L'Amour Westerns, and though they kept his body working, his mind hacked itself to kindling.

Andre arrived once on his own, Smoker having found part-time work limbing trees for the city. Pork was on his knees scratching at a vegetable garden. King observed him from the shade. The dog's hearing was suspect, but he sensed the vibrations of Andre's truck motor and the cab door shutting and he rose arthritically and sniffed, then his tail began to wag. Together they went to Pork.

"Good year for the tomatoes," Pork said. "We'll have baskets of them."

"And the squash in fall," Andre said.

Pork nodded. "You got time for a drive?"

Andre had become accustomed to short visits and at the first awkward gap in their conversation began to hunt an exit plan. In a vehicle, escape was impossible. He agreed finally when he could not come up with anything legitimate to argue. They passed through the agency and Nespelem; outside of town there are few paved roads. Ancient foundations dotted the fields, their siding and studs dust in mounds next to them sometimes. The place looked postapocalyptic. For Andre, the country was still more idea than physical place and without a map he'd be hard put. Pork's memory was failing, but here he recalled property lines and low spots that filled once every ten years with enough water for cattle.

A sign indicated an abandoned church that had commenced in 1902 and closed in 1959. Pork exited the cab for the adjacent graveyard, fenced with barbed wire to dissuade cattle, though badgers and groundhogs had burrowed plenty.

"Here," he said.

It was Andre's grandfather's stone, not extravagant in the manner of giant icons or family markers but fine white marble and etched with his name and dates.

"Figured you might be interested," Pork said.

"You sure it's him?"

"I'm not shoveling to check."

Three months later, Smoker discovered Pork ensnared in a barbed-wire fence, gaunt and hallucinating. They hurried him to the emergency room, and the doctors stitched his wounds but had no thread to patch his mind. Pork ended up in the county nursing home where he mumbled day and night and refused visitors. Most there had thirty years on him, but it wasn't years that had chased the sense from their heads; they added differently:

rheumatism left by a stack of snows and Chinook thaws; a logged-out mountain; the dead, in general; sometimes just the liquor store closed Sunday.

Pork quit eating two months into his stint and a couple of weeks later died. The service was in the longhouse. The minister chanted medicine songs, then read from Matthew. At the town cemetery, well-groomed and minded by a caretaker—unlike the portion of dirt and weeds where Pork's father lay—the mourners, cousins and uncles and nephews and nieces neither Smoker nor Andre had seen since childhood, lined in rows three deep.

The pallbearers hoisted the casket onto straps suspended over the open grave. The minister offered one last prayer.

"This concludes the service," the minister said. "There will be a dinner following at the church."

A squat man in a blue suit cranked a wheel. The crowd stared as the casket descended. The pallbearers tossed their boutonnieres into the open grave. Another man climbed onto the tractor. It coughed and started. But Smoker was already spading dirt into the grave. Two more shovels leaned against a caretaker's shed. Andre took one and a cousin another. Some families returned from the parking lot to the grave site. A few hunted trucks or car trunks for more tools. Soon six were undoing the pile, then eight, swapping shovels with one another. They finished the mound and bladed it smooth. Andre propped the flowers against the dirt.

Returning to the community center for the wake, Andre caught the smell of the kitchens as they drove through Nespelem for the church. TVs blared from open windows. High schoolers passed each other in their cars, the air-conditioning and music on high, nodding their heads like junkies.

Smoker paused for half a rack of beer at the Ketch Pen. From the tavern's rear porch came gunshots. An early goose hit like a sack of flour atop the roof. The truck turned left and Smoker saw two locals in lawn chairs armed with shotguns. A boy lifted himself up the eave to fetch the goose.

LAMENTATIONS

June 1986

The second time Andre and Claire traded vows was in front of the middle school. The newspaperwoman Claire hired steered Andre to one knee and deposited Claire's hand in his to kiss, an act he'd never considered but once instructed he gentled her ringed finger to his lips so Claire would recognize it was imagination not tenderness that he lacked.

Determined on a fairer start this time, Claire towed Andre to a desolate line shack half up Bonaparte Mountain to honeymoon. They packed in food and drank water from a spring. The first day lay close and humid, but the night sky cleared. In their doubled mummy bags, Andre pointed out landmarks and silhouetted shapes and stars and planets. One dot in the sky, off-color, Claire claimed was Mars. It was in the wrong quadrant, Andre knew, but accuracy seemed a tiresome constriction. He began to pretend for her random myths of this rock or that animal, stretching Indian stories for evidence, and when he ran short of those, he called upon Hans Christian Andersen. She was asleep before he wearied of lying, and alone in the quiet, he congratulated himself on taking marriage into a second day.

———

Smoker had witnessed the newly married surrender friends and family for recliners and TV sets, and it concerned him enough to insist Claire and Andre break bread with him Wednesdays. Smoker selected a café that boasted lacy tablecloths and the right forks but served only passable chow. They would have feasted better and cheaper on tavern fare, but Smoker insisted on a restaurant that accepted reservations and paid the bill. At first Dede joined them. She ordered a salad and drank red beer to back her bourbon and said little. Soon Smoker arrived alone.

"I'm shed of her," he announced.

Andre laughed.

"I got good reason."

"So does she."

Smoker lit a cigarette then looked at his surroundings and stabbed it into a saucer. The food arrived. Andre requested a lukewarm ham slice be warmed. It returned black. Smoker pitched plate and all through the order window. The kitchen cooks hollered. Smoker wielded a table knife. "I'll skin the bastards."

"Not with that," Andre said.

Smoker advanced on the kitchen anyway until he reached water glasses on a tray and changed tactics, hurling them into the order wheel where they shattered and rained on the cooks underneath. The manager scrambled for the check stand. Smoker put a plate between him and the phone.

"Cops ate here, they'd rain all over you, too, goddamnit," Smoker shouted.

Andre looked to reassure Claire his brother was only taking a joke on a wide loop, but she was busy emptying a salt shaker onto the floor.

Drinking glasses depleted, the three of them broke for the door. Half a mile toward Claire and Andre's apartment, they encountered a police car, which had neglected the lights. The three of them concluded the kitchen packed little weight with the authorities.

Inside the apartment, Andre tore lettuce, Smoker cut tomatoes and a sweet onion, and Claire boiled eggs and sliced lunch meat into squares. They ate chef salads in their jackets on the duplex balcony. When Smoker excused himself for home, an hour after, Andre and Claire cleaned the dishes, then she constructed an ice-cream dessert to treat Andre. He asked her reason. Needing one was part of his silliness, she told him.

"Your brother's thoughtful," Claire said.

"What makes you say that?"

"He knows we have to work in the morning. He leaves at nine. You didn't notice?"

At the beginning of the new year, Claire began studying the ads for a house. She thought Andre was uninterested until he purchased one without consulting her as a surprise. The house occupied the butt end of a dirt street that held three similar abodes and an apartment development for the indigent. Diapers that roaming dogs had rooted from their contents scattered the gravel. The hard-packed lot rebuffed even dandelions. The stoop sagged. On the exterior walls tongues of pink paint unlicked the wood siding. Inside, nicotine pasted the walls except where the summer heat had sweated it into long brown beads.

The first night, in the vacant lot behind, Claire heard children swear like sailors and dogs bark and whine and howl. Claire wadded cotton into her ears. One child's howl, however, could not be suppressed, a four- or five-year-old girl, Rose, with ratty blond hair. She wandered all hours, face blank as a white sky, a doll as unkempt as herself in one hand to clobber the troublesome dogs.

The next day, Claire purchased paint and rollers and unpacked old bedding for drop cloths. She primed and enameled the rooms. Andre assisted when she required him, but possessed only a menial commitment to the project. By the end of a month, Claire edged the last wall and unmasked the switches and baseboards and reapplied the outlet covers. She tapped the walls for studs and drove nails for their photographs, then mounted shelves to hold the knickknacks of her childhood and was pleased it was hers.

When trouble between Smoker and Dede thickened, Smoker occasionally took nights with them. He would arrive late and sleep on the couch, fully clothed. If Andre was awake, he'd roust Claire and press her to love him. He became hungrier, knowing Smoker might hear, and roughed her a little. Instead of shrinking, Claire met him in the same place, drawing quick breaths and making hissing sounds. Mornings, she would leave an afghan over Smoker and a spare towel in the bathroom and reset the coffee timer for noon.

October, Claire informed Andre she was pregnant. The next

day, she had cedar slats delivered and began to fortress the house with a tall board fence. To her surprise, the sawmill made a second stop that evening and unloaded planks and two-by-fours. Andre and Smoker constructed forms and mixed and poured concrete for deck footings. Andre toiled on the structure until dark each evening after.

Bedtime Claire tended a list on her nightstand notepad and nights she and Andre swapped names and she let Andre touch the shifting baby through her skin but Claire recognized the conjuring sensation that turned women to mothers was her own.

Andre continued on the deck, though Smoker abandoned him for elk season in the Blue Mountains. Not long after, Claire discovered the child, Rose, clasping a measuring tape while Andre marked his next cut. Andre fed her what was left from dinner and at evening's end paid her with his pocket change. She became steady help and Andre propped the fence gate open for her after work each day.

"What's a fence worth if you keep the gate open?" Claire asked him.

A week later, Smoker loaded their deep freeze with an elk's hindquarter. The first roast was sweet as beef, not gamey and about as good as food got. Claire took a few minutes in the evenings following to assemble meals with meat, rice, and vegetables on paper plates that Smoker could heat when he was inclined. The Wednesday following Smoker exited the house with two heaped boxes.

"She tired of feeding me?" Smoker asked.

"You bringing meat mean you didn't like what she's cooking?"

"Meant I was thanking you all."

"Maybe it's like that, then," Andre said.

Andre carried on with the deck flooring. Rose hammered short nails and delivered the tools. One Saturday afternoon, he took her ice fishing where they caught perch and drank hot cider. He'd asked Claire to join them, but she demurred, busy with baby clothes and a cross-stitched facsimile of the birth announcement in a neutral color, awaiting name and date.

He and Claire started Lamaze classes twice a week after school. Andre was habitually late, as he felt compelled to deliver Rose a sandwich and some pocket change on the days he couldn't work. Claire practiced with the instructor until Andre arrived and turned short with him when he did.

Andre accompanied Claire to her doctor appointments. He read the alpha-fetoprotein test results that declared the child's spine had developed correctly and that Claire was clear of gestational diabetes. Together they listened to the child's squishy heart thump. The nurse bathed Claire's belly in warm jelly and put something akin to a magic wand on it until the child's shadowy image floated in a monitor. She inquired whether Andre and Claire wanted to know the gender. They could not choose. They did not disagree; they simply did not know, had no resource for determination. The question troubled Andre deeply. To him it was his first act as a parent and he feared stepping wrong from the onset and not being able to walk himself or the child back from it.

Mid-March, an early thaw melted the last of the winter's ice and snow over a long week. Andre continued the deck with Rose. One afternoon, Claire complained about Andre's cooking and pressed him for a dinner in town. Andre set a sandwich on the wood piling with fifty cents for Rose, but Claire latched the gate behind them. It was a slight cruelty, not directed at the urchin but at Andre for dividing his attentions.

The dinner was the most enjoyable evening they'd had in months. They sat on the same side of the booth and held hands. Afterward, she directed him to stop in a darkened parking lot, where they kissed and hugged and whispered to each other like the early days.

The car lights illuminated their driveway then the house and fence. When he eased up the garage pad, a shape lay heaped against the metal door. Andre recognized the bloody jacket shredded by the dogs. He lifted Rose and carried her to the car then delivered her to the hospital emergency room.

The next morning, Andre returned to the hospital but only family was permitted to visit. Afterward, he saw her when he passed the bus stop while she waited with the other children. Scars wandered her face and she stared past him with stone eyes, and if Andre lived to a hundred he knew he could not outlast the silence she meant for him, a silence that seeped into his house and marriage, though neither Claire nor he spoke of it.

12

EXODUS
August 1991

Andre continued to examine the picture. He understood he'd become fixated on it, wandering through its simple lines and colors like he had been his own thoughts. He desired to know the difference between Bird's work and the others on the wall. He recognized it was different. What troubled him was naming it.

The dogs scratched and Harold let them in. They circled the fire. One came to Andre and he rubbed its ears. Another rolled by the fire and began licking its scrotum, reminding Andre of an old joke that he was too tired to recall completely.

"Goddamned Calvin," Harold said. "Excuse me. I'll see about him."

Harold was gone. Smoker examined Andre closely.

In one of his last lucid moments, Pork had signed the ranch's deed over to the boys. Smoker and Andre both considered transplanting the dog to town, but he was a farm dog. A fenced yard would be foreign country. Those leasing the farmland promised to watch him, which was the best proposition they could manage. Not long after, Smoker's pickup threw a rod and he traded his stake for Andre's four-wheel drive, just a year old.

Hunting season, Andre met Smoker at the place in a truck new off the lot.

Andre shouldered his rifle and started for the rocks. He never brought home much meat. It wasn't that he lacked the stomach for blood; he lacked a mind for it; hunting made you unlearn yourself; and Andre could not back out the screws.

Half a mile and they hiked out of the wheat into a streambed busted wide by spring thaws. They rested on the cliffs above the ranch. Below, a pickup stopped in a wide spot on the gravel road. A man got out one side and two boys tumbled from the other. One walked with his feet straight, taking long goose steps like the Nazis in old high-school documentaries.

"You coming?" Andre asked.

"You go on," Smoker said. "Think I'll work my way across the side of the canyon to that big rock."

Smoker tracked Andre's orange stocking cap as it scaled the bluff into the shale slides, a bright dot in a season that had quit on color. He envied his brother's view from that promontory. Up there, a person could see the whole of the country. It was hard to hunt; there was so much to sort through. You got lost just looking. At least Smoker did. He could only guess about Andre. Smoker closed his eyes. The scent of burned fields, disked and turned, rested over him. He didn't open his eyes until something stirred the rocks. He waited on the rhythm of steps. In his rifle scope, the deer poked through the shadows, just a two-point but solid from a summer of green wheat and lazy afternoons. Smoker watched the deer skyline then let him amble the wall break. Twice the buck pitched his ears and halted. Two does joined him. He let his harem lead. They wove through the draw bottom single file. Once the lead doe jerked into a trot. The buck faced the other direction, leaving nothing but an ass shot that would ruin the meat. Smoker waited. A noise in the rock above drew the buck's attention. The deer turned. Smoker found him in the scope, put the crosshairs over his shoulder, but the deer collapsed before he could fire.

The does bolted over a barbed-wire fence, but the buck kicked dirt and weeds. A black stain blotched its stomach. It buckled then staggered to its forelegs. Smoker slowly pulled back on the trigger. The buck dropped hard and didn't stir. Above, a boy slipped in the silt and slid down the grade, one of the two from the truck at the house.

"You shot my deer?"

"You knocked him down," Smoker said. "I just finished him before he ran off."

At the hill's break, they saw the deer, still, tongue caked with dirt. Smoker sawed his knife through the windpipe gristle. Steam lifted from the deer's throat. He handed the boy his knife and showed him how to notch his tag with the month and date, then puncture the buck's ear and tie it. Ten minutes later Andre appeared over Smoker's perch. The boy could see it was two against one. "We gonna share him?"

Smoker grinned. "Which part you want?"

"The horns," Jack said.

"I think you could probably talk me out of the antlers." Smoker split the deer's belly. The boy rolled the guts onto the ground. Smoker separated the liver and slipped it back into the empty chest. They dragged the deer toward the house until a man and a smaller boy crested a bluff in front of them. The boy's father shook. "John Miller," he said.

"I shot this deer, then he got up." Jack, the boy, turned toward Smoker. "He shot him so he wouldn't get away. He said I could keep the antlers, Dad."

John cocked a thick eyebrow at Smoker. "Awfully generous with your deer."

"He got to that brush, he'd belong to the coyotes," Smoker said.

"You say," the man replied.

"Folks got to have permission to hunt this property. It's private," Smoker told them.

John fumbled his wallet from his pocket. He dug out an orange card and held it up. The boys did the same.

"That's Fellers's card," Smoker said.

"Yes," John said. "Harvey Fellers."

Smoker told him, "This isn't Fellers's land. He just leases."

John blew a breath. "Jesus. I didn't know."

The boy stroked the antlers with his forefinger. Andre looked into Smoker's face. "Ain't your land," Andre told him.

Smoker eyed his brother.

Andre knocked dirt off one boot with his rifle butt. "It's Fellers's land. I sold it."

Smoker gazed off a long while. No one spoke. Finally he kneeled and stared at the deer a long time then patted its haunches with his palm. The hair bristled and swirled where they'd rolled him. Smoker rubbed it flat and considered the animal dying: its busted gut and open nose full of gunpowder and the smell of its own blood. He imagined a wild, frantic brain trying to recall how to beat a heart or blow open a lung, a knowledge of a kind so useless and necessary it seemed impossible to recall.

Before the sun fell, Smoker and Andre hunted the creek drainage together. A cool wind leaned the weed tops in gusts. A line of does worked its way to the wheat. Fifteen, Smoker counted. The deer were jumpy and broke into a trot whenever the wind shifted enough to throw their scent line. Andre fastened his jacket buttons. They stayed quiet awhile. Smoker's legs stiffened from the walk. He stretched them and enjoyed the tight muscles unbunching. Andre stared west to the river and the lighted line of the coulee. He pulled a weed from a tuft of dirt. His teeth worked it flat before he rested a hand on Smoker's shoulder and pushed himself up. "You traded."

"Yep."

"I ain't taking your blame."

"I'll let you blame yourself," Smoker said. He found the moon, pale in the still blue sky, just a thin melon slice like they served in the café. He felt his brother's shadow over him, and then he knew it was not. He listened to Andre's steps until they'd played out and no sound at all was left in the grass.

"Don't you fall asleep on me, goddamnit," Smoker said. "You look only half here."

"My powder's dry," Andre told him. "Make sure yours is similar."

"How you think it's going so far?" Smoker asked.

"Swimmingly," Andre said.

"I don't know what that means."

"Me neither. It's not going at all," Andre said. "When Bird gets here. That's when we'll see."

They were quiet for a while.

"How'd you get women?" Andre asked.

Smoker shrugged. "There ain't no trick to it," he said. "Past hello and a joke that makes yourself look silly, it's just listening. She can read the phone book if she's inclined. It's better if you don't know the topic. Leaves the questions easy to ask." Smoker drank. "Smooth talkers are overrated. Woman's got to be convinced and the only person can sell her is her. Just doing a different kind of math. You'd be good at it." Smoker looked at him. "You're starving for love songs, though."

"What you're describing doesn't seem fodder for them."

"Sing it long enough and it passes."

"How come Dede runs off twice a year with you so tuneful?"

"Keeping them is another matter."

"That's why you fucked Claire? You wanted to know what a stayer was like?"

Smoker kept silent.

"And now she isn't one anymore."

"Ain't her leaving," Smoker said.

"She filed papers."

"You were already gone. You can blame her and me all you want but don't get the afterward turned around. She kept with you. Even before me and her you moped in your head by your lonesome. I crossed where I never should have one time and so did she. But that's all, one time."

"That's felony logic. You just don't want to own up."

"I have owned up. I just owned up again. So has she. Your problem is owning up isn't enough. None of us can rehang the goddamned calendar and put days back. We're stuck and so are you."

"That ain't enough," Andre said.

"You want to hit me?" Smoker asked.

"That's not enough, either."

"You want to hit her?"

Andre shook his head. "I want to know why."

Smoker sighed. "It happened is all."

Andre shook his head again. "Wasn't any earthquake or tidal wave nor act of God. Something you did."

"Yep. Me and her," Smoker said. "And it wasn't no act of God, you're right. Just something two people did."

"To me."

"To each other. Wounding you wasn't the goddamn purpose."

"You were aware it would bust me up and so was she. Tell me that isn't your fault and I'll tear your ears off your goddamned head."

"I got no excuse," Smoker replied. "All you said is true." He paused. "You know you're the smartest of us, but you get the bit between your teeth about something and logic nor horse sense can dissuade you and that doesn't seem so intelligent. It's my fault, yeah, and hers, too. And yours. That's why you can't add it up. You're not hunting a reason. You aren't even looking to blame. You want me and her to make it so it didn't happen. I'm not much of a thinker but Claire is. Don't you figure she's been studying it as hard as you? Hell, likely harder. She's got no sum for that kind of math, either, and you're back where you are."

"Back where you put me, you mean."

Harold returned not long after without Calvin. "He won't be long," Harold said.

Andre rose for the door.

"I said he'd be here anytime," Harold said.

"Okay," Andre said. "I'm just going to check the camper and get me some air."

"Dogs'd hear anybody fussing with it," Harold replied.

"I'm a worrier," Andre told him.

Outside Harold's house, the bear lumbered to the camper window. Andre retrieved the pint from the cab, then fashioned a loop from their rope and unlocked the camper door. He passed it over the animal's head as it lumbered out. Together man and animal climbed the bluff behind the house. Their breaths smoked in the clear cold air. After a hundred yards, Andre paused on a flat rock. He'd shouldered his rifle to provide an equalizer if the bear turned hostile, but instead, the animal crawled the distance between them and put his head at Andre's feet, then lay on his back like he wanted scratched. Andre recognized a tiny plastic tag on its ear with numbers and a circus icon. The bear pawed Andre's hands for more attention. He had no claws, Andre saw. His teeth, too, had been filed flat as a horse's. He'd be hard-pressed to kill a squirrel.

The animal curled around his hands. Andre tugged the cork from Smoker's whiskey pint. The bear rolled to his back and extended all four limbs. Andre dangled the bottle over him. The bear clamped it with both forepaws and employed a foot to gently tip the bottom. The bourbon trickled into his mouth. The bear coughed, then shuddered and extended his tongue. He hoisted the bottle again and whiskey glugged into his mouth and spilled out the corners. He steered the bottle upright, blinked, paused a moment, then dropped it. The glass clinked against a rock. The bear lifted his paws and bleated, and Andre realized this was one of his circus duties, though alcohol was likely a new addition.

Above, enough moonlight remained to silver the trees and rock outcroppings, but shadows draped the driveway portions where the outside lights couldn't reach. The hard ground was blue and the sandpit behind looked like waves from a million years ago. Andre sang himself a lullaby then hummed other songs, just threads he recalled from the radio. The bear tipped with the rhythm until a motor scooter lumbered the road below.

LAMENTATIONS

August 1987–January 1988

A month after Rose's encounter with the dogs, Andre and Claire's child breached in her womb then stymied and died within Claire. The obstetrician performed a cesarean section. Finished, he withdrew the dead infant from Claire's incision and a nurse weighed and measured it as she would a live, breathing child. It was a girl. The name they had chosen was Charlotte. Another nurse wrote it on the birth and death certificates and had Andre sign each. Later, a nondenominational adviser whispered to them of funerals and caskets. He placed a sweaty pamphlet in Andre's hand before going. A sad-looking cartoon couple occupied the cover, no bubbles. Nothing existed for them to say or think. Inside contained a list of grief counselors.

Claire recovered two more days in the hospital, Andre next to her in a reclining chair. They watched cable television. The nurses forced Jell-O and gravy and potatoes into her until the doctor signed the release.

The undertaker lay Charlotte, whom the coroner determined was strangled by her own umbilical cord, in a cedar casket. He had dressed her in the gown Claire intended for her baptism. Claire's parents purchased three cemetery plots. Charlotte was interred in the center with the notion that Andre and Claire would bracket her for their final rest.

Andre had only recently considered the possibility of a child of his own; he was ill equipped to consider one's death. The thought was so immense that, like the child, it stuck crosswise in his mind and remained fixed there, neither a thought nor not one. Sometimes he believed he'd opted for a closed casket because he no longer desired a child of this world. Seeing her would cement the curve of her round cheek or the tiny bump of nose or thin black hair combed back like a Mafia boss, and his remembering those physical details would tether her to a place so fucked up it saw unfit to permit her entry. Other times, he thought it cowardice. Without her fixed in his memory, the tiny dress and matching ribbon in her hair, the lace shoes that he could fit his pinkie finger into, his loss was less intimate, less a daughter to lift and hold and speak to and hear, less a mystery of warm flesh; instead he opted for the idea of a child, not one he could forget but one he could recall on terms he could steer.

Claire had no such option and he worried that on top of the sky of grief over them she also endured tangible, physical pain like those with amputated limbs who ached in their absent places.

They did not speak of their mourning. Words would reduce it to the trivial. The mail brought Hallmark cards and notes with inspirational sayings as consolation. Andre bore them with a furious silence. He did not drink. That was as demeaning a cliché as words. He refused to fall into any recognizable pattern of mourning or sorrow that would shape his grief like others and his child like others lost.

Claire donated the baby's clothes and blankets from her showers to Goodwill. The crib she boxed and shipped to a Spokane orphanage. She painted the room beige and furnished it with the cheap nondescript items that typified guest rooms. She sealed other things in boxes and placed them high in a closet. A week later, however, she grew dissatisfied with the results and returned the furniture and painted once more an eggshell color and purchased a rocker and old desk and hung photographs of their parents and grandparents on the walls. A month later, she painted a backsplash and opted for green curtains and plants on nightstands and the dresser.

Smoker brought playing cards and a cribbage board and once a week they dealt three-handed and ate takeout. He was little comfort for Claire or Andre, but they were of no more to each other.

At recess four months later Claire fainted. A fever she had failed to mention had passed 101 degrees. She complained of stomach cramps. Chills shuddered through her. Antibiotics sometimes eased the symptoms but only for a day or two and afterward they circled back angrier than before. Andre burned his sick days nursing her. She began to discharge oozing puss pellets. The GP finally referred her to a Spokane surgeon, who discovered Claire's obstetrician gouged her bladder during the Cesarian and overlooked the error. Another surgery was required to stitch the leaking organ.

Claire's temperature leaped to 105 degrees before she left the OR. She was wet as a hard-rid horse. The nurses drained a sour-smelling tube from her side. Her pain was such she couldn't tolerate a bedsheet. The doctor insisted on a cold room to fight staph so Claire's skin goosefleshed and she shivered constantly. The drip antibiotics didn't perform. Claire's stomach, filled with gas, neared what it was pregnant. Three times her heart stuttered, honking the monitors, which alarmed the doctor enough to speak to Andre about medicine's limitations.

Smoker visited twice a day. He prodded Claire to weak laughter with tavern stories, but she requested more morphine and he and Andre ultimately settled for patting each of her hands. When she was asleep, Smoker bent to hear her body under the machine hum.

"I ain't ever going to think of breathing the same," he said.

Andre refilled their coffee cups from his thermos. "I been turning loose of her," he said.

"What does that mean?"

"When I get home, I walk a room in the house. I stay until I got it in my head without her. The upstairs is nearly finished."

"You quit her that easy?"

"It's nothing like easy," Andre said.

Later that night, Claire suffered a nightmare. Andre bent and whispered to hush her until she butted him with her head hard enough to raise a knot. Her eyes flew open. She hunted his face. Andre understood he'd relegated his daughter to something that would comfort him and was betraying Claire even before death could force his hand. Happiness was full of waiting for the other shoe to drop. Charlotte was the first and Claire the second. Their loss would return him to the familiar.

Then, two days later, Claire's fever broke. In ten more, she returned home. Another week and Andre was in front of a classroom again, though he left school to feed her lunch and administer her medicines. Mornings, she'd prop herself on the pillow for a kiss, but he cited the school's contagions.

Once he arrived home to find Smoker with an electric drill and a coping saw opening his living-room wall. "You adding to my house?" Andre asked him.

"Just an outlet," he said.

Under the end table was a perfect hole waiting for a junction box that would keep the lamp cords from dangling over the heater. Before her illness, Claire had hounded Andre to perform the chore but electrical work left him like a monkey working calculus.

Another week passed before Claire stretched across Andre's heavy stomach and fooled with him for a while. After a time, she stopped. Morning as he woke, she steered his hand to her and slapped herself with it. "I'm not going to break," she told him.

The next evening Andre lay in their bed, listening to Claire breathe beside him. Her bare spine bent like water meandering through a groove in a pale land and her shoulder blades rose into flattened mounds. Andre opened his hands over her. Each breath,

Claire's skin rose near enough to warm his palms, then dropped away. She would wake if he asked her, but it seemed his hands didn't have the question in him.

Smoker continued his Wednesdays with them. He delivered the tavern news to Andre and to Claire a housebroken blue heeler pup. The dog slept on her pillow and watched Andre with unblinking eyes.

The week following, Smoker cooked elk sausage and eggs. Afterward, Andre rinsed the dishes. He listened to Claire's laughter. In the entryway where neither could see him, Andre watched the dog battle Smoker's coat sleeve. Smoker tugged enough to elicit a growl. Next to them, Claire tucked her feet under her. Her color had improved and the skin on her face no longer appeared slack. The dog rested a moment then Smoker tapped Claire's wrist like he was danger itself, and the dog lit into him and broke skin before Claire could encourage a retreat.

Andre recalled the two of them dancing in the tavern last New Year's Eve. Smoker requested permission and Andre was pleased to give it. His brother had been bucket man in the wet T-shirt contest an hour before, but dancing with Claire in the darkened room, he looked stately. Andre had seen it then as a pleasant moment, one as much his own as Smoker's or Claire's.

That night Claire kissed his neck then his forehead. She was attired in her panties and his T-shirt, white with pockets because he preferred those without for himself. She parted the bedding then enveloped it around her. On her nightstand were framed photographs in two rows, mostly of himself and her, though one was Smoker displaying a trophy deer rack. Andre lurched enough for Claire to start. He wiped all save Smoker from the flat surface.

"What's gotten into you?" she asked.

He steered her hips until she couldn't see him. She turned to argue, and he slapped her haunches then twisted her hair and aimed her head at the photograph. He touched her mouth with his free hand, and she kissed his fingers and sucked them. They made damp streaks and traveled to her nipples. Her back muscles fluttered and her shoulders folded into his chest. He thrust his fingers inside her then his erect self and listened to her screech and cry.

The next morning, he left for work before first light. His students greeted him, but he didn't reply. He printed an assignment on the board that they could never finish in his hour. Through the window, he studied the cloudy sky and, under it, the passing traffic and crossing guards returning from their morning escorts. Andre held the position as a kid. The teachers made him lieutenant, which meant he got to boss three others. Smoker was two years behind and wouldn't attend the morning meetings, so he was never considered. At an assembly near the end of the year, the principal awarded Andre a silver badge for completing the year with honors. It had been lost long since between his father's and mother's houses.

After school, Claire took Andre in the stairwell, barely allowing the door to shut. Before bed, she backed into him on the couch, reaching behind herself to undo his belt. When she turned, he studied her face's fine bones but failed to recognize her.

The following day, Andre issued tests to every class. His students prodded him for hints, which, as a rule, he offered, but this day he volunteered none and told them they knew what he knew. His break, the teachers' room was empty and he spent his preparation time correcting. On the wall, Claire's school box held a month's mail, mostly catalogues and memos from the district; he'd been afraid to disturb the contents until after she'd passed, then doubly so when he knew she didn't. Below, the label's raised letters held her first name followed by his own surname. It appeared to be spelled incorrectly but he could not find the mistake.

He left school as soon as class ended. In his driveway Smoker's truck rested, idling. When Smoker recognized Andre, he set the emergency brake and stepped from the cab. He extinguished his cigarette and pointed to his chin. "You better hit me till I quit getting up."

Andre walked past without answering. In the living room, Claire stood, dressed.

"My brother's in the driveway."

"Ignore him."

"Seems a little late for that."

"It's a little late for a lot of things, goddamn you." She shook her head then held it with both hands and cried. "It wasn't good." She fought to catch her breath. "Don't leave," she whispered. "Not now."

"I won't," he told her.

"Let's have another baby," Claire said.

Andre nodded. "Sure," he said. "We'll have a baby."

He filled a tall glass with the whiskey he'd hid from himself in the top cabinet and went outside to drink it. Claire didn't follow. North were the reservation's mountains and the country the river broke through. He sat staring at it. Later, the stars cleared above him. He blinked his lids until his eyes grew too murky to see through, leaving him blind and awake until, eventually, he was not. Morning, the light stunned him, and for a moment he forgot why he was there at all.

13

EXODUS

August 1991

Bird had wrapped both arms around Calvin, who steered past the camper to the house. If she recognized the truck, she didn't let on. Calvin halted the scooter with his feet, then propped the kick-stand. Calvin helped her down and Bird took his hand. He whistled and Smoker and Harold hastened to the porch. The mounted light left them in sharp relief. Andre lifted the rifle and peered through his scope. Calvin remained opposite the others, his back to Andre. Bird, though, ran to the steps toward Harold until she recognized Smoker next to him.

"Get in the rig, honey," Smoker said. "Time to go home."

She lowered her head. Harold disappeared inside and returned with her coloring book and a can filled with crayons. He offered them to her, but she shook her head no.

Smoker extended his good hand and Bird took it. He limped toward the truck, Bird in tow, examining his bloody pant leg. Suddenly Calvin grabbed her other hand and tugged. Bird danced on her toes to keep from splitting in two.

"The money!" Calvin shouted. He pulled with both hands. Smoker nearly tipped but held on. The money was in a gym bag behind the truck seat. Andre waited for Smoker to say so. He put the scope on them.

"Calvin!" Harold shouted. Calvin let go of the girl, but he thrust his rifle butt across Smoker's nose. Bird scampered for the truck.

Calvin glared at Smoker. "Where's your brother?"

"I don't know," Smoker replied. He looked at his blood-spattered shirt.

Perched atop his rock, Andre watched through the riflescope. He'd neglected the bear until he heard bushes thrash and branches pop. The grade's thick underbrush quivered then a lower portion did the same. The dogs sounded. Andre lifted his rifle and shot three times, lifting the dirt under each animal until they retreated into the dark woods.

The bear shambled into the light, roared then bent and shat. Bird peeked through the truck window. Smoker reached for his belt and pistol. Andre found Calvin just as Calvin shoved his rifle barrel into Smoker's ear. Andre squeezed the trigger. Calvin's cap jumped. His skull peppered Harold with blood and bone.

Harold stroked the bloody hair out of Calvin's eyes.

"We never done nothing to you. Not one thing," Harold shouted.

"Get clear," Andre warned.

Harold wobbled into the shadows toward the barn. He lifted a bicycle from its rack and pedaled out of the light and Andre let him go.

Smoker gimped to the truck, broken several places. The bear bawled and pawed a knot on his temple. Smoker and Andre dragged Calvin's body into the camper. The bear followed as Bird looked on. Inside the cab, Smoker stuffed his nose with napkins and added another bandage to his ass. For his finger there was no medicine. Bird stroked his hand with hers. Andre took the wheel. The bewildered bear peered out the windows and Calvin banged across the narrow floor at every turn.

The truck struggled over the road out and turned when Andre figured they had discovered one more traveled. He didn't know why Smoker chose not to part with the money. Perhaps he thought he could manage both; perhaps he was tired of trading what wasn't his; perhaps, too, he simply forgot.

LAMENTATIONS

January 1988

The light shone on Smoker's face from his brother's half-curtained bedroom window. The rest kept to the shadows, as in movies.

"You look like a Greek god," Claire said. She lay naked beneath the sheets. Smoker had pulled on his underwear.

"Which one?"

Claire stared at the ceiling a moment. "Apollo, maybe," she said.

"He sleep with his brother's wife?"

She sighed. "They slept with their sisters even."

"I'd fit right in."

Smoker fished his cigarettes from his shirt on the floor and lit one, then let loose a smoky cloud.

"What god's he?"

"Hephaestus," she said. "His mother tossed him off Mount Olympus when he was born and crippled him. Work was all he was good for. He made Achilles's armor."

Smoker stabbed the cigarette into the dregs of his brother's morning coffee. The butt and ashes floated. A newspaper folded to the crossword lay next to the cup.

"Between a buck and two. That's Adams."

"There's a pen in the drawer," Claire told him.

"He might recognize the handwriting."

"He's not that observant."

"That's a little unkind, ain't it?" he said.

"Seems we're both open for some criticism where he's concerned." Claire propped herself on a pillow, revealing one smallish breast, the nipple as brown and unremarkable as the rest of her.

Smoker wrote in the word.

"I'm not stupid and I don't confuse truth with fantasy," Claire said. "This," she patted the bed, "wasn't love. You don't have to chase me off with a list of my husband's virtues."

"Truth what you want?" Smoker asked. "Truth is I wouldn't've given you much consideration if you hadn't been married to him."

"It seems that would be the one reason not to," she said.

"Seems." Smoker studied the crossword and tapped the pen against the paper. On Claire's nightstand were pill bottles in a line and a half-empty water glass. "How is your health?" he asked.

Claire laughed.

"You are going to live, I assume," Smoker said.

"The doctors think so." Claire collected her clothes. Smoker watched her twist her socks on and fit each breast into its bra cup, then reach behind her back for the clasp. She unrolled her underwear and slipped it over her thighs, then buttoned her blouse, hands moving together like children's fingers playing the spider-in-the-waterspout game.

"You ever see anything die?"

"Houseflies."

"Then you never killed anything?"

"Houseflies," she said again.

"Something that could live ten, twenty years if you didn't."

"No," Claire said.

"It don't die right off."

"Dress, if he scares you," Claire said.

"He don't scare me. He scare you?"

"No," she said.

"Then scared isn't what I'm talking about, is it?"

Claire had put the crossword in her lap. She chewed on a pen and counted squares, then slowly tore it into confetti over the garbage pail. Smoker lit another cigarette. He offered the butt end to Claire. She dragged then hacked out a lungful of smoke.

"What'd you take it for, then?" Smoker asked her.

Claire didn't reply. Anybody not smoking thought cigarettes settled something in a person when they really just welcomed you to what was unsettled.

"I could put a seven-millimeter round into an elk or deer heart eight times out of ten. Blow it to pieces. They're still breathing and kicking, working to get loose."

"You're full of shit," Claire said.

"I am," Smoker admitted. "Let me try again. The deer or elk. It's kicking and foaming."

239

"Does your story have a point?"

"Animal ain't ever been as alive as when it is dying."

"That how you see this?" Claire asked. "You and me shooting a bullet into him."

Smoker shook his head. "Andre's been gutshot from birth."

"And now?"

Smoker shrugged. "It seemed humane to finish him."

Claire laughed.

"What?" Smoker asked.

"Your humanity."

"You think this is playing my brother false?" Smoker asked. "I found you out."

"You really believe he'd see it like that?" Claire asked.

"He will."

"What makes you think so?"

"Because I know he's more than work and thrown off a mountain."

"That's unfair."

"To him or you?"

"It was unfair of me to say. I didn't mean it."

"How come you said it, then? How come you undressed when I did?"

"It was unfair of you to come here," she said quietly.

"I don't see no gun against your noggin."

"You want my guilt just to cover up your own," Claire said.

"Nope," Smoker said. "He's done the feeling for the both of us. Made two stops at the confession box every week. Said double Hail Marys. I've always been sorry I couldn't return the favor."

"Why this then?" Claire patted the bed. "Why me when there's a line a block long for your attentions."

"I guess I been mad about it, too."

Smoker could stare a woman skittish or gaze one bold. The most beautiful in town unburdened themselves to him in long quiet talks until they felt like they owed him. The next day they'd come around grinning and wearing tight clothes, everybody in the place knowing why.

"I just wanted it clear," she said. "I wanted to know, not guess."

"Well, it figure now?"

"Yes," Claire told him. "But not the way I worried." Claire looked at the cigarette still in her hand. "My husband is all I want."

"But you lacked faith."

"All right," she whispered. "I lacked faith. But now I don't." Claire took his T-shirt and socks from the floor and set them next to his jeans. "He'll be home soon," she said. "You want him to know?"

"He already knows," Smoker told her.

He watched her ash drop to the carpet and smolder. He was barefoot and let it be. Outside, a passing car disturbed the gravel. Smoker pulled his white T-shirt over his head. Claire handed him his pants and shoes.

"Hurry," she said. "Please. Hurry please."

14

EXODUS

August 1991

Andre recognized trees and sky in the flat headlight beams. Hours passed. He watched for following lights and saw none. They ran out of road near dawn. A creek trickled across their path, sand on both banks. It was in its summer track, shallow and clear over a gravel bed and less than two feet deep. Andre and Smoker stopped and drank from it, then found a Styrofoam cup in the floor's trash and filled it for Bird. Andre dished out a handful of aspirin and Bird fed them to Smoker who lapped the pills from her hand like an animal. She had said nothing since the mountain and Andre wondered if she'd surrendered speech for good. Smoker patted her head and she looked up at him with only doubt.

Nothing remained but to cross the creek. Andre turned in

the wheel hubs and shifted the truck into four-wheel drive. Water splashed the grille. Andre could hear it against the metal undercarriage. He opened the door to check if the exhaust was submerged. The motor coughed and he dropped the gas feed hard, jumping to higher ground. They drove the opposite bank fifty yards south, for no reason other than that the truck ended up pointed that direction, then rocked through a manageable break into a field and onto a road that led around one mountain then another and returned them to pavement. Smoker slept. Bird counted his breaths; Andre watched her mouth in the mirror. The radio played songs from the fifties and sixties.

Hours later, Smoker asked, "What day is it?"

"The day after yesterday," Andre said. He caught himself in the rearview mirror. It was his own face staring back, not some wicked stranger.

He no longer knew how to construct a reflection that didn't include regret, and his brother, though he whistled by the graveyard admirably, handled such matters by simply not looking. Andre knew the earth would continue twirling them. He wondered if it stopped suddenly and reversed itself, if that would be a kind of forgetting he could do. He saw himself spitting whiskey into a glass, then pouring it in the bottle under the bar, then the hospital machines that sucked the last poison from Claire and the doctors feeding the child medicine until it was blood and fluid and free of them. He saw he and Claire unmeeting, even he and Smoker unfastened, his mother's ovum and dad's seeds uncoupling until the slate was clean and he was where he could place each safely where they needed to be.

The highway looped between a cavalry fort and campground where the Spokane River met the reservoir. It climbed again into more wheat, reservation ranches, where the tillable soil remained wedged between the rock and draws that held pine stands too thick to hew and be profitable. They passed Fruitland—three houses and an abandoned service station—and drove onto an unimproved gravel road along a creek bed into a flat above. There Andre unhitched a wire gate and followed a rutted dirt track against the wheat's edge. The sky had blued and the day warmed. They halted behind a piece of basalt and an enormous bull pine. Dark, he and Smoker dragged Calvin half a mile to a fallow dip. There they dug a grave seven feet deep in the soft earth and interred him.

Andre discovered a tractor, keys in it, as was most farmers' habit. He started it and lifted the cultivator so as not to cross its careful loops. At the grave, he dropped the hinges and turned the earth in the same concentric pattern covering their work only twice, recognizing that his conscience not his common sense pressed him to make another turn, and a thousand turns would never satisfy that portion of his mind.

The evening sun spilled across the river bend before they returned to the car and he and Smoker and Bird repeated their path the opposite direction, then bearing north and east to the Gifford Ferry through Inchelium and into the Okanogan Mountains and the reservation and finally back to the coulee.

It was fifty miles out when Smoker woke.

"Isn't any way to know if or when we're clear of this," Andre said.

"We won't ever be clear."

"Likely not," Andre agreed.

They let five miles pass.

"You ever think Penny killed herself?" Andre asked.

"What the hell makes you say a thing like that?"

"What did she tell you right before?" Andre asked.

"I'm not going into it again."

"She hated the big water?"

"Turns out she had some reason," Smoker said.

"Seems scared is more a little kid's word. Hate's for broccoli or bedtime."

"Maybe hate's what was handy."

"Could be," Andre allowed.

They drove awhile farther in the morning gray. A doe and two fawns stood at the road shoulder. Andre wondered if the bear saw them.

"She told me she hated me a few days before," Andre said.

"Well, you probably earned it."

"I brought her ice cream. She took it and looked at me and said I hate you. Then she took a bite and said she hated you, too. And Pork and Peg. Then she ate some more. I asked why but she just handed me the empty bowl and watched more TV."

"Hell, she was the only one in the family everyone catered to and we did without letup. You'd think she knew she was a short-timer and so did we so we heaped love upon her."

Andre entered a turn and then accelerated. "Just because she was the apple of our eye, don't mean she saw it the same. You've got plenty experience at others taking to you and you not feeling anything back."

Smoker seethed. "Bust me in the chops and make a finish of it."

"She hated the water because it was going to swallow her. Maybe she felt the same about her kin."

Smoker lifted his pistol from under the seat. "I swear I will shoot you someplace it hurts if you don't leave off."

Andre nodded to the sleeping child between them. "You know what I'm suggesting?"

"Yes," Smoker said.

"Good."

"I don't like it a bit."

"Didn't expect you would."

Andre crisscrossed the wheat and rock in silence until he made town, then parked the truck at his wedding house.

15

EXODUS

August–September 1991

At three in the morning, Andre rang her doorbell until Claire answered. Bird stood next to him on the porch.

"I better sign those papers," Andre said.

Claire blinked. "You're back?"

"Not for long so I need to sign."

"I was thinking you and I might talk it over first," Claire said.

Andre shook his head.

"What happened?" Claire asked.

"It went bad," Andre told her.

"Bad?"

"The cops will visit you. I tell you more, you'll have to lie or tell them what they want. And I know you'll lie."

Claire glanced at Bird.

"Will you take her?" Andre asked.

"Where's Smoker?"

"In the truck."

"How about Dede?"

Andre shrugged. Claire bent and wiped a hair from Bird's forehead.

"How long?" Claire asked.

"For good," Andre said.

"Okay," Claire said.

Andre kicked one shoe with the other. "Tell Reynolds to draw them papers up," he said. "And some for Bird, too."

Three nights later, past midnight, Andre approached Claire's place once more. He parked at the Almira water tower under a willow that disguised his rig then hiked two miles to the house. In the twilight, he watched Claire and Bird on the couch. Claire was reading, he recognized her body rocking with the words. The girl remained perfectly attentive. After Claire put Bird down for the night, Andre whistled. Claire saw his cigarette ember and smoke rising behind the tree. She opened the door. On the table were several documents he signed, forging Smoker's name when necessary. Claire brought him a foil-lined box. Inside she'd put a leftover roast, some spuds, a loaf of bread, and a package of salami. She'd found his bottle and threw it in, too. Then Bird appeared in the bedroom doorway.

She looked at Andre and blinked.

"Can I sleep with you, Claire?"

"Sure, kiddo," Claire said.

The girl raced into Claire's bedroom. Andre heard the bed bounce. He patted Claire's hand.

Claire walked him to the porch. He stopped her from switching on the light.

"You don't know where we are," Andre told her. "Keep it simple when they come. Tell the truth. If they press you, tell them you want your lawyer. I dropped some money with Reynolds. It's not enough if things get sticky, I'll find more."

"What about school?"

"I'm done with it. I didn't want that, but there it is."

He listened to the wood screen door clatter and shut behind her then lugged the food and bottle toward his truck.

Andre parked the truck at the house but Smoker and the bear and King were absent. The next day he waited until evening then walked to the spring. At an unkempt willow he looked for sign of them. Finding none, he forged a trail through the heavier brush, the food in a knapsack over his shoulder. He unhooked a barbed-wire gate and angled through the alfalfa. The dry air held the sagebrush scent, a tougher smell than things that required rain. A sound through the low grass startled him. King broke through, his hair matted and tongue flapping. The dog nosed his leg. Andre patted him.

Half a mile farther, Andre made a coyote call and waited for its return. A small fire burned inside a ring of stones where Smoker turned a scrawny rabbit over a spit. He had resorted to green wood that smoked and burned grudgingly. The bear, a few feet away, pawed his eyes.

"More chow," Andre said.

King whined and lay down at Smoker's ankles. Smoker divided

a wedge of fat and gristle from the roast and fed both dog and bear. They woofed their scraps then eyed each other. The bear whined and King circled him then lay beneath Smoker.

"They partnered up?" Andre asked.

"Tolerating each other, at least," Smoker said.

Andre uncapped the bourbon and offered the bottle. Smoker pulled deep then returned it. Andre held up his open hand.

"Still dry?" Smoker asked.

"Guess so," Andre told him.

Smoker set the foil in front of King. The dog's tongue scoured it.

"Some sandwich stuff in there, too," Andre said.

Smoker built the bear a sandwich to keep the animals even. Andre lit a cigarette and tossed the package to him. Smoker rested his arm against a high spot of grass. His finger was still crooked and a knot bent his nose in a manner that the bar folks might identify as character. The bird shot in the ass would strain his gait and he would treat it similarly.

"You did right," Smoker told him. "Goddamn, I'd like to talk it through with Birdy, though."

They remained quiet awhile and smoked. Andre lay on the ground. The lowering sky attached to the coulee in gray wisps. The birds hushed and the coyotes quit their evening shouts. The bear snored. Andre recalled that he and Smoker once owned this country.

"I wish it would rain," Andre said at last.

Smoker laughed. "Look at you. A heathen praying for the flood."

That night, Smoker and the bear and King fell into their dozes, while Andre remained weary but awake, his mind fluid and teetering toward unconsciousness. Sleep was trust and he wasn't sure he had courage enough for it.

Epilogue

EXODUS

October 1991

Smoker didn't recognize the washout; it was as simple as that. The pickup hood disappeared into the cleft cut by spring thaws eight months ago, then the cab with them inside. Smoker shoved through the gears even as they dominoed the grade. Partway, he lost Andre through a window. Smoker twisted his head to see how his brother fared, but forward was backward too quick for a good look.

The truck finished with its tailgate up a tree and grille in the dirt. Smoker shoved himself from the steering column and examined the divot his skull made in the windshield. Rainbowed light twisted through the spider cracks and hurt his head. He bumbled to the sprung door then collapsed onto the pine straw below.

"How'd you do?" Andre shouted from above.

Smoker took inventory. The glass nicked his forehead, which bled steadily, but a little time would fix it. He attempted to stand but his ankle took no weight. His split sock filled with blood and a deep cut exposed gray bone. "I'll manage," Smoker hollered.

"Any way you can get up to me?"

"Be easier for you to slide down than me crawl up."

"My leg bone's come out," Andre shouted.

"Guess a leg trumps a foot," Smoker replied.

He hunted a stick and hobbled across the hill. His ankle throbbed and his breaths cut him so that he limited himself to short puffs of air, which left his head dizzy and his vision unreliable. He paused and inhaled deep to catch up and his lung felt like it hooked a rib. He paused in a tree well but remained so long his starry thoughts could not recall why he had halted nor why he should keep on nor, if he had reason to move, which direction he ought to pursue.

"Come on, then," Andre hollered.

Ten feet up a tree, Smoker saw a bloody smear. He climbed toward his brother's voice and found him several feet above heaped against a tamarack, shoeless. Both halves of his femur split his jeans. The skin shone and he shivered. Smoker unbelted his hunting knife and hacked his brother's pant leg. Blood pasted the denim to Andre's skin and the blade caught hide. When Andre didn't yelp, Smoker ordered him to wriggle his toes. He couldn't.

"Try the other," Smoker told him.

They answered. Smoker peeled the pant leg to Andre's calf. Each bone end had furrowed a trough coming out. Red, quaking muscle and fat sided the wound. In its gutter, blood fluttered then drained to the middle where it spilled out, then stopped a beat before repeating itself.

Smoker lugged his sweatshirt off, wincing at his aching sides. He looped and knotted it and made ready to throttle the bleeding.

"Tourniquet might leave me losing it."

"I thought you was crippled a minute ago. Losing just one should be a relief."

"Things tight?" Andre asked.

"It ain't milk spilling out of you."

Smoker cinched the shirt taut and knotted it. Andre's heart beat more blood from him. A low branch was near. Smoker tore it free, then tied both ends to the shirt sleeves and cranked until the stick could bear no more. The bleeding kept on.

"Get a bigger stick," Andre told him.

Smoker shook his head. "It ain't the pressure, it's the muscle padding the artery." Smoker had watched the ground blacken under deer and bear he'd killed; he'd listened to the last of it ticking. He wondered if he'd end up seeing his brother go over in the same way. He pressed his fingers to Andre's neck. His pulse was fast but steady. Fear paled him. Shock wouldn't be far behind.

Smoker's ankle had fallen apart hiking up so he got himself lengthwise along the grade and rolled. The hard earth and rocks battered him and pinecones tore his undershirt and back. He extended his arms to steer himself toward the pickup.

Under the seat, Smoker found the ripsaw. He pulled it over a tree's trunk to clean it then hunted another walking stick and hobbled Andre's direction.

"Don't watch," Smoker told him.

"It's my leg, I guess I'll see what happens to it."

Smoker began sawing. Andre's flesh opened. Smoker's breath tore through him with each pass. More skin and fat parted. The muscle sheath fought the blade, but once through, the saw cut deep, separating the tissue like slicing steaks. The only catch was tendons, which snapped and popped under the blade.

Near halfway, Smoker got to the bleeder. The artery flailed like a worm. Smoker plucked it and squeezed the end shut. He'd brought a rubber band from the truck and, on the way up, cut a green twig and scraped it of bark. He sliced the artery clean with his pocketknife, then stretched the limp end of the vessel over the wood stopper as far as he could without splitting the flesh, then wrapped them both with the rubber band. Finished, he sat against the tree trunk and vomited.

"We weren't even drinking," Smoker said. "I never once wrecked drunk."

"Maybe we had it right all along," Andre replied.

Smoker spit then cleared his throat. "We're a long way from anywhere," he said.

"And I don't seem to be good for hiking out."

"You'd be hard put."

"How about you?"

Smoker shrugged. "I ain't near as beat up as you, but I won't win any races."

"Well, I guess you better get to it," Andre said.

Smoker shook his head. "I ain't comfortable leaving you."

"Well that's kind of you, but we'll be a long time waiting for the next bus."

"Goddamnit, you think I haven't thought of that."

Andre said nothing, just stared at his ruined leg. It was near four o'clock as best he could tell. The sky was blue and hot. Gnats hovered over his face. He swatted them.

"It worse than a hangover?" Smoker asked.

Andre shook his head. "Hangover feels guilty. This doesn't hurt as much as it's supposed to. It's kind of interesting to tell you the truth."

After a while, Smoker sat and put a hand to his chest. His paled skin was damp with sweat. Breathing was difficult, Andre could see. Smoker leaned against the ground and slept aimed backward down the hill. It would leave him a headache, Andre thought. He was going to remind him of it but drifted off before he could. When he woke, Smoker had no pulse or breath in him.

Andre stared into the dusk and then the rising night. The sky seemed on top of him. He'd heard the most amazing thing about space is the amount of nothing in it, but tonight it looked like it might hold all it was rumored to. He longed to be just a salt speck flashing across the great rock walls, the yellow prairies, the pine, tamarack, elm, and white-barked birch lining the breaks. He felt a thrill of lightness. His stomach cramped then let go. He vomited but felt fine after. He heard the blood flow then tick from him until his heart lost its prime and he died.

A month passed before hunters found them. The coyotes had had their share and the magpies. Their faces were meaty blanks, and it was only through the contents of their wallets that anyone might've guessed who they were at all.

Acknowledgments

Many thanks to the following, who helped wrangle these strays into a herd: Nicole Aragi, Sean McDonald and all the MCD/FSG folks, Jeff Sanford, Charles McIntyre, Chris Offutt, Max Phillips, Desi Koehler, Elizabeth McCracken, John Whalen, Bob Ganahl, Jim Preston, Darren Nelson, Stevens County Libraries, and the Washington Center for the Book, as well as my family.

A Note About the Author

Bruce Holbert is a graduate of the University of Iowa Writers' Workshop. His work has appeared in *The Iowa Review, Hotel Amerika, Other Voices, The Antioch Review, Crab Creek Review,* and *The New York Times.* He grew up on the Columbia River and in the shadow of the Grand Coulee Dam. Holbert is the author of *The Hour of Lead,* winner of the Washington State Book Award, and *Lonesome Animals.*